MURDER AT THE MET

E. W. COOPER

INK DOG PRESS

978-1-7352449-4-5 (paper)
978-1-7352449-5-2 (Kindle)
978-1-7352449-6-9 (EPUB)
978-1-7352449-7-6 (WebPDF)

INK DOG PRESS
634 W. Cavalcade Street
Houston, TX 77008-9998

Cover design and illustration and interior design by Lindsey Cleworth

Printed in the United States of America

For my father, whose love of opera inspired me to write these books

and

For my mother, who shared her love of a good mystery

1

Niels Rask cut his eggs with precision, even as he paused to consider Lund. Every soul that crossed Rask's path received the same stony appraisal, unnerving in its concentration. Rask wore his usual trim blue suit, the lines of the jacket cut to fit his sinewy frame, with carefully polished black shoes hidden under a small and friendly mongrel named Scratch. The dog looked up at Lund, tail thumping against the thick red carpet of St. Sebastian's, one of New York's many elite clubs for men.

Lund found Rask's scrutiny reassuring. It reminded him of the happy adventures of their youth in Denmark. Niels Rask was Matthias's friend first, his solace when the little sister Matthias hoped for was, in fact, little brother Thom. When their mother died, leaving Matthias and Thom alone with a father who found solace at the bottom of a bottle, Niels would bring them to his house, where his mother made sure they were fed. And finally, Niels was there again when it was time to go to war, horrors in France too far away and too close to be real to a fourteen-year-old Lund. When Thom had appeared in the trenches at Courcelette in a stolen uniform too big for him, demanding to see Matthias with as many profanities as Copenhagen had taught him, Rask took him under his wing. They survived. Lund was never sure how Niels managed it, but they had.

Life in the trenches shook Lund's confidence that he would find his brother alive. But not Rask. If Niels had a doubt, he never let on. It took three weeks to fight their way across the bloody mess that was France. Rask's steady determination to get Lund to his brother's position willed Matthias alive for the boy. Rask's same appraising stare that took in every thread and button carried them across the trenches. To the fourteen-year-old, Rask was a hero. Time hadn't changed Lund's mind on the matter. He trusted Rask. As much as he trusted his brother Matthias. And perhaps, with Matthias half a world away in China, just a little past that.

Lund waited Rask out with patient indulgence. Returning to his eggs and sausage with a precise cut of his knife, Rask got down to business. "Matthias sent me a telegram," he said in Danish. "Seems word travels fast when it comes to Miss Penelope Harris. Only took a month for the English paper in Shanghai to find out about the Staughton matter. Matthias was a little put out you didn't call him."

Lund could imagine. "He said all this in a telegram?"

"You know how he can be," Rask shrugged, "colorful. When Matthias talks, each word doubles for a hundred."

Lund was aware. He steered his mind away from the vivid telegram he had received not three days before.

"In the photo they ran, you were holding her hand. Matthias thinks you are in over your head. Again." The knife and fork stopped their steady movement. Rask laid them down neatly, removed the napkin protecting his tie, and used it to primly dab at his mouth.

The pause allowed Lund a moment to recollect the night Renee Staughton had died, how he held Penelope's hand as they dove through the reporters to reach the car at the curb. If he hadn't, who knew what the crowd of photographers would have done to her? It was the only photo the press had managed before Penelope sequestered herself at the Excelsior. Lund kept his face blank while he sorted through a wide range of choice expletives. For weeks she hadn't left the apartment. Not even for a coffee in the Excelsior's supremely equipped tearoom. Penelope hid away in her comfortable apartment, ignoring the headlines that mentioned her husband's death or her past as the owner of an illicit nightclub casino in Shanghai's French Concession. "I haven't seen Penelope in weeks."

"So, it's Penelope now? Not Miss Harris?" Rask smiled. It wasn't unfriendly—if you knew the man. "Maybe Matthias has good reason to be concerned. From what I read in the papers, this Penelope Harris got herself into some trouble in Shanghai, didn't she?"

Lund looked around at the other tables. "I didn't know you read gossip."

"Nervous? You shouldn't be. No one here speaks Danish. Even if they did, no one at this club would sell gossip to the papers. I can't imagine what on earth would keep you from telling me your troubles. You've known me long enough. I have half a mind to get you drunk and worm it out of you."

"Is that why you called me here at six o'clock in the morning? To get drunk?"

Rask laughed. "Don't worry. Now we work." He pushed back his chair so Scratch could jump into his lap. The dog sighed and closed his eyes, content. "No one at the bank can know anything about it." When Lund didn't speak, Rask added, "What do you say to that?"

"Sounds fine." Lund relaxed. A problem to solve was what he needed. Something to keep him from thinking about her every waking moment.

"One of the board members, Wallace Peters, wants some

information about a death." Rask leaned back. "Have you met him?" Lund shook his head. "Wallace was auditing the books for his father when I started. There were a lot of late nights working shoulder to shoulder. We became friends." It was firmer praise than Lund had expected from Rask, who wasn't usually so emphatic. "His matter is a private one. It could take several days to settle. I expect you can manufacture a cover story that will be good enough to explain the time away."

"Is he in trouble?"

"No, no! Nothing like that!" An older man at a nearby table lifted his head at the loud words. Scratch shifted in Rask's lap, looking up at Lund with a reproachful air. "Wallace is straight as an arrow and about as hard as a soft-boiled egg. I've got to find a reliable investigator who won't take him for every penny. I thought of you, of course."

"What kind of trouble are we talking about?"

"His sister-in-law died a year ago. June of '27. He has some questions."

"Murder?" Lund's natural reserve hid any sign of his caution. Another murder investigation would only make it harder to convince Penelope to step out with him. Tangling with New York reporters had made her wary of anything that could draw attention.

"Nothing like that. She drowned. Police said it was suicide." Rask watched Lund carefully.

A memory so clear it was like the wheel of a train finding the rail—a woman's death, an accident or not, questions. Lund waited while the shadows of the past lengthened, paused, then retreated. "I understand."

Rask nodded and stroked Scratch's ears. "I've told him

over and over that he won't learn a damn thing, but it's no good. He can be quite determined when he has his mind set. He wants to know why she did it." Niels looked up to watch Lund. "He may be a fool, but I know Wallace—he's persistent. If you don't give him a hand, he'll go out and take his chances with the first charlatan he finds in the phone book."

"I'm not a licensed private eye in the state of New York." Lund was cautious. "I don't even have a car."

"Just ask a few questions and see how far you can get. You shouldn't need a license for that, should you?" Rask reached into his inside jacket pocket and removed an envelope. "Here, take these."

Lund looked inside. "Opera tickets?"

"I had to make it worth your while, didn't I? Your lovely songbird can't have found tickets—the performance sold out months ago. Go on. Call Miss Penelope Harris and have a night out while you're at it. Have some fun for a change." Rask nodded at the envelope in Lund's hand. "Wallace will meet you there. He insisted on the discretion. He doesn't want his wife to know about it, says it will upset her. He'll come find you before the curtain. You can talk things over with him, decide if you'll investigate the matter. If you still don't want to take him on, fair enough."

Putting the envelope in the inside pocket of his own jacket, Lund nodded. "Of course." He stood up.

"There's another matter, Thom." Rask stopped stroking Scratch's ear, making the dog shift. "I want you to take a quiet look at the books—June of last year to now."

"That's quite a bit of ground." Lund turned his head to study Rask. "Am I looking for anything specific?"

"Fair question." Rask's smile disappeared, the mask of a bank president pushing the familiarity aside. "Everything William has worked on."

William Bird. The only investigator left at the bank since Lund's first investigation resulted in the other being arrested for embezzlement. Perhaps Bird had a motive to steal, given how freely he spent money—he liked a party and a pretty girl—but he wasn't a thief. Being a fool for a good time didn't make him a criminal.

"Spread it around with a few other accounts and years. Keep it as quiet as you can."

"I investigated Bird with the others. There was no sign of impropriety," Lund said.

Rask gave Lund a careful look for a moment before he said, "Things change, Thom. Sometimes they change very quickly. You know that better than any other man I know, other than Matthias."

Lund nodded, pushing his resistance to one side. Time to go to work.

2

The problem of how to get to the ledgers dogged him all the way from St. Sebastian's. Discretion was the challenge. He'd have to wait until after the bank had closed for the day. Stay after. But not tonight, no. It would have to be at the weekend. The imperious front of New Amsterdam Bank loomed sooner than he would have liked. It was a bright morning but cold. He had just begun to feel the chill as he met the front steps. Lund took them two at a time, entering the bank with a pace fast enough to make the security guard lift his head. Lund nodded at the guard, moving quickly through the clerking desks to the back stairs. He used his own key and began the long trek up three flights, his thoughts jumbled up with clerks, William Bird, accounting ledgers, and opera tickets.

"Lund? Is that you?" A man with fair hair leaned over the banister a flight above him. "What the devil are you doing here so late? Jensen will have you for breakfast!"

"Niels had some opera tickets to give me. I had to go to St. Sebastian's to pick them up." Lund was certain he was on time, while Bird was earlier than usual. He fought the urge to look at his watch to confirm the matter. Bird was never early—or on time—to work.

"Going to the opera with the boss! Would you listen to that!" Bird's smile was too easy. "Give a pal the goods, would ya? I can't seem to make any headway with the fossil."

"Not calling him a fossil would be a good start." Lund slowed his step as he reached Bird at the landing. "What are you doing in the stairway, William?"

"Oh, the usual reason." Bird waved his hand toward the door to the balcony that overlooked the bank floor. Rask's office was there, as was the bank manager's, Karl Jensen.

Lund snorted. "A girl, then. Where is she?"

"It's not a girl!" Bird's smile faltered. "It's her father."

"William!"

Bird put his hands up and talked fast. "It's not like that, Thom. It really isn't. She isn't in any kind of trouble. The man just wants to make sure it isn't serious. And it isn't! It isn't serious in the least." Bird stepped closer, lowering his voice. "She and I just met at a party, see? We had a little fun . . ." The color drained from Bird's face.

Lund put his hand on the handle of the heavy metal door. "I have to go, William. I'm working on something."

"Wait a minute, Thom! Do a fellow a favor, would you? Have a look around and tell me if he's gone. Then come back to see me, would you? I don't want another scene. My reputation can't take it!"

"I can't do anything to save your reputation, William."

A furrow appeared between Bird's eyes. "I can't help it if a girl sets her hat for me. I've told her I'm not interested."

"Right." Lund stepped toward the door.

"Listen, Thom, just listen. She's all set to be married, but her father saw us at a party together and got the wrong idea. I don't mind talking to him, just not here. You know Jensen has it in for me. Give a fella a helping hand! I need this job, Thom! Just have a look around and let me know he's left the building. Please!"

Lund sighed. "What's his name?"

"You're a pal, Thom. Thanks." Bird slumped with relief. "Roger Warwick."

"I SHALL CALL THE POLICE if I don't get satisfaction!" Roger Warwick shouted the declaration at Karl Jensen, his voice echoing out the heavy wooden doors to the street. Even Jensen's usually steadfast nature showed a sensible caution as he took a careful step away. Lund could see why. Warwick held a heavy black cane from the middle, gesturing with indignation with every word. By accident or intention, the heavy stick threatened to strike anyone standing in front or behind him. Warwick looked angry enough to hit someone with it or, alternatively, to have a heart attack. Either way, it wouldn't be easy to send Warwick off. Lund sighed and began to descend the ornate stairs from the second floor to the lobby.

"They will tell me where my money has gone! I want to see my manager! I want to see Niels Rask!" Warwick caught the cane by the handle and struck the metal tip against the floor. The sound rang out like a shot across the lobby. Those bank customers who hadn't already stopped to look did so now. Transactions slowed to a halt.

Lund lengthened his stride, leaving his hat on a clerk's desk with one hand, smoothing back his hair with the other. He wove between the tellers to the small gate, opening it without looking down. He caught the clerk's eye. Jensen's relief to see Lund was so obvious Warwick spun around.

"Going to shut me up, are you?" The man was small, a head shorter than Lund with a slim build. From a distance, he looked like a stick a child could snap in half. Up close, the impression shifted. Warwick pulsed with a fit of quick, dark anger, veins standing out against the white of his hands, the compact muscles under his suit jacket moving like wire whips. "I want to see my accounts, right this very instant." Warwick's lips were wet with spit, his eyes wild with determination. "Someone's been stealing from me! I want to know who it was!"

The lobby held an eerie silence considering the number of people who occupied it. "I can have the books brought down, Mr. Warwick." Jensen held the distance between himself and Warwick with a wary firmness. "Our policy is accommodating regarding a review of the accounts. Although I can assure you personally, the books are in perfect order, as I looked at them myself just yesterday."

"I doubt that very much!" Warwick boomed. "You're a pack of thieves is what you are!"

A gasp rose from the crowd of bank customers lined up at the teller counter. It was past time to remove the man. Stepping alongside Warwick, Lund firmly took the arm holding the cane by the elbow. "Mr. Warwick," he gestured up toward Jensen's office door, "let's have a seat where we can discuss the matter comfortably."

Warwick pulled his arm away sharply, pivoting to glare at Lund. "Who the devil are you?"

Lund leaned down to whisper in the man's ear. "I'm the devil who will kick your arse into the street if you don't stop shouting." He straightened, adding with pleasant deference, "Would you come this way?"

"You wouldn't dare!" Warwick's eyes narrowed as he considered Lund, then Jensen. Lund spread his feet, his hands clasped in front of him as he shared the cheerless grin that haunted the dreams of Shanghai street criminals. Warwick blanched. Without another word, he strode past the tellers toward the stairs leading to Jensen's office, Jensen following quickly behind.

Lund exhaled. The lobby noises returned, occupants picking up their conversations where they had left off a moment before. Lund's eyes rose to a figure on the balcony. Rask stood with his hands on the carved balustrade, looking as much like Lund's commanding officer as ever. Niels jerked his head toward Jensen's office. Nodding once, Lund followed Warwick and Jensen.

"I HAD THE BOOKS BROUGHT up when I got your call this morning, Mr. Warwick. I've had a look at them myself." Jensen had brought them to the room the other clerks called the Library—for the quiet of the room, not for the number of books. The Library was spare and soundless, fitted with a long table where clerks could spread out the huge ledgers that accounted for hundreds of daily transactions. Jensen had arranged four such books, each open to a different account. "Of course," Jensen began, "I haven't had the opportunity to go through them as thoroughly as I would like, but the last three weeks are perfectly clear."

Warwick narrowed his eyes. "I have only the top accountants at my factory. They tell me you've lost ten thousand dollars of my money. I'm no fool, so don't take me for one! I have a firm handle on my money, and don't you forget it!"

Jensen gave a gentle cough. "I understand, Mr. Warwick. Operation of an account your size can sometimes cause confusion. I can assure you that everything is in order. A letter requesting a transfer of one thousand came four days ago. Your lawyer, a Mr. Gilmurray, made the request."

Warwick sputtered with anger, his face turning the dark

color of a plum. "Gilmurray?" He choked on the name, his body rigid with anger. The walking stick fell from his hand with a clatter. Lund caught him by the elbow before he fell, lowering him down into the chair as Jensen looked on in horror.

"Are you all right?" Lund asked.

Warwick nodded, yanking his arm from Lund's hand. "On whose authority did you move that money? If you can't tell me, you can be damn sure you'll be saying it to my attorney!" Warwick resumed his shout, his breath loud and shallow.

"But I told you . . ." Jensen looked from Warwick to Lund and back. "Mr. Gilmurray is a listed signatory on the accounts," he insisted. "It was all perfectly acceptable. He has the power to move the money but not to withdraw it. It was all within the boundaries you established with your accounts." Jensen looked as uncertain as Lund had ever seen him, shifting from one foot to the other, a light sweat breaking out on his forehead.

"If it—" Warwick had to stop and start again. "If the money was moved, it can be moved back." As he spoke, his volume grew until he was shouting as loudly as Lund had ever heard a man. "I expect you can do that much, can't you?"

"But, Mr. Warwick, I thought you understood," Jensen continued, only the slightest waver in his words. "The accounts were overdrawn. The bank must reconcile the balance per your earlier requests. There's less than two hundred dollars left."

It was too much for Warwick to take. He banged his fist

against the table. With a roar, he tried to stand. "Damn that woman! She'll be the death of me!"

He fainted dead away.

3

Penelope had thought the home charming when viewed from the street. Once inside, the narrow townhouse closed in around dozens of society women in extravagant hats, their hands busy with tea and small sandwiches. A racket of "Oh yes, dear!" and "What do you say?" and "Did you know?" rose like a cloud of smoke over her head. The crowd around them was so close that Penelope had to draw her arms in to hold her purse closer to herself. The strap of the reticule pulled at her wrist, the fabric strained by the weight of the .22 she took with her everywhere. She shouldn't have brought it, had tried to leave it at home, but she hadn't been able to help herself. The gun had been locked away in its case for months before Renee was murdered. She looked around the room and wondered what she had to be afraid of here, surrounded by women softened by luxury.

"Loud, isn't it?" Mary asked. "I did try to warn you, remember?"

Penelope looked down at her cousin. "Are we late? The invitation said—"

"We aren't late." Mary looked around them with her

practical brown eyes. "I would say they haven't gotten to it yet." She took Penelope's arm. "Come on. Let's find a seat."

As Penelope looked around, she realized only opera could have tempted her to leave her apartment. A last-minute invitation to the Hudson Valley Operatic Society, and Penelope was soon exiting the building through the kitchens distracted by daydreams of floating harmonic voices.

Mary led her into a sitting room arranged around a large baby grand piano. Taken over by ladies drinking tea, the Edwardian parlor strained with detail. Cracked, aging oil paintings and lace handwork suffering from dry rot competed with yellowing marquee posters and faded watercolor sketches. The dark colors of the heavily fringed pillows and couches clashed with each other, not to mention with the women in their tea dresses, hats, and best jewelry. The mantel was a battalion of photographs large and small in ornate frames marching from one candlestick to another. A man approached the piano just as Mary scooted around a gaggle of bobbing hats to a small couch and set of chairs.

"Shouldn't we find our hostess?" Penelope's hand tightened around the reticule as the crowd pressed in around her.

"Here she is." Mary brightened. "Patsy Galton, may I introduce my cousin Penelope Harris?"

Penelope offered her hand before looking directly at her hostess. "A pleasure, I'm sure." Her eyes swept up to Patsy's face.

"A pleasure?" The deep voice challenged. "For whom?"

As she absorbed the disordered dress with wrists and shoulders too small for her arms, Penelope wondered briefly if Patsy had meant to wear such unflattering clothes or if she simply did not care about her appearance. Glittering jewels nestled in a chaos of necklaces around her neck and in rings on her short fingers. It was as though Patsy wore a costume, awkwardly trying to hide in plain sight. Penelope felt torn between respect and affront as she wondered idly if she would be as uncomfortable at fifty. A full two inches taller than Penelope, Patsy looked down at the petite Mary in her sophisticated suit and asked, "Is this the one that can sing?"

"Yes," Mary said dryly. "You might have read about her last month. All the newspapers picked that story up. It was at that terrible party." Mary skirted the subject of murder with a practiced step.

"Wasn't that your party, my dear?" Patsy, holding a teacup, appeared unruffled, neither angry nor happy. It struck Penelope that, under the many layers of discomfort, Patsy was bored.

Mary waved a hand and said good-naturedly, "If you think I'm going to take responsibility for a bunch of gatecrashers, you can think again." They sat down on the sofa, Patsy taking a chair beside them. "I've brought her along so you can have a look at her. What do you think, Patsy? Will she do?"

It dawned on Penelope that Mary thought she was helping her. "Mary, I think you might have misunderstood—"

"I hope you don't have your heart set on singing," Patsy interrupted. "I am quite overrun with sopranos this year. I have so many we've had to settle for *Tales of Hoffmann*."

Penelope felt an uncomfortable flush begin at her neck, her quick temper rising as she opened an eye to take a better look at this Patsy person. "I—"

"Penelope isn't looking for a role, Patsy," Mary continued, unperturbed. "She's interested in *students*." She put an emphasis on the word, letting it draw out. "She wants to teach."

"Teaching. Well, of course. That's different." Patsy's manner relaxed. She caught the eye of the nearest maid. "Miriam, get Miss Staughton and her cousin some tea and sandwiches, please. It makes sense now," she continued. "You've come to see what you're in for if you decide to make a go of teaching. You'll be disappointed. No one in this company is interested in learning how to really sing." Patsy leaned back against the chair, her girdle fighting her all the way until she sat forward again, exasperated. "The cast is terrible—but that's what you get when you manage these things by a committee. Of course, I did manage one small coup capturing Valentina Carrera for half an hour. No one thought I could do it, of course, but the woman is mad for money. She'll be arriving late in the program to sing the Barcarolle from *Hoffmann*. Or at least I hope she'll sing. Knowing our luck, she'll appear long enough to drink all the champagne, then leave."

"Carrera is performing?" Penelope did not hide her surprise. "The Barcarolle? Who will sing with her? The mezzo? Who is it?"

Patsy's air was distracted. "I'm not sure . . . Someone will, you can be certain. I told you, I have so many sopranos this year that I have hardly enough solos to fit them all out."

There was movement by the piano. A lithe, attractive man with the air of an Italian maestro made a production of arranging sheets of music as he glared out at the crowd of noisy women. A young girl stood uncomfortably just beyond him with her back against the wall, looking ill and out of place. The girl had a delicate beauty haunted by deep shadows under her eyes and lines around her mouth. Penelope was sorry for her. "Who is that?"

"I believe that's Ivy. Yes, that's her," Mary replied with happy confidence. "Now you'll see what the society is all about."

Patsy Galton snorted and took a long drink from her teacup. Penelope had the distinct impression it was not tea Patsy was drinking.

Penelope relaxed with her tea, and the talented pianist began playing an ornate fanfare. Ivy stood by in a dress much too large for her, her posture slack and unhappy. A pale green, the chiffon dress was more suited for March than November, making the poor girl look even more out of place. Ivy watched the pianist with a look that verged on fear, as though every note brought her closer to ruin. As Ivy began to sing, Penelope froze, reaching a stillness she did not think was possible outside of a coma. The girl was awful. What was worse—the child knew it. Ivy kept her eyes on the ornately painted ceiling, her jaw moving obediently as she slogged through the notes with joyless tedium, a sob on the verge of breaking out at any moment.

"What do you think of her?" Patsy's small white teeth bit neatly into a cucumber sandwich, then pushed the food to her cheek so she could continue her thought aloud. "Ivy needs rehearsal. That's why I made her go first. More time to get it right. She put her name in the draw. God knows why. I should have told her no. I couldn't tell you what got into her. Perhaps her mother made her." The soprano at the piano looked up sharply, then looked down again, blushing.

Penelope was sure the girl had heard what Patsy said. Patsy shrugged and continued, "A friend of mine thought Ivy had talent. I'm not sure now."

Dipping her hat so that it briefly hid her face from Patsy, Penelope stole a glance at her cousin. Mary met her glance with a happy forbearance and winked. Penelope angled her body toward Patsy, ready to deliver her verdict on the singing, only to find Patsy on her feet, her empty teacup abandoned on the table between them. Patsy's shoulders were set back, her right hand slowly gripping into a tight, bloodless fist.

"I won't stand for it, Patsy." The cold voice traveled over the singing, loud enough to make heads turn away from the piano. "I find it extraordinary that you thought I would."

"I can't imagine what you are referring to," Patsy replied with a frosty hauteur. "Ivy entered the lottery like everyone else. If she didn't want to sing, she should have told me weeks ago, when it was possible to replace her."

Mary put a hand on Penelope's knee and leaned forward to whisper, "That's Violet Warwick, Ivy's mother."

Penelope angled her head around Patsy's girth to have a better look.

Violet's emerald velvet suit was tailored within an inch of its life, the slope of the shoulder shouting to everyone that it had been cut just for her elegantly trim figure. She wore her hair in the loose finger waves that were so popular in the salon but impossible to maintain without determination or a maid or both. Penelope had considered the style a carefree one. On Violet, however, it was anything but. The waves were too perfect, too precisely aligned. Everything about Violet was too perfect, in fact, with the exception of her hands.

They were too large for her wrists, with large red knuckles. Penelope slowly absorbed everything about Violet, from the sapphire brooch on her lapel, to the fingernails bitten down to the quick, to the strict tailoring of her fashionable suit. She was beautiful at first impression, but each moment after that, the woman became by turns hard, then cold.

The notes from the piano stopped, all eyes and ears turning their attention to the duet of Patsy and Violet. Silence spread through the crowd.

Violet sniffed. "Clover tells me that you insist Ivy sing 'The Doll Song.' Even after she offered to take it on herself."

"That's right. Clover suggested Ivy was not up to it, and I disagreed." Patsy straightened, forcing the other woman to lift her chin. "Violet, may I introduce Penelope Harris? She is my guest today. Penelope, this is Violet Warwick."

"Oh yes," Violet's drawl was cold, "I heard you can sing." She did not offer her hand.

Penelope was inexplicably angry. She opened her mouth to fire back, but Patsy spoke first. "Yes, and a good thing too. Our little society could use some new blood. And in any case, Miss Harris teaches, which will be helpful for those of us who take our singing seriously." Patsy stared down Violet, her words level. "Ivy will be quite tolerable as Olympia with more rehearsal. I understand you haven't been allowing it. That's why I asked Ivy to go first. She must rehearse." Patsy's tone made it perfectly clear there would be no bargaining. "She will improve, and then we shall have all three girls take the stage."

Penelope turned to Mary. "Three?" She found it difficult to hide her surprise.

"I have three girls, Miss. Harris." Violet turned to look Penelope over. "Is that a Chanel? Or a copy?" She swept Penelope up and down with a bored sigh. "I can never tell."

"You should watch what you say to people, Violet," Patsy said smoothly. "You'll give the impression you're nothing better than a society bitch at a kennel—all for show."

"You insufferable cow!" Violet's skin flushed an unattractive red, bringing the green in her eyes down to a dull brown.

"Some women aren't meant to be mothers." Patsy's words rang clearly over the stillness in the room, and in her voice Penelope recognized the skill of a soprano used to singing over the power of a full orchestra. The way the two women were squaring off, Penelope was certain they were about to come to blows.

A plump young woman with a pretty, round face and flushed cheeks appeared at Violet's elbow. "Mama?" she whispered. The girl looked over her shoulder at the crowd of active listeners around them. "Shall I call the car?"

"Go away, Tulip." Violet shifted her shoulders, cutting her daughter out of her view. "I won't have it, Patsy Galton. We've done our fair share for the society over the years! We've certainly given you enough money!"

Patsy replied clearly, "One aria per soprano, Violet. It is how things have always been. If Ivy cannot sing, I will cut the aria from the program. We have too many as it is."

"When Clover could easily sing all three!" Violet complained in a high, loud voice. "It's jealousy, that's what it is! You know she was meant to be on the stage."

Patsy lifted an eyebrow. "Clover should audition at the 300

Club, then. I hear they're always looking for new talent!" There was a hiss of indrawn breath from the crowd around them.

"You've lorded over us for too long!" Violet spat. "Mark my words: things are going to change soon—and you won't like them! I've been to the board!"

Penelope felt a light touch on her elbow as Mary stood up. Mary nodded to where a heavyset woman in a feathered hat made her way through the crowd. "Look who's here," she whispered.

"What on earth is happening?" Penelope heard someone behind the couch ask.

"That's exactly what I'd like to know." Mrs. Anthony Stone, the scourge of the society set, arrived with an alcoholic blotch on both cheeks and a swagger. "What on earth is happening here?"

4

MARY RUSHED THROUGH THE ROOMS, Penelope following behind her as quickly as she could.

The crowd around them shifted and grumbled as it made way for a small, round woman dressed entirely in puce, from the tip of her too-small hat to the tips of her dyed-to-match shoes. "Make way for the press, dearies!"

"Oh no!" Mary took Penelope by the arm and led her away, into the crowd. "That's all Papa needs, for me to get my name in the paper—again."

Penelope stiffened. "Is that . . . ?"

"Blast!" Mary swore under her breath. "Patsy didn't say anything about having the press on!" Mary steered Penelope through the crowd with a quick and determined step. "There's nothing for it. You'll have to hide until I find Parker and tell him to bring the car around."

Penelope looked at the crowd surrounding them. She could hardly find a wall, let alone somewhere to hide. "Hide where?"

"If there is one woman in the world who doesn't deserve a scoop, it's that dreadful Mrs. Stone!" Mary hustled them through the guests like a tiny bulldozer until they reached a door. Wrenching it open, she said, "Wait in here until I knock. We'll have to make a dash for it."

A smash came from the sitting room as if a dozen teacups had been thrown to the ground.

Mary turned toward the sound and swore. "Did you hear that? The china! Violet Warwick—that horrible woman!" She pushed Penelope through the door and pulled it shut.

"I SUPPOSE YOU COULDN'T BOTHER TO KNOCK."

Penelope's breath caught in surprise, her heart in her throat. She turned around slowly to find Ivy Warwick sitting on the floor near the toilet, the billowing tulle skirt in bunches around her feet.

"I shouldn't be surprised. Mama says most people have the manners of a baboon picking its ass."

The profanity took Penelope by surprise. From the look on the child's face, Ivy expected it to. "She's usually right." Ivy's brown eyes glared up from her position on the floor.

Penelope exhaled ruefully. It was just her luck to be stuck in the WC with an overemotional teenager. Plastering a smile on her face, Penelope tried hard not to be the type of adult she had hated so much when she had been the same age. "I'm sorry," she said. "I didn't know it was occupied." Her hand fumbled for the doorknob.

"No, wait!" The girl sniffed into her handkerchief, wiping mascara across her face. "If you open the door, they'll know I'm in here." She wiped her nose on the back of her hand. "You're Penelope Harris, aren't you?"

Penelope nodded. "That's me. Your name is Ivy, isn't it?" Putting her reticule down carefully on the sink, Penelope looked at her hat in the mirror. Bless the milliner who understood her curly hair! She tucked one wayward curl back under the hat and glanced at the girl in the mirror's reflection. "Have you been here long?" She absentmindedly made repairs to her lip rouge.

"Patsy saw you sing," Ivy replied. "At that party. The one where the girl died." She sniffed loudly, began to wipe her nose with the back of her hand again, thought better of it, and blew her nose into her limp handkerchief.

"Of course she did," Penelope said with exasperation. "Half of New York society saw me sing." Unable to help herself, Penelope looked about until she found a hand towel and gave it to the girl. "Your mascara needs fixing."

There was a loud snuffle in response. "My sister Clover said you sang without warming up or anything." Disappointment and misery stood out all over the girl as she slumped into the skirt of her dress. "You must have been blotto. Were you?"

Penelope controlled herself with difficulty. It followed her everywhere she went—that damn party. She leaned a hip against the sink, crossed her arms, and took a good look at the girl. "I was not blotto, as you so sweetly put it. Nor was I picking my ass like a baboon." Penelope saw the girl had enough sense to blush. "Were you there too?"

"Tulip went with Clover to the party. They left me at home with *her*." Ivy glared at the back of the door. Her shoulders slumped, the neck of the dress gaping open at the collar. Where Violet's clothes were tailored to her, this girl's must have come from one of her sisters. Ivy muttered, "I bet no one tells you what to do. What are you doing here? You can't tell me it's for the music." Youthful misery dripped from every word. "I would rather be anywhere but here. I hate everything."

"It's not as bad as that." Penelope repeated the platitude despite knowing that it was exactly as bad as that for every girl with a mother like Violet Warwick.

Ivy's lower lip trembled. "I hate parties. Everyone pays attention to the wrong things. No one wanted to hear me sing. No one stopped to listen. Not even Patsy. She just sat there and spoke to you. Even Mama!" Pushing herself up, Ivy stood unsteadily, her dress hanging like a sack from her thin shoulders. Penelope had the oddest sensation that the room shrank to half its size. "She said all that, and I was standing right where I could hear her! Even you! You were talking with Patsy while I sang!"

"We were talking about your voice, as a matter of fact."

Penelope didn't know why she was determined to make the girl feel better. "Patsy told me she thought you had some talent." The lie came very easily.

"She didn't say that." Ivy stared at her without blinking. "Patsy doesn't like me—she wouldn't say I was good. She hates me, in fact. Hates me like poison."

"Patsy didn't say anything like that to me. She said you were recommended to her by a friend who said you were talented."

"I've caught you lying." There was no emotion in Ivy's flat delivery. She stood close enough for Penelope to feel her breath against her neck. Penelope willed herself to be still, but it didn't matter. With the door at her back, there was nowhere to go. Ivy stared at her silently. When she spoke, the words came slowly. "I can't sing, can I? You can tell me. I don't care. Not really. Mama's right. She always is, anyway. Clover will have all three by the end of the week, you'll see."

"What could you mean?" Penelope asked. "All three what?"

There were three quiet taps on the door. "Ivy, are you in there?" Penelope recalled the plump young woman who stood at Violet Warwick's elbow, blushing through the argument with Patsy. "Mama says it's time to go. You know how she is if she has to wait."

Ivy put her finger to her lips.

Penelope sighed. "No," she called out with forced cheerfulness, "no one here but us chickens. Just another minute."

"I'm so sorry!" The voice faded away.

Penelope pushed up her hat, uncovering an ear and putting it to the door. The steady muttering of the party had resumed, although the piano had not. Penelope straightened. She hadn't been much older than Ivy when she had taken the first opportunity to escape the boredom of youth and eloped. The realization softened her.

"If you are serious about your singing, you should practice." Penelope removed a card from her bag, handing it to Ivy. "The manager at our hotel has a room with a piano he lets me use from time to time." She smiled. Ivy met her eye briefly before looking away. "If you can tolerate me sight-reading the piano music, maybe I could help you with your solo."

Ivy held the card between two fingers, stared at it with an unreadable expression. "I told you. It doesn't matter now. I don't care. Clover can have it."

Penelope fixed her hat and opened the door, slipping out quickly, then shutting it behind her. She began her search for Mary and their driver, confident she would never see Ivy again.

5

"I WONDERED WHERE IVY HAD PUT HERSELF! Violet was ready to leave her if Tulip hadn't found her. All I can say is thank goodness it was Ivy and Tulip who came along to sing and not Clover." Mary sat back into the town car's leather seat with a happy sigh. "Clover's a menace! She would have stood up to sing and never sat down again. Although Clover can actually sing, so I suppose it wouldn't have been so bad."

"So there are three sisters?"

"Yes, Clover, Ivy, and Tulip. Ivy is the worst kind of child. Ill-behaved. Well, you saw, didn't you? Her mother knows it too—keeps sending her away to finishing school. She must have just gotten back. Tulip would be the best of the three if she could just buck herself up. At least Ivy got to go away. Tulip had to stay behind and look after her mother. I see her from time to time volunteering at the library. She's nice."

"Only nice? Not the best recommendation, Mary darling."

"You'd know how high a recommendation it was if you met Clover." Mary lowered her voice. "Clover Warwick positively has the very worst temper I've ever seen. Last year she attacked one of her housemaids with a shoe. The maid lost an eye. I was certain she was going to be arrested that time—"

"That time?"

"—but she wriggled out of it again. Everyone said her father bought the maid off. Roger Warwick must have done something, because the girl had an uncle in the police. I was so certain Clover would be charged!"

"Mary, that simply cannot be true! You can't just assault a maid and get away with it!"

"Connie Whitman volunteers at the hospital and saw the maid after it happened. She said Clover could have killed her. Good lord!" Mary put a hand to her mouth. "I hope she didn't die. I hadn't thought of that. But surely I would have heard . . ."

"Are you telling me that Clover Warwick, who everyone knows almost beat her maid to death with a shoe, is singing at a society gala with Valentina Carrera? How is that possible?"

"Violet Warwick has spent thousands on Patsy's production to get Clover the best solo. Patsy says it's a drawing, you know—so everyone gets a fair chance. But everyone knows it's not. It always comes down to money, one way or another," Mary said with a sage nod. "I do wonder what happened to the maid." A furrow appeared on her brow. "I see how unfair it all was now. No one would have hired her afterward, you see. It would have upset Clover. No one upsets Clover. She retaliates. I suppose it's a good thing her father is only in manufacturing. If it had been lumber or coal . . ."

"What on earth do you mean by that?" Penelope's head was spinning with all the social rules she didn't know. Running a casino in Shanghai had been easier than learning the hierarchy of New York society. The rules guiding the criminal class had been as straightforward as they come. "Why would it make a difference where he makes his money? Isn't it all the same money?"

Mary was aghast. "It's well and good to have money when no one else does, but you can't swan about without a care in the world when everyone knows you made your packet manufacturing cheap wire hangers. I'll never use them, and I don't know anyone who would. Charles says it's just a piece of wire tied up in a knot. Can you imagine? I tell you this, Penelope: Clover can work as hard as she wants to get an invitation from an Astor, but she never will. High society won't have anything to do with something as low as a wire hanger—even if it is clever. I bet you Clover would leave town and change her name if she could, just to get away from it." She blushed. "I can barely stand to see a woman like Clover Warwick stalking about in her lovely clothes straight from the salon while I have to let my maids go—" She broke off, looked away.

Penelope took Mary's hand. "Darling, you've been going a hundred miles an hour since you picked me up this morning. What has happened?"

Mary's face pinched into a grimace. "Oh, Penelope! Papa says we must do for ourselves for now. I can't think why except that we've lost all our money! Why else would he send away all the servants?" Mary opened her purse and brought out a handkerchief. "This is the last week for the cook. I shall have to learn how to boil coffee and fry eggs. It can't be hard, can it?"

It occurred to Penelope that Mary did not understand what being broke really meant. She considered the near-steady society paper coverage of Mary's brother's excessive drinking. Perhaps her uncle was simply getting the staff out of the house while Charles dried out for a while. Uncle Harry didn't suspect anyone as much as he did housemaids. It was easy to believe he had let them go to stop the steady stream of family gossip. As for the cook, he had been complaining about her scrambled eggs to anyone who would listen at least since Penelope had arrived in New York two months before. And Mary herself was out of control regarding her spending. She had consoled herself during the onslaught of bad press with a shopping spree that included six new hats, elaborate luggage (in case she decided to take a trip), and a mink, according to the society page of the *Sentinel.* Cutting her off from the maids was likely Uncle Harry's way of teaching Mary a lesson about self-reliance—or at least coaxing her into making her own bed.

"Making coffee is not hard at all, Mary darling. I'll show you." Penelope squeezed Mary's hand. "We used to make pots and pots of it at the Jade Tiger. You have to stay awake somehow. And eggs? Eggs are the perfect breakfast when you have a slice of bread to roll them up in. Nothing quite like hot eggs at one o'clock in the morning when you're in between sets and can't sit down in your dress."

"Will you? How nice. Papa says it won't be too much longer." Mary wiped her face and looked away out the window. "I should have followed up on the girl—Clover's maid, I mean. Made sure she was all right."

Penelope took Mary's hand. "Why don't you come home with me today? Mother would love to see you. I could teach you how to make coffee." Penelope smiled.

"No students making the most of your time?"

Penelope shook her head. "I had two little girls before the party, delightful children. We had hardly begun when the newspapers carried the story about that night . . . that party—" Penelope broke off. "You know how it is. Who would want their children to be taught by a woman who at best was a notorious nightclub owner and at worst was a murder suspect?"

"But that's not who you are," Mary protested. "What about auditions?"

"It's hopeless, Mary—you know it is! The only teacher willing to take me on would be counting on the newspaper coverage, and that's something none of us need right now. No, I will just keep working at finding students until I have enough to help pay the bills. We have some savings. It will last us. And James will help as soon as he graduates from medical school. It will work out." Penelope hid her doubt under a smile. "Will you come up?"

"No, I mustn't," Mary said ruefully. "We have the opera tonight—oh, Penelope, I completely forgot!" She sat up. "Patsy must like you, my dear. She has given us tickets to see Valentina Carrera at the Metropolitan Opera! Tonight!"

6

Mary must have been nervous. She hadn't stopped talking since Parker picked Penelope up at the Excelsior. A stream of harmless gossip and society observations flowed freely as they traveled uptown to the Metropolitan Opera. In the darkness of the Daimler's back seat, Penelope held her hands together to keep herself calm, valiantly resisting the urge to lean over the middle seat and stare up at the magnificent building as it came into view. If she couldn't resist an operatic society tea party, how could she possibly resist the lure of the Metropolitan Opera? It was Mary who suggested they avoid the well-lighted street entrance complete with red carpet and a crowd of photographers. "It's the photographers, Penelope. They'll fall over themselves to get a picture of you."

Penelope shuddered, pulling her borrowed opera coat close. "Are we sneaking in the back way?"

"There is no back way into the Metropolitan," Mary proclaimed with exaggerated hauteur. "But there might be a way around the photographers if we're lucky. You can drop us here, Parker." Mary scooted across the back seat, opening the back door herself, much to Parker's astonishment, and stepped out of the car.

Penelope leaned forward across the seat. "Parker, do the photographers know this is the Staughton car?"

"They might," he admitted.

"Could you stay in the line until you reach the red carpet, stop, and open the door as though we are in the back seat?" Penelope lifted her voice hopefully.

Parker tipped his hat. "Of course, miss."

Penelope smiled and slipped out of the back seat to stand next to Mary on the sidewalk. Her eyes swept up the plain building rising eight stories above them. It didn't look like the outside of any opera house she had ever seen before. For a moment, she wondered if they were in the right place.

Mary took her arm. "Have you ever done anything like this?"

"Like what?" Penelope watched the photographers as the cars moved up the line.

"Gone to the theater alone."

Penelope was at a loss for words. She had done a dozen things young society women weren't supposed to—driven a car, sung jazz, operated a casino, eloped. Most nights in Shanghai she had run the Jade Tiger from the casino floor, Kinkaid too drunk or too bored to cope with the day-to-day attention the business needed. She had done so many things on her own that it was hard to list them all. While her cousin, she realized, had likely never gone anywhere without a male escort—unless it was a tea party or a fashion salon.

Mary blushed. "You've probably done this a dozen times at least. Silly of me."

"Mary Staughton! I'm not that jaded." Penelope put her nose in the air and intoned, "Young lady, you are not allowed to go to the opera alone! Your brother will be happy to take you." She hoped urgently Mary didn't notice her crossed fingers.

Mary giggled happily. "Does James like the opera?"

"He loathes it." Penelope smiled at the thought of her brother. Parker was almost at the front of the line, the Daimler slowly nearing the photographers gathered around the red carpet.

"Parker's still in the line!"

"Yes," Penelope kept her eyes on the car, "because I asked him. Let's wait here and watch." They edged closer to the shadow of the building. Whispering began as the Daimler closed in. The photographers got ready, each hoping to get the jump on the others. But they were too orderly, Penelope thought. She and Mary would need a bigger distraction to cover their entrance. She thought fast. It wasn't so long ago there had been a paid bounty on a photo of Penelope or Mary. Rumors persisted that there still was. "Say," she called out "isn't that the Staughton car?" The effect was immediate. Just as Parker rolled up to the carpet, the photographers rushed to get nearer to the car door, spilling onto the red carpet and knocking over the brass stations holding the rope. As the photographers pushed past one another trying to get the shot, the cousins edged around the crowd and slipped through the door, cutting off the noise and exhaust from the street as it closed behind them. They stepped up one of the carved marble staircases on either side of the entrance and into the hushed golden light of the interior.

SAFELY INSIDE, THEIR COATS WITH the hatcheck, Penelope and Mary basked in the glow of the beautiful chandeliers. Where the outside of the Metropolitan had been plain, the interior was bathed in luxury. Chandeliers hung from ornately carved gilded mounts spreading seraphim across the ceiling. The walls were covered in red silk, printed with a repeating pattern of flowering vines forming a crest. Wide-paned paladin windows overlooked the street, well above the press cameras' aim. Penelope sighed with happiness, the Metropolitan fulfilling every childhood dream she had allowed herself.

"You're going to cause an accident in that dress, Penelope." Mary giggled. "And I think you know it."

"I did wait to take off the coat until we were inside," Penelope replied sweetly. "Easier on the bumpers." She did not look down at her dress. The gold was a daring choice for the opera. In any other theater, the shimmering gold and bias cut would have set her apart. But for the first time since moving to New York, Penelope wasn't out of place. If people stared, it was from admiration, not curiosity. She was past the press, ready to take her seat to see the greatest soprano of her time, at one of the most beautiful opera houses in the world. She realized with a jolt she was exactly where she belonged.

Just to be sure they were clear of photographers, she turned back to look down at the street entrance one last time. There was something, a shadow of someone tall. For a moment she was certain she had seen Lund. Her heart quickened before she caught herself. What on earth would he be doing at the opera? She shook herself free from the longing before it had a chance to grip her. He wouldn't be alone. And seeing the woman Lund brought to see Carrera would be too much to bear. Part of her wanted to hide, the other part wanted to burst into song. Penelope grappled with her emotions the only way she knew how—studious avoidance. Taking Mary's arm, she led her cousin deeper into the lobby, away from the doors and the traffic and away from Lund. "Mary, do you see anyone you know we could talk to?" She would have a conversation with a newel post if it got her away from being polite to Lund's date.

"My dear, we are surrounded by people I know. But none of them will talk to us. It's the murder, you see." Mary looked around as they sped down the hall into a larger chamber. "Please slow down. Your legs are much longer than mine!"

"I'm sorry." Penelope came to a stop. "I'm just excited, I suppose. Carrera!"

"Carrera!" Mary smiled. Looping her arm through Penelope's, she asked, "Where on earth do you find a dress like that?"

"My guess is Shanghai, am I right?" A lean brunette with a wicked jaw cut in between them. "The Paris of the East!"

"Helen!" Penelope embraced the journalist warmly, her happiness quick and easy.

Helen Mayfield kissed Penelope on both cheeks and smiled. "Talk about cutting it close. Gil couldn't be sure of the tickets until late this afternoon." Every word she spoke had the air of rapid dictation. "One of his society gals came through at the last minute." Helen's cropped dark brown hair complemented her puckish face and small nose. Taking Penelope and Mary each by the arm, she serenely escorted them across the carpeted floor toward the gilded molding of a window. "I'm counting on you two to give me all the goods on high society. My career is counting on it!"

"Still on the society column, then? How are things at the *Sentinel* these days?" Mary asked, concern putting a familiar wrinkle between her plucked eyebrows.

"Don't give me that look, Mary!" Helen laughed. "A girl has to make money for herself, doesn't she? The holiday season is just around the corner, and my editor wants me back to my bread and butter. Even if I stumbled across the murdered corpse of Mayor Jimmy and had the killer by the ear—" She broke off. "Well, let's just say my chances of getting off the society beat are nil."

"Are you working this evening?" Penelope did her best not to catch Mary's eye, keeping her voice carefully light.

"Lord no!" Helen laughed again. "It is my official evening off! Truth be told, that's only because I didn't tell my editor what Gil had in mind. If he knew I was here, he'd have me on her." Helen's voice took on a lower register as she nodded in the direction of a gaggle of women in Edwardian lace and sparkling diamonds.

Penelope recognized the back of Patsy just as the older woman turned into the room, revealing an upright tiara holding court in a mass of stiff curls, lipstick too bright for her large mouth, and a length of pearls that reached her full waist.

"Just look at her." Helen wrinkled her nose. "Looks like she's wearing everything she had in the vault." She continued almost as though she was speaking to herself, "My editor thinks she's bitten off a little more than she can chew with this year's gala for the opera guild. It's set for the first Saturday in December and usually kicks off a bit of a run of parties.

But this year . . . well, it's the Metropolitan, really. They've loaned her Valentina Carrera, which means everyone wants to have a go at being on the same stage." Helen shook her head. "It must have cost a fortune! You never know what's going to happen at one of those luncheons. For example, I heard there was something of a brawl at the Hudson Valley Operatic Society earlier today." Her smile was merry.

"Really?" Penelope allowed the air of shock.

"I know you were there." Helen narrowed her eyes. "A nosy do-gooder told me the Shanghai songbird had been along to see about breaking into the top tier of society."

Mary gasped. "That's a lie! She was there to talk to Patsy about endorsing her as a teacher!"

Penelope took a breath, but before she said a word, Helen waved a hand. "Now take it easy, Penelope dear. I wouldn't worry too much about what these heartless society ladies say. Frankly, once they find out you're taking students, you'll be beating them off with a stick. In any event, it was probably some matron who heard you were good and was angling to protect her solo." Helen smiled. "Want me to put an ad in the paper for you?"

Penelope felt a cold shudder. "Via the latest society column? Thank you, Helen, no." Another headline and any willing students would be gone for months, maybe for good.

"Lord and lightning, girls!" Helen struck her palm with a fist and narrowed her eyes. "I need a story to break! Not more society gossip. A real story—that's what I'm interested in. Just one more chance to prove I can move to the city desk!" She leaned in close to Penelope. "You wouldn't hold out on me, would you?"

"Me?" Penelope squeaked. "There is nothing about me that would interest your readers. My life couldn't be duller. All I seem to do is give singing lessons and read books. And there aren't many lessons these days, just books."

"You keep saying that," Helen said with suspicion. "Seems to me that hasn't been exactly proved out yet. Lucky for you I want my big break to be a splashy headline in three-inch letters, or I'd be digging into your past on the double. In any case, my editor says you're played out. He's more interested in Patsy Galton than he is in you."

"Why is your editor interested in Patsy?" Penelope tried not to sound too eager to change the subject. "She seems pleasant enough."

"He can't give up his itchy palms. He's had them ever since Coralee died. Never grew out of his sense of the dramatic."

"Coralee?" Penelope cocked her head to one side.

"Would you look at that?" Helen stopped in her tracks, nodded toward the doorway.

Coming through, her head up like a regal matriarch, Violet Warwick floated forward, every inch of her glittering in the light. Penelope's first observation: Violet Warwick knew very well how to draw the attention of an audience. The second: the woman must bathe in money to have a dress like the one she wore. It was a Vionnet, had to be, the way it shimmered and moved in the light. The cut flattered every aspect of Violet. Her full outfit emphasized her elegance and class, all the way down to the diamanté buckle on her satin shoe. Violet knew it too. The way she moved put the dress to work drawing the attention of the people gathered around the entrance. Penelope heard herself say, "I'd kill for a dress like that."

"Who wouldn't?" Helen replied. "Rumor is she hides her dressmaker's bills in the mattress. From what I hear, Roger will never find them there." She winked.

Mary gasped. "Helen!"

"Is that him?" Penelope tore her attention away from the dress and nodded to the man who kept pace with Violet, a tallish man with dark hair.

"No," Mary and Helen said together, then looked at each other and giggled.

"Roger Warwick would dance on tables at the Ritz in his garters before he made an appearance at the opera," Helen declared. "That's John Gilmurray, Violet's very personal lawyer. His wife is just behind him walking next to Tulip."

Penelope found Tulip easily enough. The plump girl with spectacles looked around herself placidly, the same blank tolerance Penelope had noticed at the luncheon. "I can't see her," Penelope said. "I see Tulip, but . . ." Then she saw Mrs. Gilmurray, away from them with her back against the wall. Her black beaded gown drew out her paleness, emphasizing the dark circles under her eyes. Mr. Gilmurray walked ahead of her, his hand under Violet Warwick's elbow. "Poor thing," Penelope said.

"Roger never comes to these things," Mary continued. "Thinks they are a waste of money. But Violet? She will never pass up an opportunity to be the center of attention. She goes to all the right parties, all the right social events."

As Penelope's attention drifted, she caught Ivy's eye. Reflex made her smile. Ivy grimaced and looked away.

"The things they let that child wear." Helen shook her head. "Look at her! None of it fits at all."

As they watched, Ivy corrected a falling shoulder only to have the other side slip down.

"I met her earlier today," Penelope began. "She seemed lonely—"

"Lonely?" Helen snorted. "I shouldn't wonder. Violet is continually sending her away. This is the first time I've seen her in public in months. I don't know very much about Ivy. But Tulip's not so bad. She reads, I know that much. I'll take it easy on any society girl that carries a book around with her, just so you know. Tulip has nothing to fear from me."

Penelope glanced at Mary, who was absorbing every word with a seriousness that made Penelope wonder if she was about to have her library card renewed. "Violet and Roger Warwick are the type of people I put in my column," Helen said. "And I don't feel bad about it at all."

Penelope caught the bright flash of a quick smile, and Tulip was moving across the room, coming straight for them.

"Oh dear," Helen whispered. "Prepare for boarding."

"Penelope Harris?" Tulip smiled even as she spoke. "Don't tell me I'm wrong, because Ivy told me who you were, and she doesn't lie."

"And you are Tulip Warwick." Penelope smiled back. "My cousin Mary was just telling me you have a lovely voice."

"Isn't that nice? Thank you, Mary." Tulip blushed. "I can't stay long, but I had to say thank you for being so kind to Ivy."

"I barged in on her, to be honest," Penelope demurred. "I wouldn't have blamed her if she had shouted the roof down."

"She said you offered to help her with her singing. It was

so kind. You'll have to forgive me, but not many people give Ivy a second glance, let alone are kind to her."

A strange sort of magic was at work in the lobby of the Metropolitan, with its red carpet and red silk walls. Penelope's defenses were down completely. "It was nothing," she replied. "We were all her age once. I think I must have given my mother fits." Fits, yes indeed, a small voice in the back of her head reminded her—fits, fights, false starts, until finally an elopement with the worst possible type of man. "It doesn't take much effort to be kind."

"It is for Mama, you see," Tulip continued. "They don't get along. It's the age difference, don't you think? I keep telling Clover that any minute Ivy's going to be a little less trouble, Mama is going to unbend and be a little more loving, and it will all be so peaceful that it will be like nothing ever happened. Oh!" Tulip gasped. "I've said too much. Listen to me prattle on!"

"Of course not, Tulip." Mary smiled. "Think nothing of it."

"You should have seen her this afternoon. Meeting you was all she could talk about! It's good to see her excited about something. Lessons could be just the thing." Tulip looked over her shoulder to where Violet Warwick held court. "I must get back before she misses me." She put out her hand. "I'll ring you. Perhaps we could discuss your fees?"

"Of course." Penelope felt strangely warm toward the girl. She squeezed her hand. "I'm sure we can work something out."

A rising sound came through the crowd like a current shifting the tide. Heads turned toward the door. At first uncertain what to expect—the newest dress or perhaps a scandalous pairing of an artist and his newest model—Penelope was surprised to discover the cause of the disruption was a small man dressed in a tuxedo just a hair too large for him, looking about himself with small, mean eyes that clearly evoked a rat baring its teeth. People stepped out of his way, clearing a path across the opulent red room to where Violet stood with her hand hooked through Gilmurray's elbow. He stopped not ten feet away from Violet, lifted his arm to jab furiously with an index finger, and shouted, "I knew it! I knew I'd find you here!"

7

"VIOLET!" THE SOUNDS AROUND THEM faded as the little man bellowed, "I'd like to know where you found the guts!"

Other than the sudden white of Violet's cheek, Penelope could see no discernible change. "Roger," Violet removed her hand from the lawyer's arm, "what on earth are you talking about?" She glided across the thick red carpet to her husband. "Give me your arm, Roger. We can go in together."

"Guess I'm working tonight after all," Helen said.

The four women watched as Violet expertly handled Roger, moving him away from the stairs he blocked, back to Mr. and Mrs. Gilmurray and Ivy. Roger took up a position by his wife, her elbow cupped in his hand. Penelope thought Mrs. Gilmurray looked decidedly more interested now that Violet and her husband were so discomfited. She watched Roger Warwick like a hungry dog watches a food bowl. Beside her, Penelope felt Tulip tremble, the fingers Penelope still held turning cold.

"Gilmurray." Even though Warwick lowered his voice, the petulant growl still carried across the room easily. "I should have known you would be here." His eyes slid between Gilmurray and Violet. "With my wife."

There was a sharp intake of breath at Penelope's elbow. "Oh no," Tulip said under her breath. "Oh no."

The altercation took on the air of the sordid. Several patrons began moving toward the hallways leading into the belly of the Metropolitan. From a distance, Penelope thought they struck an odd group: Mrs. Gilmurray, her eyes shut, appearing to be willing herself away; Violet looking around herself, acting as though nothing was wrong; Gilmurray and Warwick standing across from each other like two prizefighters ready for the bell to ring. Just behind them, to the left, Penelope caught a glimpse of Ivy with her hand over her eyes, turning away from the room, her shoulders shuddering. Penelope's sudden connection with the mortified teenager was an almost painful jolt of adrenaline. Ivy's shame and embarrassment were palpable.

Mrs. Gilmurray tried to move away from the three of them, causing her husband to reach out and catch her by the elbow. He drew her closer with an awkward jerk.

"It was my wife's idea. Wasn't it, Virginia? She had the tickets bought before I could even whistle. Isn't that right, darling?" He smiled down at his wife and waited.

Virginia Gilmurray was balancing the variety of indignities available to her as her next words. It was perfectly obvious from across the room. Agree with her husband, and she would spend all night receiving Roger Warwick glares. Contradict her husband, and she would have to cope with his anger. Penelope looked from Gilmurray's hand on her elbow to his face, her fingers tightening around her purse until they ached.

Virginia's mouth compressed into a tight line, the black of her dress washing her skin out to the pallor of a corpse. John Gilmurray on one side of her, Roger Warwick on the other. She lifted her chin, staring Roger down. "You won't be wanting me," she said crisply. "I'll leave you to it, John." Then, wrenching her elbow from her husband's grasp, she disappeared into the crowd, the pink outline of her husband's fingers against her skin obvious from twenty feet away.

"I thought as much." Roger narrowed his eyes. "My wife bought you those tickets. I wouldn't mind so much if she hadn't spent my money on them."

Violet shook her husband's arm where she held it. "Roger, everyone can hear you."

"I've known for some time now that you had your eye on Violet, Gilmurray. I had you sized up from the first day we met." Roger leaned forward. "You can have her for all I care. It's the money I'm riled about. The money!"

Violet's smile remained, but an ugly pink began to creep up her neck. "Roger, you're drawing attention."

"Do you think I give a damn?" When Roger shouted, a porter on the stairs turned his head. "I've been to the bank!"

"Good God, man!" John Gilmurray stepped forward quickly and drew Roger aside, away from the crowd.

"How did you buy that dress? That's what I would like to know," Roger demanded. The little man stretched out an arm, his index finger jabbing in Violet's direction. "Didn't use your own money, did you? You couldn't, because you don't have any. It was mine! My money!" Focusing on John, Roger continued, "And you! You've been stealing from me for months! Maybe years!" He took John by his tuxedo lapels and shouted up into his face. "I'll have every red cent back and your license to practice law to boot! I'll own every bit of you, Gilmurray—right down to your custom-made shoes!"

What John Gilmurray's swing lacked in drama, it made up for in purpose. Before he knew it, Warwick was laid out on the red rug, shaking his head, wondering what hit him while Gilmurray stalked away in the direction of his wife, leaving Violet alone beside her husband.

"I . . ." Tulip began. "I have to go . . ." She hurried across the room, a pathetic figure in her worn dress. Walking a wide circle around where Violet could reach her, Tulip put an arm around Ivy and removed her down the nearest hallway. Tulip kept her head bent down to Ivy's ear. Just before they disappeared, Ivy shook herself free of her sister and sped forward without her.

"Poor Gil," Helen sighed.

"What is it?" Concerned, Mary put her hand on the woman's arm.

"He's been looking forward to giving me a solid dose of culture for months. I'll have to leave him here alone, and one of those society gals will have at him, I just know it!"

"I don't understand at all, Helen." Penelope shook her head. "What are you talking about?"

"I have to get downtown, don't I? To the paper. My editor will never let me live it down if he knows I saw the biggest scandal of the night unfold right in front of me and didn't write about it, will he?" Helen lifted herself up on her toes and tried to look over the heads around them. "Where did that man get to? Oh! Lund, just the man I need. Can you see Gil?"

"Penelope?"

She froze. The timbre of Lund's baritone made her bones quiver. There was barely a moment to brace herself before she turned. When she did, there would be a woman there beside him—a very nice woman, she told herself. Forcing down the urge to hide, she bolted on a smile and pivoted toward him. "Thom!" Keeping her eyes trained only on him, Penelope put out her hand. "How are you?"

8

LUND HAD SEEN HER FROM the mouth of the hallway. The gold dress carefully cut to flatter and drape in the most modern ways. In the bare light of day, the dress would have caused a riot, but here, surrounded by the gold fixtures of the Metropolitan Opera House and the opulent carpet and silk-lined walls, she belonged. In fact, Penelope Harris appeared to have arisen from the building itself. Lund walked toward her like a fish reeled in on a line, every step inevitable. She was standing with two other women, whom he acknowledged with vague interest that he hoped was polite. Helen and Penelope's cousin Mary, he thought. Helen seemed to be asking him something, but he couldn't concentrate. Why wasn't she turning around? Was she ill?

"Penelope?"

"Thom! How are you?"

Lund couldn't see any feature of her face except for her grey-blue eyes looking for, then finding him, meeting his stare with a sharp shock of heat. How long had it been since he had seen her in that dress? Standing on the stage at the Jade Tiger in much the same way? About to sing or having just sung? The audience at her feet, worshiping her? A year and a half ago, he thought. And she still looks the same to me, and maybe she always will. White-blonde hair wild around her head, her intelligent grey eyes reading his every thought. He was caught, captured. As surely as he had been from the first moment he met her.

He took her hand, turned it quickly, and kissed the smooth skin lightly. Did her fingers tighten? Had he imagined it?

"Lund," Helen put her hand on his arm, "do you have the time? Oh hell! Never mind that. Can you see Gil?"

Lund woke, released Penelope's hand. "I believe I saw him near the stairs . . ."

"That's good. Wait here." Helen sped to the stairs, her step quick.

"Are you alone?" Penelope asked without taking her eyes from him.

Mary giggled looking from Lund to Penelope. "Good to see you, Thom. You always seem to turn up in the most unusual places. Imagine seeing you at the opera." She leaned in. "Are you on a case?"

"No." He hesitated. "Well, yes."

"Can't talk about it? It's a secret, then?" Mary lifted an eyebrow.

"Niels, I mean Mr. Rask, gave me the tickets."

Penelope angled her head. "Tickets?"

"Yes, he thought—" He looked at Penelope and lost his words.

"Do you mean to say you have two tickets?" Mary concentrated on Lund. He could feel her willing him to answer. "Are you here with a guest?"

"No—I do, but I didn't—I mean to say, I thought—" He waited a moment, gathered his thoughts. "I had two tickets, but I left it too long."

"You're here all by yourself?" Mary frowned. "Where are you sitting? Let me see them."

He handed the tickets over and returned his attention to Penelope. "I did ring, but it was late. There was no answer, and I knew it wouldn't be enough time to—"

"Thom," Mary interrupted, "these tickets are in the orchestra. The best seats in the house." The look Mary was giving him was on par with that of a schoolmarm. "Do you mean to tell me you are going to sit directly in front of the stage, where Carrera can see you, where the whole opera house can see you, with an empty seat next to you?"

"Well, I . . ." He blinked.

"You can't." Mary insisted. "Not where everyone can see."

"I've found him." Helen reappeared, a disheveled Gil at her elbow. Lund remembered the vaudevillian pianist clearly from the Staughton party not a month before. He looked younger, or perhaps he was only more sober. If Lund's recollection was correct, Gilbert Richie had spent most of the party playing stunt tunes on the baby grand and rolling around on the floor. Helen continued, "Here, Gil, just like I promised—two unchaperoned, unmarried, and attractive women ready to hang on your every word for the rest of the night." She took in Lund. "Well, almost unchaperoned."

"Charmed." Gil looked from Penelope to Mary to Lund.

"You!" Mary stiffened, stretching herself from five feet one to five feet two and a half. "I remember you!"

"Oh dear." Gil reached for Mary's hand and patted it. Lund wasn't so sure this was a good idea. Mary Staughton might have been small in stature, but she appeared to have the temper of a Valkyrie. "I have this effect on people," Gil said. "They have mild hysterics when they see me. There doesn't seem to be anything I can do about it. It's my fame." He shared a comedic wink with Lund. "I'm sorry, darling girl," he said to Mary. "Did you send a private note? I haven't gotten it yet."

"A private note? You broke *two* strings on our piano!" Mary insisted. Lund was sure he heard her stamp her foot against the thick carpet.

"I?" Gil rested a hand on his chest with a lifted eyebrow. "Dear lady, I have no idea of what you speak." It was clear to everyone that he knew precisely.

"Mary," Penelope nudged her cousin, "Thom's extra ticket."

Mary's face flushed and set. Thom felt a sudden dread, certain he was about to find himself sitting next to the only man upon whom he would place a straight bet would rush the stage. "Yes," he said bravely, "of course. My extra ticket." There was no saying what would happen if he had to spend the entire opera next to the reigning musical comedian of New York City.

"Fine." Mary appeared to root herself to the carpet. Leveling Gil with a look of fury, she exhaled. "Thom has an extra ticket right in front. But if he gave it to you," she poked Gil in the chest, "I'm not sure you would be capable of behaving like a gentleman."

"Wait, Mary," Penelope gasped, "I didn't mean—"

"For seats in the orchestra, I can be a perfect and sober gentleman." Gil reached for Mary's hand and tried to kiss it.

"Oh no, not you." Mary removed her hand quickly, just stopping herself from swinging her bag at his head. "You don't deserve to sit where Carerra can see you. I've got your number, Gilbert Richie. Penelope, give me your ticket." Mary held out her hand. "Thom, you take Penelope with you. Gil," Mary steeled herself, "you are sitting with me."

Penelope's jaw went slack. "But Mary . . ."

"No, you go with Thom." Mary was firm. "I'm happier in the mezzanine. Really, I am. Go with Lund." She returned her attention to Gil. "You can be a gentleman, can't you?"

"You seem to be assuming I am interested in your seat." The Amazing Gilberto proceeded with deliberate humor. Lund had seen the man perform and could never be sure how he managed to make every other altogether innocent word into blanket innuendo. Even Gil's eyebrows could leer. "And where is this magnificent seat, if I might ask?"

"It's a better seat than you deserve, you scoundrel!" Mary's ears turned pink. "There's the bell. Now give me your arm."

Lund returned his attention to Penelope. "You'll have to explain it all to me, you know. Opera." He hoped his smile didn't appear as nervous as he felt. "I'm sure I will clap in all the wrong places."

She blushed. Lund was sure of it. He offered his arm and she took it.

"I BELIEVE THE RIGHT PLACE to start is with the sopranos. *Tales of Hoffmann* has three roles for a soprano, all three from Hoffmann's stories. There's the doll, the dutiful daughter, and the beguiling courtesan. Usually each role is played by a different soprano."

"But not tonight?" Lund guessed.

"No! Valentina Carrera will play all three roles." Penelope's face flushed with excitement as she spoke more quickly. "Not many sopranos could do it all in the same night." Women with their jewelry on prominent display lounged in luxurious velvet chairs, reaching over one another for the nearby ashtray. Men in tails and white ties spoke loudly with harsh barking noises of laughter. Lund led her to a wall where the smoke seemed less thick. She continued, "The opera opens in a bar. Hoffmann is quite drunk, and his friends tease him and chide him to tell them stories. So he does, growing more and more intoxicated as he expounds on the story of his broken heart. Olympia is a doll made by Spalanzani, a scientist. Coppélius, who worked to create Olympia, sells Hoffmann a pair of glasses that make the toy seem alive. He means it as a joke, you see, because Hoffman is so naïve about women."

"I can see where this is going."

"Of course, he falls in love with her! Just as Coppélius meant him to!"

"I take it that this beautiful doll sings."

"Oh yes, only one of the most difficult arias in opera. Olympia is a mechanical thing, so the musical joke is that she can hit the notes like a machine. The song also goes flat and out of key at the same time. Then the soprano has to come back to the right key and in tune almost straight away. It's tremendously challenging and quite funny if it's done right."

"I'm sure Offenbach was laughing up his sleeve at that one."

"Well, he was dead, so who can say?" She shrugged.

"Heartless woman! And what happens then? Does she blow up like a bomb or rob him blind or . . . ?"

Penelope laughed. "Always the policeman! Coppélius is so upset that he has been cheated by Spalanzani that he tears the doll to pieces as revenge."

"You see! A crime!"

"Hoffmann's magic glasses break, shattering his dream."

"That would be murder, or perhaps manslaughter?"

"Destruction of property, more likely. She was a mechanical doll, after all."

"Of course." He leaned his head back and crossed his arms as though deep in thought. "So our man Hoffmann falls in love with a doll, and she falls in with Bolsheviks and blows up, disappointing everyone. Story number one finished. What about story number two?"

"Antonia and Hoffmann love each other, but her father

doesn't approve. Her mother has died of a mysterious illness, which her father says Antonia also has. He forbids her from singing."

"I believe I can safely say that Antonia sings anyway," Lund said dryly.

"Antonia sings anyway," Penelope admitted. "But only after she is visited by the mysterious Dr. Miracle, who coaxes and flatters her until she cannot bear it any longer. She is driven to it. She must sing."

"This gentleman interests me."

"He also raises the spirit of her mother from the dead."

"Hmmm."

"And the spirit sings a duet with her daughter until she drops dead from the same mysterious illness that killed her mother."

Lund snapped his fingers. "Poison!"

Penelope was too transfixed to stop. "Act three," she began, "Hoffman tells the story of Giulietta, a courtesan who is pretending to love him on the orders of a mysterious Captain Dapertutto, who believes Hoffmann is incredibly naïve about women."

"This captain sounds vaguely familiar."

"Well, he is played by the same baritone who played Dr. Miracle and Coppélius. No production I've ever seen even attempts to disguise him. In fact, they play it up. The role is played like he is the devil torturing Hoffmann by destroying all his love interests," Penelope confided.

"Ah!" Lund exclaimed. "It becomes clearer."

"Captain Dapertutto convinces Giulietta to steal Hoffmann's reflection, which she does easily."

"What was her motivation? Money? Power?"

Penelope shrugged. "She thought it was a good joke."

"So I am assuming Hoffman dies in the clutches of the good captain?"

"Not exactly. Hoffman declares that his good friend Nicklausse will save him. Nicklausse has been there all along, you see, keeping Hoffmann out of serious trouble."

"But not quite enough to stop the destruction of property or murder."

"Some would say that was Hoffmann's mess to get himself out of."

"Would they?" Lund leaned in. "All right, go on."

"Captain Dapertutto is all set to poison Nicklausse, but Giulietta finds out. She may have fallen a little in love with Nicklausse herself when they sang a duet earlier in the act."

"Ah," Lund said sagely.

"Giulietta takes the poison instead."

"And dies?"

"And dies."

"Theft, destruction of property, murder, suicide, malicious lingering—what happens to Hoffmann then?"

"He admits to the chorus that all three women were the same one woman, the opera diva who he waits for in the pub. He's so drunk that he passes out, and instead of leaving with him, the diva exits with his nemesis Lindorf instead, who is—"

"An evil baritone."

"Quite right. The baritone. The same baritone from all the other acts." Penelope beamed at him. "Nicklausse turns into the muse and tells Hoffmann he must write poetry."

"And that's the end?"

Penelope nodded happily. "It's quite good. It will be a treat seeing Carrera perform 'The Doll Song.' And the Barcarolle in Guillietta's act! You will hear it exactly as it was meant to be heard. It's a challenging opera, difficult to sing for the soprano if she plays all three roles. Most companies split the rolls across their sopranos—makes for more of a spectacle. Carrera is singing all three parts and the Diva tonight. Which by itself is a tremendous feat. She has three difficult acts to execute as well as three costume changes. It will be a miracle to perform each perfectly, which of course is what we all expect of Carrera."

"Now I see." Lund laughed. "It's a hat trick!"

"A hat trick?"

"She's scoring three times in a row?" Lund's smile made his cheeks ache.

Penelope began to laugh.

A porter walked through the waiting area soberly ringing a quiet chime.

"Time to take our seats." Lund offered Penelope his arm. She took it.

LUND AND PENELOPE EMERGED FROM the crowded hallway and looked out at the theater's interior from the foot of the stage. Row upon row of red velveted seats going back for what seemed like an eternity until they struck a distant red silk-lined wall. There, the gilded luxury boxes—two sets of them—launched up and up, followed by the balcony, up and up, five stories high until Penelope looked straight up at the golden ceiling made rich with carved cherubs and painted murals. It was a sumptuous world filled with the brightest stars of the firmament. Penelope did not see the worn spots of carpet or the buckling of the silk wallpaper that had given way here and there. She was not on the balcony to see where the water leaked or where the rats had been. She could not imagine that she was anywhere but heaven. She gripped Thom's arm and took a deep breath of sawdust and resin.

"Are you tempted to sing?" She felt his lips brush her ear, a tingle traveling down her neck. She looked up into his green eyes and wondered if he realized. "This way," Lund said with a small smile.

The coal and manufacturing magnates had the boxes, but the youth of New York held the floor. All around them, young people chattered loudly and vigorously, waiting for the tone of the bell to announce it was time to take their seats. Penelope had never seen such a jumble of patron and artist, model and author, all discussing Carrera and her new tenor (and rumored lover) Luca Florimo. Just above the crowd, the boxes looked increasingly reserved by the moment, overlooking the riot of opera fanaticism. She searched for Mary and Gil but could not find them.

Penelope felt as though she and Lund were tied together with string, one going where the other went. It was only later that she realized he had held her by the hand the whole time, his fingers a sound fidelity among the talking and the laughter. Scanning the seats around them, she was surprised to see him look away from her and greet the man behind him with astonishment. "Mr. Peters?"

He had a round, ruddy face with laugh lines around his eyes and nose. "Niels told me you might be here," the man said, his mustache quivering with every word. "Said you might, yes." The odd repetition caught her attention as Lund turned and introduced her.

"Mr. Peters, this is Miss Penelope Harris." Lund's hand traveled to the crook of her arm, where it rested comfortably.

"Yes, Miss Harris. Yes," Peters said with a friendly wink and the heavy breath of cigars. "I've heard you sing."

Penelope blushed. "I'm beginning to wonder who wasn't at the Staughtons' that night."

"It was a good show. Yes, a good show. You shall have to sing for us again sometime. Perhaps from there?" He nodded toward the stage, ruffling her composure.

"I'm not that talented." She laughed self-consciously.

"Why not let the audience decide?" He leaned back, satisfied. "Niels suggested I speak with you about something, Lund. Told me you'd be here, so I waited at his seat. I understand that you can be discreet when the need arises." He looked around himself stiffly, his crisp white collar cutting into the soft flesh of his neck. "Only take a moment."

Penelope recognized her dismissal. She touched Lund's arm. "I can see our seats over there, Thom. We have a few more minutes until the lights go down."

The muzzy drunkenness of Lund's attention followed her as she maneuvered her way to her seat. She sat with her hands folded neatly on top of her program and watched him from the corner of her eye. It was fantasy, of course. A night at the opera, with Lund. She guarded her doubt with resolution and settled in with a warm wave of excitement.

9

"MR. PETERS—"

"Call me Wallace." Wallace Peters was not an overly tall man, but he had the presence of one. Lund supposed it was the size of his shoulders, each like a rocky knoll under the formal jacket. The rumor was, in addition to working in the bank, Peters's coal-magnate father had insisted his son work in the mines during his summer terms, resulting in the hard physique of a man who used his hands. But the most unexpected result had been that Wallace Peters was now a man with a purpose, who supported the unions. Peters had clashed often with his father until his death in 1916. Wallace Peters was thought to be an evenhanded, generous man, known for unusual acts of spontaneous kindness. Lund waited for Peters to speak. Knowing the man's reputation for friendliness, Lund didn't expect to wait long.

"See here," Peters looked over his shoulder at the boxes behind and above him, "there isn't much time before the wife notices I'm gone. She won't like me talking to you about the family business. I'll be brief. Rask says you're on the straight and narrow, and that's fine. You're also not family and you aren't from here, and that's even better. I'd rather have someone who doesn't have any connections investigate the matter. I'm sure you understand."

His face impassive, Lund nodded. Hearing the man speak without interruption would give him a better overall picture.

"You're a man of few words." Peters looked at him as though he were seeing him for the first time.

"It does make things go along more quickly," Lund replied.

"Right you are, right you are!" Peters gave Lund a tremendous slap on the back that pushed him forward an unexpected step. Peters began again. "It's m'wife, y'see? She's all in a state, and something must be done. Marital discord and all that. She had a sister. M'wife says she doesn't want to know, but she does. She just doesn't know it. My sister-in-law was a sweet girl, quiet. Lived a quiet life, if you see what I mean. Never went in for the family type of life. Said she'd rather live alone. Not that there was a man—there was, but he died, you see, in the war. She didn't mind a quiet life alone, did her part and all that. Didn't want to get her heart broken again and so forth. Everyone was settled with it. She didn't seem unhappy, not to notice anyway."

Lund glanced at Penelope in her seat. She winked at him. He returned his attention to Peters.

"Took her sailboat out a year ago June and took out all the bilge bolts." Peters exhaled and shook his head. "Sailboat sank too far out for anyone to know until it was too late. Anyway, she was dead."

Lund sighed internally. "Suicide is not a typical area of investigation, Mr. Peters," Lund said carefully. "Answers aren't easy to find."

"Wallace. Please call me Wallace. Rask told me that you handle financial investigations, looking for embezzlers and thieves an' so forth. You used to be a policeman—in China. He knew you in the war."

"Look, I want to help you, but this really isn't my area. I investigate financial crimes. This is something different. For what you need, the police might be better suited." Lund added carefully, "Or a licensed private investigator."

Peters's expression took on an element of outrage, which made him stand a little taller. "I've talked to everyone. No one is interested in a drowned woman. I know it isn't the color of my money. And I know it isn't because she was something shocking, because she wasn't. Now tell me why no one wants to follow this down?"

Lund thought for a moment. He could think of a dozen reasons and guessed that Peters could too. But of them, the most likely was the reason Lund knew best: because there wasn't a satisfying answer for suicide. Being a rich man would make getting the truth even harder for Peters. There'd be a dozen disreputable private investigators looking to cash in on his grief. "Are you satisfied that the bolts were removed? Could it have been poor maintenance? Perhaps an accident?"

"The newspapers said it was an accident, but it wasn't. I'll tell you: the poor thing killed herself. Not a mean bone in her body, couldn't hurt a fly, but she did that terrible thing to herself." Peters looked away, blinking.

"Suicide is a terrible act, so often unexplained," Lund said.

"I don't accept that. No sir, I do not." Peters took a sudden step toward Lund, his voice clear enough to draw the attention of the people sitting near them. Looking around himself sheepishly, Peters began again, his words softer. "She was as kind a heart as you would ever meet. Something happened. I want to know what it was. You will investigate the matter. Niels said you would." He straightened his jacket and cleared his throat. "I've sent the coroner's report and the note to your office. I included a letter she sent my wife about a week before. She and my wife had a trip to Boston planned—a health retreat! I tell you, it makes no sense." Peters cleared his throat again. "She had a little place in the country. We've kept it just as she left it. It might be a good place to start. My wife can't bear to go there and clear the place out. I've called the caretaker and told her I'm sending someone up to look for some papers for the estate. That should give you a good pretense. I want you to go up first thing tomorrow." Peters looked at Lund. His eyes softened. "I have to know the truth. What are your fees?"

Niels knew he would take the case, had already told Peters that he would. "I don't think that will be necessary, Wallace. Just to look around a house. It seems like a simple enough task." Lund strained under the urge to tell the man the truth: that he would never understand why she had died, and if he did learn why, he might wish he never had.

Peters put out his hand, and Lund shook it, conceding defeat. "What was her name?"

"Coralee O'Connor." Peters cleared his throat once more and peered at Lund with watering eyes. "Find out why she did it, Thom. Happiest girl in the world. I've got to know why."

"WHO WAS THAT?" PENELOPE ASKED.

"Wallace Peters," Lund said uncomfortably as he sat down. "Niels asked me to speak with him." He hoped it would be enough to assuage her curiosity. The less she knew about it, the better. Lund looked down at the program in his lap without reading it. "Family favor."

"I didn't realize Niels Rask was related to you."

"More of an adopted brother, really. He took Matthias and me under his wing when our mother died. I would have ended up in a street gang if it hadn't been for him. He moved here after the war. When I came to New York, he gave me a job."

"Instead of becoming a criminal mastermind, you became a policeman." Her eyes were a brilliant blue when she smiled. His heart beat a little faster.

"He probably thought it was a discreet place to meet." Lund observed the bedlam of socializing all around them. "I'm beginning to believe the opera might serve the same function as a dark alley. Look at it." He gestured toward a woman dressed in an ethereal dress from the House of Vionnet standing next to a woman wearing a dress made out of artists' canvas, a giant, surrealistic snake twisting its way across her shoulder and down to her feet. Men shouted across the floor and shook hands vigorously. All the while, the orchestra chattered and played as the musicians warmed their fingers and tuned their instruments. Even the timpani played over the crowd in tiny booms as the musician ensured the pedal was properly balanced. There was so much noise and bustling and rushing that Lund imagined a murder could be done quickly and easily with no one the wiser. He leaned down to Penelope's ear and whispered, "Is that why you brought a gun?"

"What?" Her voice carried with the professional power of the soprano. Several heads turned to look at her.

"I was just thinking this is the ideal place for a murder, and I wondered if that was why you brought the gun. The .22 in your purse. I would say from general experience it's a Webley. Am I right?" He looked across the audience without a care in the world.

Penelope was wide-eyed. "How did you . . . when . . . ?"

"I would usually caution you, but I know there are exceptional circumstances. Although, I have to say I'm not exactly sure why you would want to bring a revolver on an evening out with your cousin." He turned his head to look at her, his face so close to hers he could feel her breath on his cheek. "Is there any chance at all you might shoot me by accident during the third act?"

"It's not a hair trigger," she replied tersely. "The safety's on. It won't just go off."

"I am not going to mention how much it disturbs me that you can identify a hair trigger." Lund smiled.

"My father taught me how to shoot. Why wouldn't he want to teach me about how to handle a gun?"

"I didn't realize the opera was so dangerous."

Penelope sighed and looked at the purse in her hand. "I can't help it. I tried to leave it at home, but then I was afraid someone . . ."

"Your mother?" Lund suggested.

". . . would find it. So, I went back and got it. I feel safer with it. Peaceful."

"God help the mob. If they met you in a dark alley, they wouldn't know what hit them."

Penelope looked down and then around herself. "Is it so obvious?" she asked quietly.

"Only to me. Only because I know you so well." Lund turned his face away and laughed. "I apologize, Penelope. I couldn't help teasing you. However, you should know that the police in New York City don't look kindly on that kind of thing. You must have a permit for it, and it should be registered." He settled back into the seat and looked at his program. He could see the hand holding her clutch slowly relax.

"These are very good seats, Thom."

Looking at her in the seat beside him, he could tell she was in her element. The nervous veil he had sensed between them was swept aside. They had remembered enough about each other to be comfortable. Penelope smiled at him, a slow affair that started in her eyes and gave him a shimmy of happiness in his gut.

"Thank you for sitting with me. I have the envy of every man here." Just past her shoulder, he caught a glimpse of a man in profile climbing a staircase. He had the look of William Bird. Lund distantly wondered how many tickets Rask had given out.

"I hope Helen gets to the paper in time," Penelope said, shifting in her seat. "The Warwicks had a set-to right in front of her tonight. I'm sure her editor will be pleased."

"The Warwicks?" The recent memory of Roger Warwick holding his walking stick from the center of the heavy wood rose up like a ghost.

"Yes, I met them at an opera society luncheon today. The daughters sing, and it would appear the mother is something of a social climber." Penelope twisted around to look over her shoulder. "They're all here," she said. "Even the daughters. There's Ivy." She nodded to a box of seats. Lund followed her glance, careful to not appear to be looking. "I offered to teach one of them, but who knows what will come of it?"

The boy with the chimes was now passing up and down the aisles as various groups made their plans for intermission and broke apart, scrambling in the dimming light to find their seats. Lights in the hallway flickered on and off as everyone wandered about checking their tickets, looking for seats. The noise from the orchestra pit grew louder as the musicians played arpeggios and flutes hit high, fluttering notes that flew above the low strings. The lights dimmed. The massive chandelier that hung above the audience slowly rose to clear the view for the balcony seats. The oboe played his A first, every voice coming after until a rich resonance filled the Metropolitan with precise vibration. There was a pause. Then the conductor strode out from a discreet door under the stage in the pit, took a brief bow, and tapped the music stand ahead of him to draw the attention of the musicians.

The opera began.

10

ROGER WARWICK LAY ON HIS back on a red-carpeted staircase, one of his feet four steps above where he rested, the other curled behind him at an unnatural angle. His head twisted too far to the right to be comfortable, mouth agape. His eyes were open as if in surprise, but the overall expression was closer to anger. His body was flexible, with no rigor, although the medics were already threatening how difficult moving Roger Warwick would be if he began to stiffen.

Lieutenant Blake turned his head to one side as he stood over the man and considered the body like he would a picture puzzle or a crossword. Bending over the body, an elbow on his knee, he examined Warwick's head. Even without a full view, it was clear that someone had taken their frustration out on the back of the man's skull. There was bone mixed up in the hair, and brains too, Blake was sure of it.

Pushing off from the wall, he looked around. "Well?" He practically shouted the word, making the men around him snap to attention. "Where's the murder weapon?" It was a practical statement of the question rather than a polite query.

Detective Toomey called down from the top of the stairs, "Nothing up here. Looks like he was pushed."

Blake took the stairs two at a time, carefully edging himself around the body as he went. At the top, Toomey pointed at the silk damask wall. "See that?" An indentation roughly the size of a saucer staved the delicate silk. "Matches the dent on the side of his head. And look at this." Toomey squatted down beside the body and pointed to the right cheek as he spoke. "Someone took a swing at him—got him right on the kisser." Blake crouched to look closer.

"What kind of hit?" Blake stood up, Toomey rising next to him.

"Couldn't say." Toomey shrugged and spoke with the authority of an amateur boxer. "This is straight on, like they had even height. But could've been this man was standing down a step or two."

"So, man or woman then."

Toomey nodded without comment, removing a small book and pencil from his pocket.

"Okay, Toomey. Ask the medical examiner if there's a way to tell if it was a fist or a blunt object. Never know, could have been anything handy if it was a woman. Check with the attendants in the washrooms, men's and women's, and ask if there was anyone who might have come in to wash off. Anything. Hands, shoes, makeup—anything. Maybe they got some blood on their hand." Blake was silent for a moment as he looked down. Then he cocked his head up and asked, "What is that? Rain?"

"Applause," Toomey said neatly. "About four thousand people are on the other side of that wall cheering on some dame who thinks she can carry a tune."

"Didn't think she was so good, did you?"

"The attendant cracked a door so I could listen. Couldn't understand a word." Toomey looked down again to continue his ponderous notes. "They've got this hallway blocked off. The manager says it's a nuisance, but he'll force everyone the other way. Since the hallway blocks the body from view, he's just going to say it was a nasty accident."

"Four thousand people? Toomey, how the hell do we question four thousand people?" Blake shouted.

Familiar with this style of outburst, Toomey barely reacted. "You got me, boss. Maybe sort of corral them up together and get their names?"

"It would take a week!" Blake's face slowly turned red. "Get the manager over here right now!" Toomey stepped away as Blake grabbed the nearest patrolman in reach. "Get a damn sheet and cover the body up. Stand in front of the hallway and make sure no one comes down here. Post patrolmen on either side. Understand?" As he finished, the manager came trotting up behind Toomey.

"Good evening, sir, so good of you to—"

"You know that man?" Blake cut him off with professional precision.

The manager looked into the hard, blue eyes and took in the lean, athletic figure of the older man before replying, "That's Roger Warwick." And a regular bastard, his face told Blake, although the manager's dignity held the words back.

"Does he have a regular seat? People he sits with, that kind of thing?"

The manager looked around, thinking and patting his pockets as though there were a list in one with all the answers. Finally, he replied, "He has a box. A family box. Typically his wife comes to the performances and brings friends." He seemed to be choosing his words carefully.

"Are they here now? Tonight?"

"Why, yes. They were not sitting together. Mrs. Warwick brought guests with her this evening. Lovely people, the Gilmurrays." Blake was keeping a mental list of the lies the house manager told. It was perfectly obvious to anyone watching the man speak that the Gilmurrays were not lovely people at all.

"Where are they—I mean, which box?"

"I can show one of your men." The manager waited for a beat before asking, "Would it be reasonable to ask when the body will be moved?" Holding his hands in front of him, he made patting movements in the air as though to soothe the lieutenant before he erupted. "I only ask because it seems so disrespectful to have a dead man lying out where everyone can see. The last act will be over in less than half an hour . . . There are ladies . . ." Sputtering to a stop, he backtracked, adding, "What I mean to say is that surely there are ways to remove Mr. Warwick before he is seen by anyone?" The manager trembled. "I'm not sure if you have noticed, but there are photographers who wait outside the stage door. I'm not sure, but they might have seen your police cars—"

Blake exploded. "Oh, for God's sake! Toomey!" Running back with a patrolman just behind him, Toomey was too breathless to answer but stood still to listen to his instructions. "Get a sheet and cover him up!" Pointing at the patrolman, Blake spoke with more familiarity than the manager of the front of the house expected. "I don't care what kind of magic you use, McCain. Get to that box and keep them there. You!" He pointed to the manager. "You're going to block off this floor." Blake held up a single finger when the man began to protest. "You're going to block off this floor all the way from the washrooms to the end of that hallway."

"But those are boxes—" the man sputtered, "our benefactors."

Blake's voice was quiet, equal parts nursery logic and asylum management. "They will be perfectly comfortable in their boxes for a little longer while we take names and addresses. Seems reasonable to ask them to stay long enough for that. Then one of my men can escort them to another staircase." The manager watched, mesmerized, his lips moving along with Blake's as he spoke.

"Sir." The quiet voice just behind Blake had a weight of its own.

"What is it, McCain?"

"The Warwick box. It's on the other side."

"What, McCain? Your legs can't walk that far?"

"No, sir." McCain slowed his words down and said again. "The Warwick box is all the way on the other side of the building. It's on the other side—straight across." He pointed his finger at the wall.

Blake stood for a moment as the incredible dawned on him. With a vigor Toomey had come to fear, Blake bellowed, "Shut down the floor—no one in or out! We'll have to talk to them all!"

11

"I JUST MINDED MY BUSINESS, which some of us have to do, you know. But don't tell that to the management. No, they don't understand the regular person at all." Sergeant Poulhaus nodded in the silent, knowing way of a man who knows when not to interrupt a witness. "They make us go down and all the way to the back when we have business to do ourselves. Doesn't matter if we're in the washroom all night or not! No! The management says we have to use the ladies' at the back, so that's where I was, at the ladies' in the back."

She was hot and flustered, even in the cold, damp air of the opera house. Her eyes locked on his like she were a sailor swimming for shore with sixteen sharks and the whole pirate army coming on quick behind her. Poulhaus made a note. "So, that's when you found the body. On your way back?"

Looking at him oddly, she seemed confused. "Well, I was right back there, right at the door, see? And I had a feeling. Do you know how you have a sense of something? Something wrong?"

"What door would that be, miss?"

"The washroom door, right there." She looked over her shoulder, then back at him quickly. "I supposed you aren't worried about nobody finding the body because the whole floor is blocked off. But there's a stair right there you might want to put a man on."

Poulhaus sighed, stopped taking notes, and looked across the wide corridor to the door she indicated. "That's all the way on the other side, miss. No one is going to be sneaking up on us by those stairs."

"But it's all right there . . . it's . . ."

"Why don't you tell me how you found things?"

She looked up at him, blinked, and thought for a moment. She opened her mouth to speak again, shut it, and cocked her head to one side. The woman gave him a look that told him she sympathized with the whole of the New York City Police Department.

"Well, I went up to the door of the washroom, like I was telling you." She said the word *washroom* very carefully and paused before continuing. "And I had a feeling something wasn't right. Too quiet, if you know what I mean. Everything sounded differently, like there was someone in there but there was no sound."

Poulhaus was nearing the end of his rope with her slow-moving pace and the strange looks she was giving him. He made a noncommittal sound and kept his eyes on the notebook. She was a lovely thing, a bit on the matronly side, but not too old for a matinee or a walk through the park. Poulhaus sensed she was waiting for him to say something, so he said, "Go on. You had a strange feeling . . ." and tried his best to keep the majority of his circumspection out of his tone. But when he looked at her, she was staring down the hallway at the group of detectives and policemen standing at the bottom of the stairs.

"What's that?" she asked with dawning horror.

"Now, don't go having a dizzy spell. You've already seen the worst of it when you came up on him sudden like. You told the sergeant that you found the body without shedding a single tear or passing out once. Now, don't go breaking your streak." Poulhaus reached over to pat the woman on the back with the stiffness of a man who had no sisters, daughters, or aunts. "Pull yourself together, woman," he said in what he hoped was a consoling way.

She seemed a great deal more shaken than he had first thought as she reached out her hand to grab the arm of his uniform and asked shrilly, "You mean to say there's two?"

SHIFTING UNCOMFORTABLY, POULHAUS GAVE HIS report rapidly as he walked beside Blake all the way along the promenade, through the irate society families giving their names and addresses, and past the medical examiner, who had just come down the stairs to have an eyeful of the body. "She had just come back from a break, sir. The management asks the employees to use a bathroom at the back of the facility, and it was quite a long walk. She said she couldn't have been gone more than twenty or thirty minutes." Blake's stride was just slightly longer than the detective's, causing Poulhaus to trot along beside the lieutenant.

Blake stopped in front of the door and searched his pockets for a handkerchief. Covering his hand with it completely, he swung the door open. The sitting room with several small makeup tables was empty, mirrors staring out blankly in the quiet. Blake walked through, barely looking around him at the luxury settee or the gilded mirrors and taps. He saw only the marked sole of a worn shoe dangling from the toes where it belonged, the stockinged foot of its owner limp beside it. He followed the foot to the hem of an orchid lace dress. She lay on her side. One leg out stiff, the other slack. Her hands so tightly balled together that he wondered if she had cut into her own palms with her nails. Her face was pallid and covered in mucus and vomit. Her eyes were shut. His own eyes traveled down her body to where the belt of her dress pushed up on her round belly. He took in her swollen ankles and wrists and sensed a wave of anger growing in him that would shake the walls.

Opening the stall door carefully with the handkerchief, Blake stepped inside the stall, mindful of avoiding where the girl had been sick. He wasn't thinking very clearly except to tell himself that, until he knew for himself, there was truly no way to tell for sure if she was dead or alive. Rage was blinding him as he steadied himself against the stall wall and crouched down. Removing the handkerchief, he felt for a pulse and held his breath.

Exhaling, he ordered Poulhaus with exacting fortitude, "Get the M.E. and tell him we have a live one. I want him here two seconds ago. Prop that door open when you come back and don't let anyone touch anything. Run!" Poulhaus was gone, sprinting his way back to the stairs. Blake kept his hand on the girl's neck as he said to her, "Now you listen here. I have three girls myself, so I know life can be hard. And cruel. And mean as hell. But there's never going to be enough reason to give up on it when you're carrying a child. So you listen to me and hang on. Do you hear me? Hold on!"

Phil Mercer reached over to put his hand on Blake's shoulder. "I'm here, Nate. Let me through."

Blake stood up as he said, "I found a pulse, Phil. I'm sure it's hers and not mine . . ." Poulhaus caught his breath and wondered at the man staring down at the girl. It was a new man in front of him. Truth be told, it was a father and a grandfather who stood there with his hands on his knees crouching down to watch the M.E. work over the girl.

"She's alive," Mercer said crisply. "Roger Warwick will have to wait. Nothing beats the living. Get the stretcher over here, Nathan. They can bring up the spare on the bus for Warwick."

"But that's a Warwick!" The washroom attendant was at the door, a tissue clutched in her hand, her eyes red from crying. "That's Tulip Warwick! I'd know her anywhere!"

Blake and Mercer looked at each another for a moment before the M.E. turned back to the girl and Blake returned to Poulhaus with the full force of his temper. "Well, what are you doing standing there?"

"But, boss . . . Mr. Warwick is already on the stretcher."

"Then take him off! This is his daughter, and she's still alive. Get him off!"

12

"I THINK THE MANAGEMENT HAS turned off the furnace." Penelope shifted her feet, standing a little closer to Lund. "The police could at least let us go down to the lobby and get our coats. What do you think has happened?"

"A dowager has lost her pearls, perhaps? She'll find them in her purse after berating the staff for an hour and a half." Lund looked down at the top of her head. Penelope looked away down a wide hallway filled with members of the audience. He shook his arms free of his tailcoat, his shoulders relieved from the strain of the fit. He held it out to her, inclining his head.

"Won't you be cold?" Goosebumps stood up on her arms as Penelope rubbed them.

Lund leaned toward her. "I'll keep my arms around you to stay warm." Three acts of Valentina Carrera, not to mention their hands meeting between the seats during the Barcarolle, had done the necessary work. Lund was drunk with romance.

Penelope flushed a rosy pink and giggled. The bright,

sparkling sound made his stomach do a backflip. He held out the jacket by the shoulders as Penelope slid one arm in, then the other, the tips of her fingers appearing just past the cuff, the tails reaching the middle of her calf. Looking down at them, she said, "I must look ridiculous."

"Don't worry. The police won't mind." Lund peered at the policemen clustered around the far end of the hallway. "I certainly don't." He stared down at the back of her neck, resisting the urge to reach out and touch her skin. He looked for and found the bottom of the faint scar that came down her left cheek and disappeared behind her ear. Kinkaid Ambrose's parting gift to his wife was meant to mark her forever, but the scar was nearly faded. It had taken money, a year in Munich, and a wealth of surgical talent. "You always look beautiful to me," Lund said, "from the first moment I saw you."

"Oh?" Penelope stood close enough to brush his chest with her arm as she turned to look up at him. His rebellious heart gave a flutter. "When was that?"

"You were down at the docks cleaning out a sailboat. You were determined to go out in it."

Her brow wrinkled with concentration. "An irritating police officer stopped me. Told me the boat was—"

"A decrepit nuisance," Lund finished for her. "And it was. You wouldn't have lasted ten minutes in the bay."

"That was you." She studied his face. "I was fit to be tied for days. I even went down and complained."

"To Matthias, yes. He told me." The memory was so clear Lund thought he could hear the harbor boats, even feel the warmth of the sun. "Matthias also said that he told you a proper boat with a proper license was required in the harbor."

"Yes, well." Her nose went up. "So what if he did?"

Lund laughed. "That was the first time I saw you. I thought you were lovely, even if you did have a wicked temper."

Time spun down around them, slowing until they shared one world apart from everyone else. Lund thought she could feel it too, all the best parts of China appearing like a mist around their feet: the people, the beautiful bright green Lund had never seen anywhere else in the world, the ancient gates of civilization rising up all around them.

"Oh, that boat!" Her face lit up with recognition. Penelope tapped a finger against his white shirt like the fabric were a map of the memory where she could mark the exact spot. The warmth of it made him shiver. "I remember now. It was a menace. I bought it from a boy on the wharf."

"Wasn't even his," Lund replied, content. "I probably could have had you up for theft on top of the nuisance charges. That's how Matthias knew. He plainly stated that if it had been anyone but a child, an abandoned kitten, or my true love, I would have locked them up for stealing that boat." The words took him further than he had expected. The swirl of memory faltered. Lund resisted the urge to look around him.

The pause was only for a fraction of a moment. She showed the briefest recognition—she had seen him waver; he was sure of it. Penelope's blush deepened, her hand flattening against his shirt so he could feel the heat through to his skin. She said, "What do you mean? I bought that boat fair and square."

Lund relaxed. "So you say, but you couldn't show me a receipt. And you couldn't find the dirty cherub either."

"He was small! And surly!" She couldn't help herself. A giggle became a laugh until they were both leaning on each other, laughing with no concern about what the people around them might think.

Lund kissed her.

A slow and gentle kiss. Her hand found his, her fingers winding through his own. They parted. When he looked at her, it was as though he were looking straight into her. He could see it flash across her face: her terror of love. Penelope was so terrified by the prospect after the spectacular failure of her marriage that it stood out all over her, from her wide eyes to the hand that tightened its grip on his vest.

She looked up at him and tried to make her lips move. She struggled with what to say as his heart fell. It was too early. He had rushed her. Regret and hope all jumbled together. Lund could see the words were impossible. He could say them, but she could not. Whether she loved him or not, the words would not come. He exhaled.

"I apologize, Penelope." Lund looked down at the floor as he straightened up. "I shouldn't have presumed."

"Thom . . ." Penelope looked down at her purse.

"There's no need to hold a gun on me." He smiled ruefully. "I went too far. I realize it."

"Thom." She leaned into him, her voice quiet so no one else could hear. "It's not that. You just caught me by surprise. I trust you." She took his hand again, the gun in her purse a heaviness pulling their palms together.

"If you could count on one person, anytime, anyplace, I would like it to be me." Lund smiled. "If I fail in that, I would much rather you shot me."

"Don't worry." Penelope nodded and gave a half smile. "I will."

Even before Lund kissed her again, he heard, "Outrageous! At the opera!" causing him to turn suddenly and demand, "Be silent, you old baggage!" unaware that he had spoken in Danish.

"Mother isn't expecting me tonight. I told her I would stay with Mary." Penelope breathed the words into his ear.

A deep flush followed by a rush of blood gave Lund a jolt. "I have an early train in the morning. Six a.m." He spoke more suddenly than he would have liked.

"Almost not worth going to sleep, is it?" The fingers holding his hand traced up his wrist." Police or no police, criminal behavior be damned! Lund was ready to sweep Penelope off her feet and knock the group of patrolmen down like pins to get to the taxi line.

"Penelope!" A shrill cry from across the lobby shuddered across the crowd. Lund and Penelope stood apart, both turning toward the tremulous voice. "Oh, Penelope!" Ivy Warwick stumbled across the floor toward them, falling forward into Penelope's arms. "I need your help! Oh, please, I need your help!"

13

LUND LEANED AGAINST THE NURSE's desk in the hospital foyer, his exhaustion getting the better of him. He wearily recited his movements of the evening to a third policeman. The young patrolman wrote everything down carefully with a small pencil, his printing laborious and slow. Lund exhaled his frustration and reminded himself of the first few years he had been a policeman relegated to the night shift or traffic duty. The young man in front of him couldn't have been more than nineteen or twenty, the same age Lund had been when he walked his first beat.

"Just a minute." The patrolman concentrated on his writing, the sound of the pencil against the paper audible in the quiet.

"Take your time." Lund meant it. The idea that she would go home with him had disappeared around one o'clock with the first policeman's questions. It was three now. He'd have just enough time to see her safely home before he left for Wallace Peters's property on Long Island. The keys to Coralee's house felt heavy in his pocket. Rask would expect the matter resolved, or on its way to a satisfactory resolution, by the end of the weekend. Then there was the matter of the books. And Bird on top of that. Lund had work to do.

"I've given you my exchange," Lund offered to the patrolman's bowed head. "Perhaps we can return to the discussion at another time. I would like to take Miss Harris home."

"Just another minute." The young man didn't look up from his writing.

Lund hoped Penelope had found a way to separate herself from Ivy without a scene. The girl had been nearly hysterical in the car ride to the hospital, eager to get to her sister's bedside but oddly uninterested in her father. When the police had explained that Roger Warwick was dead, Ivy looked at

Penelope as though expecting Penelope to tell her what to do. Lund told himself it was shock, but something about it struck him as odd. He had seen all kinds of strange behavior when confronted with death—both as a policeman and a soldier. What he had not seen before was the blank disregard Ivy displayed when McCain broke the news. It was as though Roger Warwick were a man she had never met. Tulip was Ivy's only concern. Once at the hospital, Ivy hadn't allowed anyone or anything to get in her way, clinging to Penelope as she made her way to her sister's bedside.

"Thom!"

The bellow woke the patrolman up. The young man straightened, his ears turning bright pink. Lund dropped the hand he was leaning on and slowly straightened his posture as well. "Morning, Nathan."

Lieutenant Blake barged down the hospital corridor with the usual burst of electricity he brought to an investigation. Every officer and detective within arm's reach tensed as though Blake might reach out and grab them without notice. "What's the idea of the tails, Thom? You taking me to a wedding?"

"Are you bringing the ring?" Lund shot back.

Blake laughed, slapping Lund's shoulder hard enough to make his teeth rattle. "Is he done here?" The lieutenant's focus shifted to the patrolman with the notebook.

"I think I have it all, sir. Movements accounted for through both intermissions. I have to check it with McCain, but I think—"

"You think? Better to know, not to think." Blake jabbed a finger into the officer's shoulder. "Make sure you get all the statements typed up tonight—no excuses. I want them all complete and on my desk before the next shift comes in." Gesturing for Thom to follow, he walked away before the kid could answer.

"Being a little hard on him, wouldn't you say?" Lund asked quietly as they walked.

"Not hard enough, if you ask me. The boys missed a body on the sweep through the floor after they found Warwick. There was a girl on the bathroom floor, sweet as you please, almost dead from something she ate."

"Coincidence?"

"Unlikely." Blake stopped and looked Lund in the face. "Since when did you believe in a thing like coincidence?"

"Wishful thinking," Lund replied casually. "I'd rather it wasn't murder."

"Who said it was?" Blake was wary. "Roger Warwick, maybe murder. Couldn't say so soon. But the girl? That's suicide."

Lund thought back to Ivy in the cab. "Penelope's upstairs with the younger sister now. Ivy's her name. Did you know?"

Blake shook his head. "Is she? I didn't know that. Been questioning the staff at the theater. Someone must have seen something, but we couldn't shake anything loose." He started up the stairs. "From the sound of it, getting up and moving around during the performance is typical. Especially in the boxes."

Lund opened his mouth to speak and stopped himself.

Blake gave him a knowing nod. "None of your business, is it?"

"None at all." The relief was immediate. "We were there, but it's none of our business."

"McCain says you knew the man."

Lund thought back over the day. The morning seemed a long time ago. "I met Roger Warwick at the bank this morning. He struck me as highly strung."

"He wasn't the only one." Blake put his hands on his hips, straining the buttons of his tweed vest. "Wife came straight away to identify the body. You never saw such an act! Screaming and crying and carrying on. Hanging on the morgue attendant like he's her personal bearer. I seen a lot of women cry over the years, Thom. This lady, she was a professional at it." Blake said in a brittle falsetto, "'Was it quick? Did he suffer?' You should have seen the attendant when she went into a faint. He didn't know where to put his hands!" Blake began to walk again, Lund falling into step beside him. "I had the nurses standing by with the smelling salts when we told her about the daughter and her delicate condition. What does Violet Warwick do? She goes the other direction. She's a wet cat, throwing things, screaming. I can tell you, Mrs. Warwick has a strong set of lungs. If the ward attendant hadn't been there, I would have had to arrest her for assault. She was that angry!"

"Over the daughter?" Lund's first thought was Penelope. Was she still with Ivy? Had she been there? "Tulip?" He shouldn't have left Penelope alone with the girl.

"That's the one." Blake shrugged. "Pregnant and unmarried. Might set me off too if it were my kid. But not like her! She was like a punch-drunk prizefighter swinging away on a crowded subway car!"

It didn't take much of an imagination to draw a picture. There was something unwieldy and off-kilter about the family, something just out of reach he couldn't put his finger on. Lund should have stayed with Penelope. If anything had happened to her, it was his fault. It wasn't that he didn't trust her, and God knew the woman could take care of herself; it was the Warwicks he didn't trust. "Couldn't have been that bad, surely."

Blake shook his head. "It was exactly as bad as I said. Ask Miss Harris when you see her. She'll back me up."

"She was there?"

"The Warwick woman lunged at her. I had to stay between them. And Miss Harris hadn't done a damn thing."

Lund exhaled his displeasure. Why was it the Warwicks were reminding him increasingly of a pit of vipers? "Was Penelope . . . ?"

"I wouldn't worry about your girl, Thom. She's got a practical head on her shoulders. She stayed good and out of it, even when Mrs. Warwick started going in on the sick girl. Miss Harris let the matron handle everything."

"Violet Warwick attacked her own daughter?" Lund shook his head.

"Gave her a slap right across the face, then went in on her. Bet you're glad they aren't your problem." Blake leaned in, lowering his voice. "I'd like to say I'm surprised to see you, but the truth is I'm not. Seems like you and your girl always turn up when this lot gets up to something interesting. Were you there for the opera or business?"

"The opera." It was an easy lie. "Listen, Nathan." Lund stopped, pivoting toward Blake. "Tell me what Penelope and I need to do so we can go home."

"All right, Thom, I get it. You win. It was all pleasure tonight." Blake continued up the stairs, Lund following behind. What can you tell me about Roger Warwick?"

"Not much. He came by the bank, put up a howl, and left."

"What got him howling?"

"One of his accounts was short on cash. He had the idea someone had been pilfering."

"Did he have an idea who?" Blake reached into the inside pocket of his jacket and removed a small notebook.

"It was just an impression, but I rather thought he might be on about his daughter."

"The one in the hospital?"

"No, Clover."

"Clover Warwick. Now that name brings back memories." Blake started the second flight of stairs. "I've got the boys looking for her right now. Trying to keep it off the radio so the newspapers don't get in our way."

"Penelope saw her in a box opposite Warwick's. She was sitting with her fiancé." Lund dredged his memory. "It was before the curtain went up."

"Clover Warwick has something of a reputation at the precinct. Did you know?"

"I heard something," Lund admitted slowly. "Did she hit a maid with her slipper?"

Blake nodded somberly. "The girl lost an eye. Her father paid a pretty penny to keep it quiet."

"My god!" Lund was aghast. "I thought it was party gossip. Do you mean to tell me the girl actually attacked a maid?"

"Beat the poor girl half to death. Whoever told you hit the nail on the head."

Lund could see Blake's train of thought clearly. "You think Clover lost her temper and killed her father?"

"Just an idea," Blake replied. "What do you think of it?"

Lund thought for a moment. "Warwick got up from his seat for a reason. He must have been meeting someone. If it was his daughter, why go to the opera at all?"

"Maybe it was the only place he could see her?" Blake narrowed his eyes. "Or are you thinking a woman couldn't kill a man in cold blood?"

"A woman could do it, no doubt about that. But it's a long stretch from going after someone with your shoe."

Blake thought a moment. "Could have been blackmail that ended with Warwick dead."

Lund shrugged. They were on the floor where Tulip was being treated. "In any case, it's your baby."

"Say, Thom, what were you and Penelope doing here anyway?"

"Penelope met Ivy Warwick at an opera society. Valley Opera—something like that."

Blake turned right down a darkened corridor. Walking ahead, it looked as though he were talking to himself. "Why is that name familiar? What was it? Hudson . . . ?"

"That's it." Lund snapped his fingers. "The Hudson Valley Operatic Society. Patsy Galton is the person in charge—"

"Patsy Galton?" Blake turned to face Lund. "What's she got to do with it?"

"Nothing I know of, Nathan, but that's where Penelope met the girl—Ivy, I mean."

"Huh." Blake's face smoothed as he considered. "Of

course, she would want to do something with the opera, wouldn't she?" He said seemingly to himself.

"She had hoped she would meet someone with a connection to an instructor. I'm sure she would like to sing a little if she had the chance."

Blake leaned in, putting his hand on Lund's shoulder. "Take my advice, Lund. Penelope should stay away from Patsy Galton—not her quality of person at all," he said with a snort. "Come on. I want someone with me for this. The doc always seems to behave a little better if I'm not alone."

14

"WHY ARE WE HERE?" ELEANOR hurried along the empty hallway behind a young orderly. She hardly knew what she had put on or how she had gotten to the hospital. The phone call had been short and breathless. "Come at once." Eleanor had done exactly that and walked straight up to the main desk, announcing she was there to see Dr. Mercer.

"Dr. Mercer wanted your daughter closer to the lab," the orderly said over his shoulder, not slowing for a minute, even when she had to speed her step to a jog. "There's a small room on this floor where your daughter could be comfortable." Eleanor looked around wondering where all the patients were. Every room was filled with scientific equipment and darkness.

"My daughter?" If there was hesitation in Eleanor's step,

it hardly showed. "Has something happened to her? Why was she brought to the hospital?" When the orderly came to a halt, Eleanor reached out and took him by the arm. "Young man, you should answer my questions! I'm her mother!"

The orderly sighed without looking at Eleanor, casually shaking her hand from his arm. "Dr. Mercer, I brought her up like you said."

Eleanor let go of the orderly's arm and looked first at the door to the doctor's office, the glass in the door absent, then down at the broken glass around her feet, her astonishment growing. "What is the meaning of this? Why have you brought me here? Where is my daughter?"

"This is my lab. My name is Dr. Mercer." Fine white hair puffed around the man's skull like mist.

"What on earth?" Eleanor's temper cooled her nerves. "I want to see my daughter this very minute!"

"Now, now, Mrs. Warwick," the orderly raised his hands as if he were calming a horse, "there is no reason to lose your senses. I brought you up here on Dr. Mercer's say-so, but if you can't keep your temper under control, I can take you back just as quickly."

Eleanor could feel the warmth traveling up the back of her neck. Every part of her quivered as she spoke. "My name is Harris, young man. My daughter called me from this place forty-five minutes ago. Penelope Harris. Where is she? Has something happened?"

"Here, Mother." Penelope stood in the drab hallway, her gold dress incongruous against the sterile, white-tiled walls. Eleanor reached out for her daughter's hands. Penelope continued, "I'm simply fine. Everything is fine. Well, for me at any rate. It's Ivy's sister Tulip." She turned into the room so Eleanor could see the small bed in the corner with an unmoving mass of sheets. Tulip's orchid lace gown was in a paper bag, which Penelope was determined to throw away as soon as she had a chance. A small lamp on a bedside table illuminated the girl's white, strained face. Ivy was nearby in a chair, her legs curled up under her and her head leaning against the wall.

"This is Tulip Warwick, Mother," Penelope said quietly. She nodded at the girl in the chair. "And her sister Ivy." Turning her back to the room, she whispered so only Eleanor could hear, "Tulip has been poisoned. I didn't know what to do."

"Could I speak to you for a moment?" The doctor coaxed the two women back out into the hall, pulling the door shut behind them. "Exactly who are you to this girl?"

Eleanor bristled. "I'm sure I couldn't tell you, Doctor. I got a message that my daughter was at the hospital, and I came. That's all I know."

"Oh no!" Penelope put her hand to her mouth. "I told the night manager at the Excelsior to let you know I was here in case you were worried. He must have gotten confused! I didn't mean for you to come here. It's so late."

Eleanor hadn't looked at her watch when the telephone had woken her up. She had put on the tweed suit she always kept clean, and had the desk clerk call for a cab. For the first time, she looked down at her watch. Eleanor did not hide her astonishment. "By God! It's four a.m.! Penelope, are you all right? Where is Mary?"

"She went home hours ago. Lund is here with me. He's

downstairs making a statement to the police." Penelope leaned forward to whisper, "The police let me come with Ivy because she told them I was her chaperone."

"The police?" Eleanor's alarm was growing. "What on earth does a sick girl have to do with the police?"

Penelope said quietly, "Ivy's father died earlier today in between acts. He fell down a flight of stairs."

It wasn't so early in the morning that Eleanor had lost her wits—men didn't just fall down the stairs at the opera and break their necks. But saying so would embarrass Penelope and these two young women. Eleanor looked from her daughter back through the doorway to the girl in the bed. "Where are her people?" she asked. "They should be here, not you."

Dr. Mercer sniffed loudly. "Exactly who are you to these girls?" he inquired with crossed arms and disapproval. "You aren't their family. I already met them, and you aren't nearly loud enough."

"A friend," Penelope said quickly. "Ivy asked me for my help. It seemed the decent thing to stand by her."

"But who is this girl Ivy, Penelope?" Eleanor asked. "You haven't mentioned her before."

"I met her this morning, Mother—at the luncheon."

"This morning?" Eleanor's mind rebelled. What had Penelope told her when she came home from the luncheon? Had she mentioned a girl? Or poison? Penelope had known the child less than a day. She could hardly mean anything to her. "What on earth are you talking about?"

"Mother," Penelope put her hand on Eleanor's arm, squeezing it warmly, "Ivy needs help."

"No one but family is allowed with someone so ill," Dr. Mercer declared. "I'm sure the police would agree with me. I must ask you to go."

Penelope put her chin up. "I heard Violet Warwick quite clearly an hour ago," she said crisply. "Tulip doesn't have anyone to rely on but the girl sitting in that room, and she can't be older than seventeen."

"I can't help that. There are rules." It did not look to Eleanor like Dr. Mercer had a firm grip on the rules he took such store by. He couldn't meet Penelope's eye when he spoke. Even the matron at his elbow seemed to be giving him a disapproving glance.

Eleanor could see that the man was not indifferent, only caught between what he felt was right and the shock of Tulip's condition. "But what has happened here? Where are the girls' family?"

A furrow appeared on Penelope's forehead. "They don't want anything to do with Tulip, Mother. They've disowned her." The faint noise of Tulip retching reached them beyond the door. The three of them shifted uncomfortably as the matron passed behind them to enter, shutting the door carefully behind her. After a moment, the noise stopped. Penelope took a deep breath. "Dr. Mercer, after what we both witnessed an hour ago, wouldn't you agree that these two girls need a friend? You heard what Violet Warwick said. She won't have them in her house. It sounded to me like she meant it."

The doctor rubbed the white stubble on his chin and glared at Penelope. "You can't hold what a person says against them when they are that emotional. The woman was hysterical!" He gestured to the glass on the floor, telegraphing a scene that must have caused the damage. Eleanor stiffened. What kind of people were these Warwicks?

Penelope continued, "I'm not here to replace her family, Doctor. I am only here to help if I can. I will sit in the hallway if you would prefer. I just don't agree that I should leave. At least not until Ivy has someone from her family she can rely on."

Dr. Mercer looked down at the floor and pursed and unpursed his lips while he thought. "Tulip will need round-the-clock care. I'm not sure she's out of the woods yet."

"Will she lose the baby?" Penelope asked softly.

Eleanor felt a sharp jolt. It was all coming at her too quickly. A baby?

"I wish that was the only thing I was worried about." His anger dissipated rapidly. "Arsenic can be tricky. The truth is we don't know much about it. Could be she will be all right after a transfusion and," he paused delicately, "some other steps. Or she might go into kidney failure and die, or her heart might give out. If she makes it through, then maybe her baby will. Not sure what else to say. Have to treat the mother first." Putting his hands on his hips, he looked up at the ceiling, then down at the end of the hall where a policeman was slowly walking up, his hands behind his back. "Violet Warwick can't tell me what to do," Mercer added. Turning to Eleanor, he exclaimed, "Imagine telling me to throw out her own daughter when she might be dying! Refusing to pay the bill and disowning her in front of witnesses?" The doctor's face was red, and his voice rose. "This is my floor, and what I say goes!" He shouted, "You want to stay and help, that's good enough for me."

The matron, who had quietly returned to the hallway,

turned to Penelope and Eleanor after Mercer stomped back to his lab. "Don't worry about Doc Mercer, he's all bark on the outside and soft pudding inside." As she reached for the doorknob to let them in, she said, "See if you can get her to tell you what she ate yesterday. I can't get her to say a word, which is frankly not surprising given what her mother just put her through. We found some chocolate in her purse. It's at the lab. But in the interest of public health, we need to know if there was anything else. Can you do that?" Penelope nodded, and she was alone with her mother.

Eleanor whispered loudly, "Arsenic? Babies? Penelope, what exactly goes on at the Metropolitan Opera?"

15

"LUND, THIS IS DR. MERCER. He's one of the city pathologists—sorry, medical examiner. How many are there now, Phil?"

"About ten of us across the city," Mercer said reluctantly. "We always seem about to hire more, but we never do."

"Phil, this is Thom Lund. He helped me with the Gott case last October." Blake clapped Lund's back once with a loud cracking noise. "Knew the victim—Warwick, I mean. I want him with me for your preliminary findings."

Mercer's face turned the color of a cooked beet. "What exactly is going on in this hospital?" he burst out. "I am overrun with civilians!"

"Now, Phil, take a seat, would you? Lund isn't precisely a civilian. Besides, he knew the victim, was hired by him to investigate a money matter." Lund made a mental note to correct the lieutenant later when the coroner was out of earshot. He hung back, trying to look as inconspicuous as a tall man in a formal tailcoat could.

"I've had enough of the public for today, thank you very much." Mercer glared at Blake.

Blake held up both hands in mock surrender. "This one will be on his best behavior, Phil. Scout's honor."

"Well, he'd better be. That woman put my best microscope through my office window!" He gestured to the door. A few small pieces of glass still lay near the wall like a trail of breadcrumbs. "The hospital doesn't like scenes like that one. I'll have some explaining to do in the morning."

"Feel free to lay the blame at my door. Probably should belong there, to be honest. I should have realized she was loony when she pulled a faint in the morgue."

"It is your fault," the doctor said firmly. "I don't like civilians in my medical rooms."

"You want me to take the girl with me when I go? I could—"

"No, no." Mercer waved a hand and shuffled papers on his desk. "After what I went through? She's staying right where she is." He ran his hand through his hair. "I'm sorry, Nathan. It's been a long night." Looking up at them from the desk, he declared indignantly, "Not here. Can't give you a report in front of an open door. Wouldn't be private, then, would it?"

Dr. Mercer led them next door. Turning on the lights, Lund saw two long tables with microscopes and weights and burners. An undefinable smell mixed with bleach and scouring cleaner. "Have a seat," Mercer said as he took a stool, balancing on it like an irritable cat. "Warwick was killed by a blow to the head."

Blake had taken a small notebook out of his pocket and began taking notes. "From the stairs or the hit he got before he fell?"

"The hit. It was a clean hit right to the chin. Lucky, or someone who knew what they were doing. Warwick was dead by the time he hit the stairs. The bruises from the stairs were on the outside of the arms. If he had been conscious, he would have put his hands out to catch his fall." Mercer threw his arms out in front of him with his fingers splayed. He held them there for a moment. "Like that. If he were conscious, he would have fallen, and the stairs would have struck him on the inside of his arms." He crossed his arms and glowered at Lund. "Instead, he slid down the stairs and landed facedown."

Blake looked up from his notebook. "He was faceup when we found him."

"I know it." Mercer used his hands as he spoke. "Someone flipped him over."

"Man or woman?"

"I need to do more measurements. Don't have enough data now to say. Could have been either one."

"You think a woman could have made that hit?"

Mercer shrugged. "Sure. Anyone can get lucky. But not likely."

"Determination? Anger?" Blake asked.

"Who knows? Motive isn't my area."

There was a moment of quiet in which the only noise was

Blake's pencil moving around the page in his notebook. Mercer watched Lund as he slowly walked down the long table, taking in all the instruments and books.

"Okay, Phil," Blake said finally. "What about the girl?"

"That's a bit more interesting. Arsenic, it's got to be." Mercer took a small tray from behind him and lifted the towel. Resting in the pan were two chocolates, one with a bite taken out of it, the other one whole. "You can see where the chocolates were tampered with—here." He pointed at the edge of the chocolate. "Wasn't the most professional job, but it was thought out. Whoever did it could have cut out the bottom, but this person broke off some of the chocolate then replaced it and tried to smooth it over. You have to look for it, but it's there. It struck me as an amateur, but frankly," he stopped for a moment, putting the tray down on the table so Lund and Blake could see, "I wonder if this is someone who has tried poisoning before."

"Anything specific?" Blake looked up. "Or just a feeling?"

Mercer shrugged. "Just a feeling."

"Do you think they were attempting to kill the girl or just make her sick?"

Mercer shook his head. "I couldn't say. Hitting a man with a blunt instrument? I can understand that, but arsenic poisoning—I'll never comprehend it for as long as I live. Horrible way to die. Painful and unrelenting all the way to the end."

"Where could they have picked it up?"

"Anywhere." It was Lund who replied. "Most rat poison is made from it."

Mercer continued, deep in thought, "I'm sure she ate at

least one chocolate. It made her ill, too ill to go on, and she collapsed where you found her. Maybe if she had eaten all three, she would have died straight away. I have to examine the chocolate, of course, but if I had to say at this point, it was attempted murder."

"Could it have been suicide?" Blake pressed his case when Mercer sighed and rolled his eyes. "Look, she was pregnant." Blake counted on his fingers. "She can't tell anyone, can't do anything about it. It wouldn't be the first time that a girl tried a home remedy to take care of an unwanted visitor."

"Yes, Nathan, perfectly sensible conclusion, and I would agree with you but for one thing: that girl didn't know she was pregnant."

Blake stiffened, pausing to look at Lund over his shoulder. "I looked at her once and could tell immediately. What do you mean she didn't know?"

"Listen, Nathan. There are young women out in the world who know hardly anything about themselves. It wasn't the first time I've had to explain the birds and the bees to an expecting mother, and it won't be the last. But I can tell you with my hand on the Bible that the girl down the hall had no idea she was pregnant until I told her earlier tonight."

"What did she think she was?"

"It's straightforward. She thought she was fat. Her mother has her on a slimming fad and is hardly allowing her any food at all. The poor girl told me she couldn't understand why she wasn't losing any pounds. I'd say she's about four, maybe five months."

"But the other symptoms!" Blake protested.

"The faintness and nausea she would put down to her

restricted diet. There are similar explanations for the other symptoms too."

"Have you ever heard anything so incredible?" Blake turned to Lund.

Lund replied briefly, "It isn't unheard of."

"Don't believe me!" Mercer was sarcastic. "I'm only the doctor."

"Alright, Phil, keep your temper."

"It could have been suicide for a different reason," Lund said quietly. Both men turned to look at him. "Remorse for killing her father."

16

LUND LEFT MERCER'S OFFICE WITH a heavy step. It was almost 4 a.m. and his body screamed from exhaustion. The night shifts he had worked in the Old City of Shanghai's French zone were a distant memory. Soft, that's what he was now. Lund stretched his back, shaking his head to wake himself up. He found a young orderly leaning against the wall with his eyes shut and asked him for directions to Tulip's room. The orderly pointed down the hall toward the nurse's station, where a flash of gold caught his eye.

He stood still. "Penelope."

Her head lifted, blue eyes boring into him as he stepped forward quickly to take her hand. "Oh, Thom." She looked at him as though she was about to cry.

"What are you still doing here? You must go home." He put his arms around her, holding her as tightly as he dared.

"I will." Penelope wiped her eyes with the back of her hand. She shook herself and began again, "We will. Mother is arranging a cab. Ivy is just cleaning up. She has . . . her dress has . . ." She pressed her face into Lund's arm. "Oh, Thom, it's been awful!"

"But why are you here? Go home. Surely Ivy has someone who can stay with her. Family friends? Her sister Clover?"

Penelope laid her head against his jacket, pulled his white handkerchief from the outside pocket. "Ivy's told us she's been away at school. She only just came back. She doesn't know anyone who would help her. Her mother isn't any help, that's for sure. She told Ivy not to come home. Clover? God knows where she is. I'm sure she'll turn up when the newspapers publish."

"Perhaps the hospital has someone who could—"

All at once she stiffened and took a step away from him. "Next thing you'll say the police should sit with her!"

"Penelope, Tulip took arsenic, or was given it." Lund was too tired to find the right words. "Something's wrong here. In most cases, the police are the best suited in a situation like this one. There is a reason for that."

"She's just a child." A furrow had appeared in Penelope's brow as he spoke, her eyes suspicious. "Half the time I don't think she knows what she is saying. She's lost, she's alone, surrounded by strangers. I can't leave her like this." She was upset, but he couldn't understand why.

"I could ask Nathan if there's a female police officer who could sit with her or . . ." He trailed off when he saw her face.

The paleness had given way to anger, bright pink spots coloring her cheeks.

"I'm taking Ivy home with me." Penelope straightened as she spoke. "She needs to change her clothes and have a rest. Then I'll bring her back. By then Violet will have had some time to think it over. I'm sure she'll be back once she realizes the press are onto the story."

He had made her angry, but he couldn't see how he had done it. "I can take you back to the apartment, but I can't stay. I've got some business on Long Island I have to deal with."

"Business?" Penelope's mood darkened further. "You mentioned that last night. What business do you have on Long Island that is more important than a girl on her own?"

"It's for the bank, Penelope. You know I can't talk about it."

For a moment, he could see the hurt in her. Penelope took a step away from the nurse's station, her head up. "No need to escort us. Mother and I can handle things with Ivy from here." The words were stiff. After stepping away from him, she turned as though she couldn't make up her mind and said, "Will you call when you come back?"

Impulse guided his hand to reach for hers. She allowed him to take her hand. Raising it up, he kissed it. When he looked up, the angry pink spots on her face faded into a blush. "Of course."

She smiled. It was small, and probably against her will, but it was there. Lund's heart leaped. As he stepped away, he pushed all his misgivings about the Warwicks to the side. Penelope was her own person, with better judgment than most men he knew. She'd do what she said she would and take care of the girl, then take Ivy back to her family and finish with the matter. There was no sense in telling her what to do when she couldn't stop herself from looking after a hurt and broken thing. Penelope had too much heart to walk away when someone needed help. His instinct told him it was more than just helping a fellow soprano. Penelope had been a woman alone in Shanghai, tied to a drunkard who separated her from her family and her operatic career. What if someone had taken her under their wing in those first few weeks? Helped her the way Penelope wanted to help Ivy? What harm was there in helping a girl who was alone?

But his suspicions lingered. Ivy was different from Penelope. In what way exactly, he couldn't say.

He took the steps down to the taxi station two at a time. He could trust Penelope to do what was right. But all the same, he wouldn't spend too much time on Rask's assignment. Penelope had a way of finding trouble. By dinnertime, she could be up to her neck with venomous Warwicks.

Lund hurried. Just in case.

17

Perched on the edge of her chair, Ivy wiped the sweat from Tulip's forehead. Tulip's face was white except for her lips, which were a strange shade of purple. Penelope remembered a child she had once seen with hypothermia. He had fallen through the ice at her grandmother's estate in Scotland.

When the estate manager pulled the child out, his lips were deep purple, his body quivering with the cold. Tulip looked so much like the poor boy that Penelope had to resist the urge to rub her hands against Tulip to warm her. Tulip's hands trembled. Penelope was sure she was in great pain. She did not cry out or make any sound, which somehow made it harder to watch. An unhealthy smell hung close in the small room. The smell and the silent woman in her sickbed made Ivy and Penelope seem bizarre in their evening gowns. They sat silently waiting for a turn for the better, or the worse.

Penelope leaned into the light. "Tulip, what did you eat this evening?" Tulip turned her face into the bedsheets and writhed.

Ivy's voice was barely above a whisper as she answered for Tulip. "Mama has had her slimming. Tu can't have anything but cold cereal for breakfast, broth and lettuce for lunch, and nothing for dinner. She didn't eat anything else."

Penelope waited for a moment and then spoke again. "Tulip, the lieutenant found chocolate in your purse. He's testing it now, but it will take some time. Was there anything else?"

Tulip shook her head no.

"Where did they come from? Where did you get the chocolates?"

Tulip grew weaker before their eyes. She shut her eyes and covered them tightly with her hand. The door opened, and the matron came through with a small cart.

"I have to get her ready for a procedure. Dr. Mercer says it's definitely arsenic. We need to move things along a little bit."

"Come along, Ivy. The matron will take good care of Tulip." Penelope stood and led Ivy from the room.

The matron leaned her head close to Penelope. "Find out anything?" she whispered.

"Just that the chocolates were hers." Penelope's exhaustion went straight through to her bones. "She wouldn't say where she got them."

"Well, that's something at least. If the poor thing didn't have too much of it, maybe she has a chance." The matron nodded to herself, straightening her pinafore with a brisk tug. "Got to have hope in times like these. She should have known better."

"What do you mean?" Ivy's voice was shrill. Penelope put an arm around her shoulders and pulled her close.

Growing fussier by the second, the matron answered primly, "Didn't she know there are lots of people who would want a child if she wasn't ready for it?"

"What?" Ivy's eyes grew wider. "What child?"

"You heard me," the nurse answered briskly. "I must return to my patient."

"A baby? She wouldn't have done that! She wouldn't have a baby. That isn't something Tulip would do . . ." Ivy's voice rose with growing hysteria. "You have to tell her that Tulip wouldn't have done that! Penelope, you have to help me!"

Penelope led Ivy to a chair and gently lowered her into it. She said to the matron, "My mother and I can take her home and see that she gets some rest and clean clothes before we come back." She searched for words but couldn't find any that felt right. "Is there time?"

The matron considered and her face hardened. "It's her heart we worry about. Does she drink alcohol?"

"I don't know," Penelope replied, wishing she had gotten to know Tulip a little better earlier in the day when she had seen her across the room. The scene at the luncheon came back with vivid clarity, all the Warwicks' neuroses on display. All but one. Where was Clover?

"Perhaps, if it's just the arsenic . . ." The matron shook her head. "Honestly, sometimes I wonder what the world is coming to. You've just got to have hope in times like these. Got to believe she has a chance."

"Does she?" Penelope asked. "Does Tulip have a chance?"

"I've seen stranger things. Now, run along with the girl. She doesn't want to be here for this. Go on."

Penelope took a step back, and the matron shut the door. Her last view of Tulip was her quivering hand gripping the sheet. "Come along, Ivy." Penelope looped her arm through the girl's. "Come home with me. I'll get you some breakfast and some clean clothes. We'll be back as soon as you've had a rest. Tulip will be better then. You'll see."

It was plain that Ivy did not believe her.

18

The train to Sea Cliff would take a little over an hour and a half, most of which was travelling through underground stations. The warmth of his coat and the rock of the starting and stopping train coaxed Lund into a light sleep. As the train bounded out from the underground track, he awoke to see either side surrounded by farmland undisturbed by the crowding city just to the west. Absorbed by the sudden change, he stared out the window. The train blew her whistle. A flock of birds rose up like a sheet shaken out straight over a bed, twisting across the sky. He leaned back against the seat with his hat resting on his knee and watched the birds as he thought about Wallace Peters and Coralee O'Connor.

Coralee, daughter of the textile O'Connors, was an experienced sailor, yet had drowned in June 1927. He pulled a black-and-white studio photo of her from the inside pocket of his coat and studied it. A woman looked back at him with light eyes and softly waved hair gathered at her neck. The train whistle drew his eyes back to the trees that lined the rails. He looked for birds to rise from the branches, but there were none here. Only leaves shaking themselves free in a cold wind. Putting his hat on the seat next to him, he returned the photo to his pocket.

Coralee had been thirty-five when she died, a grown woman. He wondered again about Wallace Peters and his relationship with Coralee. Had he been friendlier than a brother-in-law should be? Had they been lovers? Lund hadn't sensed anything like that when he had spoken to the man the night before. And Rask hadn't said anything. But that didn't mean it wasn't possible. Lund shook himself clear. Exhaustion was muddling his logic. He focused.

The police report had not been helpful. The county police suspected suicide and said as much in police alerts during the search. Lund wondered who had notified the coast guard to keep an eye out for the sailboat she had taken out the night before. It took two days to find the *Fancy-Free*, three weeks for her body to appear on a beach. The one-man police department found her body washed up near Orient Point and then took her to the local coroner, who declared her death a suicide. The missing girl's story filled New York papers for weeks, and the last note she had sent her sister featured prominently in every story. Sold to the *Examiner* by a member of the household for an undisclosed sum, the note clearly stated the intention of suicide in simple prose that lent well to lurid headlines. It read, "Tuttie darling, don't be angry with me. I've tried so hard, but I can't make a go of it. I'm not going back. Love, Cora." Instead of performing a close examination, the deputy dutifully sent the body straight to the family, no questions asked. By the time the New York medical examiner reached the body, it had already been embalmed. Lund was captured by the note, which held his attention even through the physical exhaustion.

Lund had read the folder's contents through twice before boarding the train, committing them to memory. In the late evening on June 18, 1927, the harbormaster saw a woman in white sailing pants, a dark shirt, and a wide-brimmed sun hat prepare the *Fancy-Free* for a night sail. He knew Coralee was an expert sailor, and wasn't worried. She had taken the boat out many times before, sometimes at night, and always came back safely. When she didn't return that night, he concluded that she had dropped anchor when the clouds came in. When midday came and went without a sign of Coralee, the harbormaster took a skiff out to search the bay. He found nothing.

Police found the *Fancy-Free* at the bottom of the drink,

her ripped sails loose and all her screws removed. She had been scuttled with no witnesses to say why or how. Photos showed Lund a boat that had once been beautiful, her mainsail ruined, her cabin filled with sand and mud, her bow cracked by rocks the current found to beat her against. Even the compass had been smashed. Before or after the sinking, the report didn't say. It was a miracle the sailboat had been found at all.

Coralee had left the bulk of her estate to her sister upon her death, her husband, Daniel O'Connor, having died in the war. During her life, she had been generous, friendly, outgoing. The society pages frequently covered her because of her congeniality. Perhaps there was something helpful in the society columns? Lund made a mental note to ask Helen what she could recall about the woman. Could be a hidden scandal had driven her over the edge. He would send a note to Peters asking for access to her banking records, but he couldn't imagine what she could have done to be blackmailed. Peters had been clear she lived a quiet life.

Lund stared out the window, thinking. He understood Peters's confusion. With any luck, he would find something to give the man to hang on to. But, more than likely, the answer would always remain unclear, unsatisfying. Lund knew this better than anyone. It was surely the reason Rask had chosen him for the job. He had found no easy answers when his mother swam out into the surf and did not return. No note. No explanation. Without a body to bury, Lund began to think of her as merely away, as though she were always somewhere just outside of his line of sight. A wraith. A ghost. Courcelette had cured him of her haunting, replacing her with a steady concentration on survival. Lund wondered if he had given up on his search for answers or if he had simply settled on blaming his father.

The train whistle blew. Birds rose from the trees. He dreamed his mother was still alive.

The sharp cold of the day pricked his face as he left the train car at Sea Cliff station. From the platform, the small buildings around the station reminded him of villages across Europe, each huddled around the rails like a family around a fire. Lund took his time as he walked past the ticket office, looking for the stairs, absorbing the charm of the small town square and the quiet. He found a cabbie leaning on his car and eating a sandwich. "You know the way to Piping Rock?"

"Sure I do." The man put his sandwich down on the hood of the taxi. "What do you want going out there?"

"I'm here on behalf of the owner, Dale Wilcox." The map put Coralee's house several miles away. Perhaps the cabbie had known her, but he couldn't be certain. Lund pushed up the brim of his hat and squinted at the man. "He said this was the closest station."

"He had you on, then. If you're going on to Locust Valley, you had three stops yet."

Lund had no answer for this. He had taken the route Peters had given him in the file, the same one Coralee took to reach the cottage.

"Not if you take Frost Pond." The driver in the next cab over leaned across his seat and gestured to Lund. "You got the address written down, Mac? Give it over." There was a grunt as the man pulled a map from his glove compartment.

Lund leaned one arm on the second cab and studied the cabbie with the sandwich. "Nice day," he said placidly. "Don't get to see too much of the sky in the city."

The cabbie with the sandwich watched him suspiciously, absorbing Lund's expensive suit and wristwatch. "I should have known you was from the city." Gesturing with his thermos cup, he added, "Better watch yourself out here. You'll get lost."

Lund leaned a little deeper against the car, loosening his right hand. "That right?"

"Yeah, there's a lot of city people coming out here to Sea Cliff these days, getting themselves lost. Wasting everyone's time. I say they should just go home." The cabbie took a bite of his sandwich and watched Lund without blinking. Lund gauged the difference between them as about four feet and twenty years.

"Shaddap, Chrissy, or I'll knock your lights out," the other cabbie said peacefully from inside the car. He winked at Lund and then continued, addressing the other cabbie, "This man, he don't know how you run your mouth all the time. Maybe he don't know you're kidding." Peering at the map without looking up, he followed the road with a heavy finger. "Here it is," he jabbed at the thin map, "right where I said. Chrissy, you owe me a nickle."

"I'll give you a nickle all right, old man." Chrissy put his sandwich down and grinned at Lund, all his front teeth showing. Lund slowly stood up from his position against the car, relaxing his arms from the shoulders with careful suspicion.

"C'mon, Mac, get in before Chrissy tries it on you and you have to biff him one." The second cab driver reached behind his seat to open the back door.

Lund kept his eyes on Chrissy for a long moment. There was no way around the cabbie but to walk past him. Inside the car, the second driver finally got the door open and sat forward to start the engine. Lund sighed and began for the door. He took three steps before Chrissy tried to hold him with his left arm and punch him in the kidney. Lund caught the kid by his wrist and pushed him against the car with his body weight. Chrissy cried out, and Lund released him, allowing the man to fall back against his taxi, holding his wrist.

"You broke my arm." Chrissy's face was red, and he looked as though he was about to cry. "You broke my damn arm!"

"Jesus, mister!" The second cabbie looked from Lund to the kid with his mouth open. He thought hard for a moment while he looked Lund over from inside the cab. Seeming to make up his mind, he called out, "Don't be a crybaby, Chrissy! If he did break your arm, you had it coming. Trying for a man like that—anyone would have taken a swing at you! C'mon, Mac, get in the car." Lund slid into the back seat and shut the door, watching Chrissy gasp for air as he held his arm, the half-eaten sandwich on the hood of the car next to the thermos.

"My name's Paolo," the driver chirped as he pulled the taxi out of the train lot. The kid back there's my nephew Christopher."

"I suppose I should apologize?"

Paolo laughed. "For what? He's had it coming all week, that kid. My buddy Jerry let him run the cab while he takes his wife to see her mother. He's not going to be happy when he comes back and finds out the kid ran off all his regular fares being so nasty. It's been on my mind to pop him one myself!" Paolo cackled. Putting his arm across the seat, he spoke over his shoulder. "So why are you going up to Piping Rock? I know for a fact no one's been there for a year. It's that woman's house, the one who offed herself. Am I right?"

"The estate sent me up to look for some papers." Lund settled back into the seat and watched the driver's eyes in the reflection of the rearview mirror. "The caretaker knows I'm coming."

"That would be Wanda Wilcox. Caretaker is just the right word for her too. She was downright devastated after Coralee died. Treats her place like a shrine and never moves anything. Been plenty of times since last year that people asked if they could go in, newspapers and the like, and she wouldn't hear of it. I hope you aren't lying about permission, because her husband, Dale, will fill your backside with buckshot if you are."

"I guess you're going to tell me you don't like strangers here."

Paolo laughed. "There are no strangers in these parts. Everyone knows everyone else. We are all in each other's business all the time. That's what happens when you live in a small town like this one—no privacy." He looked over the back seat and winked.

"Did you know Coralee?"

"Of course I did. We all did. Coralee used to come out here nearly every weekend. I used to ask her, I'd say, 'Mrs.

O'Connor, why d'you want to give up New York City and all that class for our tiny little town?'" Paolo turned the car down a street lined with trees so tall and dense that they blocked most of the sunlight. Lund felt a sudden chill.

"What did she say to that?"

"Oh," Paolo turned right and shifted as the car began to pick up speed, "she said that it was the best place she knew to hide out."

"What did she mean by that?"

Paolo turned to look at Lund. "If you don't mind my asking, did you know her?"

"No." Lund didn't hide his curiosity. "I've heard she was very outgoing."

"Now where did you hear that from? New York City? I bet they said that because that's what she wanted them to say." He laughed. It was friendly and warm. "That's who she was hiding from—all those prancing ponies in New York City!"

"So she was solitary, then."

"No, she had a friend. They would come out together and take care of the place. She didn't come every weekend, but pretty steady. In the summer when all the windows were open, you could hear them singing." He began to slow the cab down and pointed out the window. "My friend's mother lives down that road." Paolo indicated the woods with a nod. Lund could just make out the roof of a house in the shadows. "There's an inlet there that opens into the bay. Coralee lived on the other side. On a calm day, we would sit outside and listen to them sing. You'll see what I mean when we get there. Just a few more minutes."

Lund was silent as he looked out the window and realized Paolo had driven him deep into the countryside. The transition from the small town center with businesses and a fire station to the country had happened so quickly that he had hardly noticed.

"Here we are," Paolo said as he turned down a dirt drive. "Just down there at the end of the road. Looks like Wanda is waiting for you. Can you see her?" Lund looked over the man's shoulder at the distant house and saw a figure in a dress standing in front of a white cottage with red trim. About a hundred yards away, a second house with grey shiplap sat dark. Beyond both, a waterway sparkled in the November sun, its banks dotted with ice and snow.

"How do you know that's Wanda?" Lund could barely make out the woman in the distance.

Paolo laughed. "She's the only one who would be out here, isn't she?" The cabbie turned down the drive, taking the road slow. The woman walked out to meet them, her hands deep in the pockets of a heavy peacoat.

They reached the end of the drive, and Lund got out of the back, coming around to the driver's side with his wallet out. Handing over a five to Paolo, he added one to it and asked, "Can you take me back in a couple of hours?"

"Sure!" Paolo took the money and put it in his pocket quickly as he looked past Lund at the woman.

"Don't you give him anything extra! He'll just spend it on a drink like he always does." Wanda Wilcox stepped up to the car and leaned down. She said through the window, "I'm gonna tell Rose you just got ten dollars. I will."

Paolo took on a serious look. "Now, look here, Wanda."

"I see her tomorrow at the Women's Auxiliary meeting. It won't be any trouble at all." She stood up straight. "And don't come back here expecting to rob Mr. Lund blind. He's working. Do you hear me, Paulie? He isn't up for any of that flimflam you and your nephew get up to. Do you hear me?" She took a step back and said to Lund, "Dale'll take you back when you're done here."

Paolo screwed up his face in a grimace and sucked his teeth. "That isn't the right way to speak to a man, woman. I have a mind to have a word or two with Dale."

"Well go to it—he's right over there." She pointed to a small boathouse just off the creek, about a quarter of a mile from where they stood. She crossed her arms and turned back toward the small white cottage. "See you later, Paolo." She walked toward the house without looking to see if Lund was following. He walked behind her, around the front of the cottage to the back of the house.

The place snuck up on a person, he thought. First forests that hid the sun on a perfectly clear day and now cottages that hid open water. The sun that had lulled him in the train shone on the water without restriction, the color of the water a deep, dark blue mixed with black until the shore, where it turned a dark green. The dense woods that lined the inlet were lit up with gold. Lund imagined the canopy of leaves during the summer was thick enough to cover the sky completely. He wondered what Penelope would make of it.

It was a remote spot. Secluded, that was the word. The two cottages were the only buildings he could see near the water, and they sat a thousand feet apart. Lund counted four houses about a nautical mile away, each one separated by dense tree growth. When the trees were heavy with leaves, he was sure the two cottages in front of him would be hidden from the water and from the road. He tried to imagine how it must look in June. It would be dark, even with a full moon, difficult to see.

"You coming?" Wanda had turned to watch him.

"Private sort of place you have here." Lund fell into step alongside her as she led him around the back of the smaller cottage. "Must be beautiful in the summer."

"Some say so." Wanda kept her mouth tight and looked away at the cottage.

"Can you see the water from the house in the summer?"

Wanda gave him a look that told Lund she knew exactly why he was asking. "From this house? Yes. Not from ours." She turned her face away from him, her thoughts hidden.

A screened-in porch faced the water, the skeletons of chairs stacked one on top of the other. Wanda looked at the porch and sighed. Lund looked at her in the light and saw she was younger than he had first thought. She had freckles across both cheeks. Her hair was held back at her neck. He thought she might have been crying. "Mrs. Wilcox?" he asked politely, and she nodded, staring through him with brown eyes as hard as flint. "Thank you for meeting me."

Taking a deep breath, Wanda seemed to steel herself. "Is he going to sell?" she asked abruptly. She nodded at the white cottage with the red trim. "Coralee's house, I mean. Is he going to sell it?"

"I wouldn't know anything about that." Lund looked down at her and wondered what it could be that had her so upset.

She insisted, "Mr. Peters said this was about the estate. Doesn't that mean he's going to sell?"

"I'm just here to look for papers, Mrs. Wilcox. I'm not here for anything else."

She sighed and wilted. "Sorry, mister. It keeps me up at night thinking about having a neighbor so close. Especially someone I don't know. We don't like strangers." Lund glanced at the grey house in the distance and thought he saw someone pass in front of the window. "Don't see how you're going to find any papers. She burned them all before she went out that day. Did they tell you?"

Lund shook his head. "I'll just have a look around. You never know. Have to check everywhere."

She nodded. "Come and get Dale when you're ready to go back, and he'll drive you to the station."

"Did you know her well? Coralee O'Connor, I mean."

Wanda looked at the ground for a moment. "My whole life, if you must know." She indicated the distant house with a quick nod of her chin. "My mother sold her the land after my father died. She wouldn't have done that for just anybody." She paused and hugged herself tightly as though she was cold. "Mrs. O'Connor was the nicest lady I ever met. All the same, I wish Mr. Peters would sell it back to us before he sells to someone else." She watched him from the corner of her eye. "I told him so."

"Paolo told me Coralee came out here nearly every weekend."

"Paolo!" She spat on the ground near his feet. "He's wicked." She stared out at the water behind him.

"I can see why she came out here so often. It's beautiful."

"Takes some people that way. She said it was heaven to her." Looking down, Wanda shifted on her feet. "She didn't do it," she said flatly. "There's no way she would have."

"Kill herself?"

"I meant scuttle that boat. That's what the police said Coralee did. They said she took out all the bilge plugs from *Fancy-Free* and scuttled her." She shook her head stiffly. "She would have never done that to her boat."

"Why do you think that?"

"Because it was cruel and mean!" Wanda stopped herself and looked down at her shoes again. After a moment, she wiped her face with her cardigan sleeve and handed him the keys. Then she turned without another word and walked toward the distant grey house.

19

THE PORCH DOOR OPENED TO a small, serviceable kitchen. The lights, still functional, bathed the stove and counter in a warm yellow light. The countertop around the sink was clear, yet the room still gave the feeling that the cook had just stepped out and would return any moment. The place lacked the smell Lund usually associated with houses that had been closed up. He had the strange sensation of being watched, listened to. It made the hair on the back of his neck stand on end.

On the other end of the kitchen was a small table with

two chairs. A vase with cheerful silk flowers sat between two brightly painted yellow chairs. Lund wondered who such a private person would be having over for dinner. He stood over the table for a moment, touching the embroidered flowers on the placemats with the tip of a finger.

His thoughts were fitful and chaotic. Lund found that he could hardly face leaving the kitchen to see the rest of the house, his sensation of being watched was so strong. He set his mind to it without thinking and found himself in the living room, a large, open room with a phonograph, a piano, and a fireplace. Comfortable chairs that were worn, patched, and worn again sat on either side of the fireplace. One low and flowered, the other leather. Lund wondered who Coralee could have taken as a lover, and made a mental note to speak with Peters about it.

Behind him chest-high bookcases lined the walls, filled with books of every kind. Along the tops were photographs and mementos, all carefully dusted as though the owner had just left. Again Lund had the strange sensation of living in another world where Coralee had not died. He found the stairs and climbed them slowly, hearing each squeal and creak under his feet.

The bedroom at the top of the stairs held two twin beds neatly made up with white chenille covers. A garden window seat looked out over the road. Each nightstand had a lamp, one in the figure of a shepherdess, the other a shepherd. Lund got down on one knee and examined the floor, finding deep scratches where the beds had evidently been repeatedly pushed together, then separated. Who had she been hiding from out here in the middle of nowhere? The closet was empty except for a pair of rubber boots, some hatboxes, and pieces of luggage. The boots might have been worn by a man with small feet or by a woman, over her shoes. The hatboxes and monogrammed luggage at the top of the closet were empty. Lund removed his hat and jacket and dropped them on the nearest bed, walking with more purpose.

The washroom had been appointed with a small sink and toilet, both pink. The tile was an eclectic mixture at best but distinctly feminine and heartily sweet. On the wall hung a painting of a mermaid combing her hair with a shell. Opening the linen closet, he found sheets but no towels. It seemed odd that they would be missing when everything else seemed present and accounted for. He stared at the bathtub, with its small window looking out into the woods, and thought.

There was nothing for it. He would have to search each room.

Following little more than an instinct that the house had something to give up, Lund decided to start with the smallest room first and set to work on the washroom. As he felt the tile, testing each for looseness, he thought through his next steps. He could only confirm the assumption that Coralee had burned all her papers if he searched the house for more. Her secretive life and the uncertain clues that she had a lover made him believe firmly that there was more to be found. Signs that a man had lived here with Coralee were everywhere, from the chair in the living room to the boots in the closet.

The best hiding spots, in his experience, were those in plain sight. Matthias had hidden cash in his father's bookshelf for years under a cover that read, *Sermons from the Antilles*. There really was no better way to keep the old drunk from stumbling upon the accumulated wealth. Until they ran away to join the front, their father hadn't a clue there was enough money to drink himself to death just a few feet from where he slept.

Lund stood in the middle of the bedroom and cast his eyes along the baseboards, the heavily waxed floor, and the nearly empty closet. He was turning in place, his eyes scanning the windows, when he was drawn to a small building outside the house by the drive. Picking up his hat and coat, Lund went down the stairs and out through the front door, striding across the lawn with a quick march just short of a run.

After making short work of the lock, he pushed the heavy door open and stared into the boathouse. Empty now, except for the long poles and wedges used to prop the *Fancy-Free* upright when it was out of the water, the boathouse had a mournful air of loss and barrenness without the sailboat to cheer it. Shelves scaled the wall, covered with tools, rope, gloves, paint, sailcloth, repair kits, motor parts, and broken paddles with accompanying glue. There were cans of nails, screws, nuts and bolts, and all the tools to properly use each in every kind of box imaginable. He found chocolate tins covered with dancing women repurposed for kerosene-soaked rags and a single red mitten. He had searched only half the boathouse when he found a pair of small coveralls soaked in oil and stiff with cold. Holding them up, he shook them out roughly, then methodically searched each pocket. When he felt the paper in the left breast pocket, he already knew he had found gold. Extracting it carefully, he unfolded the note. Lund leaned back to put it in the light from the window.

The note read, "I'll tell them everything."

20

"It's a wonder we aren't running an animal hospital for stray dogs and cats," James grumbled from the comfort of his bathrobe. "Please tell me that she won't be here all morning. I simply must study or I will fall behind."

Penelope stole the toast from his plate and took a bite. "You should have a little fun, brother dear. It would suit you." Other than to take off her shoes and her opera coat, Penelope had done little to adjust her appearance since they had brought Ivy to the apartment. She sat down at the small round table and sighed with relief. She glanced down at her dress. "I've worn this dress too long; the fabric will lose its shape."

"You come home with a stray and all you can worry about is your dress?"

"Be quiet, James. She can hear you!" Penelope reached out to slap his arm. "I can't afford to buy another dress like this one. I have to keep it nice a while longer."

James took another piece of toast from the rack and began to butter it. He lowered his voice. "When do you take her back?"

Penelope glared at her brother. "Your mind is a one-way street. Anyone ever tell you that?"

Eleanor appeared from the kitchen with a pot of coffee. "Behave, James." She waved a hand at her son as she set the pot down on the table. "Penelope and I just spent all night in the hospital."

"I know your lovely heart is in the right place, Mother. But I must ask if you and Penelope plan on bringing any other strange women to our humble apartment while I am still in my bathrobe."

"I really have no idea where these thoughts come from, James." Eleanor patted Penelope's hand. "Your sense of humor has positively degraded since we returned to America."

"It's the lethal booze," Penelope said in a stage whisper.

"More like these medical texts." James snorted. "In addition to driving on the wrong side of the road, Americans do everything differently. By the time I become a licensed doctor, I will have learned two different methods for every surgical practice known to man."

"You're happier than you've been in months. Admit it." Penelope prodded him with a finger and stole another piece of toast.

"The damsel speaks the truth!" James declared. "Finally!"

"Before you know it," Penelope said, "you'll be supporting Mother and me with your excessive doctor's salary."

"Don't make me laugh! By the time I have my degree, you'll be rolling in it from your singing career. Say!" James sat forward. "How did that shindig go yesterday? The rehearsal thingummy. Find any students?"

"It was a bust." Penelope turned her attention to the coffee pot at her elbow. The rehearsal felt to her as if it had been a year before. She and Mary had such plans and schemes. More than one of the opera society ladies would have happily spent a little cash on a lesson or two ahead of the performance, they were sure. It had been a good plan, smashed to oblivion with the appearance of Violet Warwick and Mrs. Anthony Stone. Penelope tried to put some enthusiasm into her words. "I shall think of another way. There's more than one way to peel an orange."

James sighed, patted her hand. "Oh darling, I'm so sorry for you. Well," he stood up with a brisk brush of his lap, "I'd better go study if I'm going to support the family. Penelope, knock on my door when the girl is gone, would you? I don't want to emerge in my suspenders and shock the gal."

"Shock her? James, that would shock me!" Penelope replied with a grimace.

"So long, toots!" He lifted the pot of coffee from the table and disappeared into the hallway. A moment later, Penelope heard the door to his room shut, followed by a loud click as he shot the bolt.

"Well I never!" Penelope sat up straight.

"What is it?" Eleanor pushed through the swinging kitchen door and sat down at the table.

"James just locked himself in his room."

"Hmm." Eleanor studied the table. "And from the look of it, he took the coffee with him. Mrs. Reynolds?"

A large woman with forearms like turkey legs leaned into the room. "Yes, Mrs. Harris?"

"James has run away with the coffee again. Is there another pot we can use?"

"Just a moment, Mrs. Harris."

Eleanor returned to Penelope. "I can't say I blame him. I'd lock myself in my room, too, if I thought the girl would leave on her own."

"Mother, hush! She'll hear you."

"It doesn't bother me in the slightest if she does or doesn't—and that isn't a common occurrence for me." Eleanor sniffed. "She couldn't have been more unpleasant in the cab if she had tried. I've seen young girls in trouble many times, and whatever that child is going through has nothing to do with anyone but herself."

"You would feel differently if you had seen how her mother talked to her. She blamed Ivy for everything, came about as close as she could to saying it was Ivy's fault Tulip was in the hospital."

Eleanor shook her head. "Violet Warwick may not be much of a mother, but as long as that child is under the age of eighteen, she is her mother. Not you, and certainly not me. Ivy can't stay here, Penelope. I agreed to bring her home for a change of clothes and to get her away from that place while the doctors do what they can, but that is all. We will have our breakfast, we will clean ourselves up, then we take her back. Even as I sit here, I regret it. She should have stayed at the hospital."

"By herself?"

"With her sister." Eleanor met Penelope's eye with steady calm. "Didn't you tell me Tulip was disowned by her mother? She's there alone right now. She might even be dying, and she's all by herself. If you can't see it, and Ivy doesn't know it, then I will tell you quite plainly: that child should be by her sister right now."

"Of course, you are right. I'm not thinking clearly." Penelope glanced over her shoulder at the hallway leading to her bedroom, where Tulip was changing. "I can't imagine what it must be like for a girl to have a mother like that."

"I will happily take that as a compliment." Eleanor reached for the newspaper. "Now, I must remind you. We have the indomitable Mrs. Reynolds once a week on Saturdays for two things: a decent breakfast with bacon and help with the laundry. You'll forgive me if I leave you to take care of that feral child while I enjoy these excellent eggs and coffee for the one meal I am not required to make myself." Eleanor turned her attention to the front page. "You had better get out of your dress and change into something more appropriate for the hospital."

21

Penelope collected her opera coat, purse, and shoes as she passed the front door to the apartment. The purse was heavy in her hand, the gun reminding her suddenly of Lund. The flush grew from her neck, warmth moving up her cheek like the stroke of a finger. The recollection of his kiss followed suddenly, catching her unaware. With little effort, she remembered the slow exhale of his breath against her parted lips, her heart beating a little faster. Why had she allowed Ivy to interrupt them? She had been asking herself the question since Lieutenant Blake had stepped out from the phalanx of policemen and greeted Lund like a brother. She should be at Mary's right now settling in for a good long gossip about Lund, the Warwicks, and Gilbert Richie. Penelope had looked for Mary and Gil at the intermission and had seen neither hide nor hair of them. There was a story there, she was sure of it. She sighed. Staying up all night would have been worthwhile with Lund. But this child, this angry child—Penelope regretted her compassion. Lund was right. She should have let things be.

In the grey light of the morning, Penelope knew she helped the girl for all the wrong reasons. She was entirely unable to keep herself from seeing the similarities between Ivy and herself at the same age. The frustrating life as an expatriate in a foreign country hadn't been the first choice for a teenage girl set on a career in the opera. Then when her father moved them all to Hong Kong, putting him closer to his shipping business and Penelope further from her dreams, she freed herself from the tedium the only way she could think of. By eloping, she destroyed her chances at a career in music and saddled herself with a past the newspapers couldn't get enough of. But Ivy . . . this child was not a younger Penelope. She was a stranger. Ivy would have been fine under the matron's care, and it would have been better to not leave Tulip. The cab ride home from the hospital had been uncomfortable. Even more so when Ivy had taken Penelope by the hand and clutched it tightly enough to make her fingers hurt, all while keeping her body strangely tense and turned away.

Penelope knocked on the bedroom door. "Ivy? Have you dressed?"

The silence from the other side of the door was too still, too quiet. Was the girl gone? Penelope looked behind herself at the apartment door at the other end of the hallway—still latched from the inside. "Ivy?" Penelope opened the door.

Her room was small but warm and happy. A window spilled light across the bed every afternoon without fail. The yellow striped wallpaper with tiny rosebuds wasn't Penelope's usual taste, but after two months she had begun to think it sweet. It certainly suited Ivy's youth. The yellow was welcoming at any time of the day or night. Ivy's dress lay on the floor in a crumpled heap, the clean suit Penelope had put out for the girl on the floor next to it.

Penelope felt her exhaustion all the way down to her toenails. It seemed hardly possible that just the day before she had been on her way to the luncheon with Mary, the Warwicks not even a dot on the horizon.

Ivy lay still under the covers with her hair swept back from her forehead and splayed out on the pillow, Penelope's favorite silk coverlet from China wrapped tight around her shoulders. She looked a good deal younger than seventeen in the light from the window. Penelope stood there for a moment, puzzling over the differences, and chalked them up to exhaustion. She laid the coat and her other things on the dressing stool and sat down on the edge of the bed. "Ivy, breakfast is ready."

The girl opened her eyes. "I was so tired," she said. "I thought I would lie down."

"Perhaps when we get back to the hospital, the matron can set you up with a cot in Tulip's room." Penelope put her hand on Ivy's shoulder.

"Would she do that?" Ivy's tone was strange, as though she were revulsed by the idea. "I don't want to go back. I shouldn't have to." The girl sulked, furrowing her brow and pushing out her bottom lip. "I don't want to see Tulip. I don't. She doesn't want me there either."

"Ivy, I was sick for a long time." Penelope pushed aside the memories of the convalescent wards that haunted her dreams. "When I was in hospital, all I hoped for was to have my family there by me. You may not understand now, but you will regret it very much if you aren't there for Tulip. You don't have to stay in the room with her, only let her know you're nearby."

Ivy sat up and rested her chin on her knees. "Are you saying I should go to the hospital because it's what's expected?"

"That's only part of it." Penelope searched for the words. "Ivy, Tulip is very sick."

"You mean she might die?" There was a strange flatness to her delivery. "I don't care about that."

The coldness took Penelope by surprise. Did the girl know what she was saying?

"No one understands me. They all want me to go away. Even Tulip. Ask them. You'll see."

"Tulip cares about you." Penelope remembered Tulip's earnest, round face. "I know she does."

"You don't know anything about my family. You don't know what they've done. Mama doesn't want me there. I get underfoot—she told me so! Tulip doesn't want me either. I know because she told me too. I'm not upset she's sick. She brought it on herself! They all did. Horrible people. Terrible people. Dreadful things happen to people like that." Ivy brightened, lifting her head. "Like Papa. He died, didn't he? He fell down a flight of stairs."

"Ivy, how could you say such things?"

"Mama was going to send me back to that place. As soon as she could convince Papa." Ivy jutted her chin out. "It's a horrible place. Everything I do there is wrong. I can never do anything right. And no one likes me." Ivy's voice rose, insistent and angry. "You want me to leave? That's where they are going to send me. It's on you. That's what it is. Anything that happens to me is on you!"

"You can't stay here, Ivy," Penelope insisted. "You need to be with Tulip."

"You're just like the rest of them." Ivy's face turned red. "You don't really like me! You don't want to help me!"

"That's enough."

The cool voice from the doorway sent a flash of relief up Penelope's spine. Eleanor stood at the door, every inch of her in command of the household. She met Ivy's petulant stare with the control Penelope had feared as a child and admired as an adult.

"Ivy, you will get dressed in the suit my daughter has put out for you. Then we will return to the hospital, where we will wait until someone from your family comes to get you."

"No one is coming!" Ivy protested.

"You have another sister, don't you?" Eleanor did not blink. "Her name is Clover. She can get you, take you home. If you tell us where she is, we could call her for you."

"I don't know where she is." Ivy sulked. "Clover left during the third act, just before the end. She and Tulip don't get on."

The comment was hardly surprising. From the look of things, none of the Warwicks could stand one another. Penelope stood, picked up the suit from the floor, and laid it back on the bed. "Perhaps your mother will send a car for you."

"Didn't you hear what I told you? Mama doesn't want me! And now neither do you!" Ivy swung her legs over the side of the bed and stood up. Penelope was struck by how small the girl was—all bony elbows and shoulders. "You can take me back to the hospital if that's what you want." She picked up the suit skirt. "I don't care."

22

McCain hesitated just outside the door to the hospital room, his hand hovering above the doorknob. He told himself he was being impractical, but it was the heebie-jeebies and he knew it. It began in '20, when he lost Marie and Robbie to the influenza. Hours sitting next to Marie, waiting for her pain to end, holding her hand while the nurses came and went. He hadn't been able to shake his fear of antiseptic since.

"She won't bite." A practical but not heartless voice materialized at his elbow.

"Matron," McCain just barely kept himself from flinching, "how is she?"

The matron looked about thirty-five to the patrolman, sturdy and strong but still pretty, with jet-black hair tucked under her cap. Her eyes had a twinkle that encouraged him. McCain liked women with spirit. He couldn't help liking her even before she said a word.

"She's lucky to be here," she said, deftly dodging the question, an answer by itself. "Dr. Mercer is an expert in poisoning. If anyone can help her, he can." She studied McCain for a moment before continuing. "I suppose I should tell you," she sighed, "the doctor has done all he can, plus more that he thought of along the way. If she can rally, she'll survive. Her sister was here earlier. Her friend rang just a little bit ago to say she was bringing her back within the hour. Good thing too. That girl in there could use a friendly face." The matron studied McCain. "She's a young thing. Have you seen her?"

"No." McCain reached into his pocket. "What's your name?"

She studied him. "Juliet Jones," she said finally.

"Well, Matron Jones, I have to ask her some questions."

"She's had a rough night. It's almost certain she lost the baby." She put her hand on his arm. "Can't you wait? Let her sleep for just a little bit longer?"

"I have to get her statement. Boss's orders." He felt himself blush as she studied him. "Do you believe she tried to harm herself?"

"You mean because of the baby?" The matron considered him, then looked back at the closed door. "No," she said finally. "I don't mind telling you that earlier this evening I was convinced of it. Her age and that far along without telling a soul? I've seen too much of it. But she was surprised when we told her. Genuinely surprised." She straightened the front of her dress with a tug. "That's not evidence, I know. It's just a feeling. I wouldn't be able to stand up in a court of law and say she didn't try to kill herself, if that's what you're looking for." She watched him warily. "But it's the truth. That child didn't poison herself." She held his eye without blinking. "All right. I'll let you ask your questions. But when I say it's over, you stop. Agreed?"

"Yes, matron. Just as you say."

She sighed. "It's been a long night. Why don't you just call me Juliet?"

His nervousness retreated in the face of her steady practicality. McCain relaxed. "M'name's McCain. And you can call me Jasper."

CORNERED WITH A PERFECT SQUARE and stretched taut across Tulip Warwick's body, the ironed white sheets glowed bright and crisp in the dim light of the table lamp. McCain briefly wondered how often they had been changed in the last few hours. The odor of vomit and metal settled just below the smell of ammonia. The matron put a wooden chair next to the bed and nodded at it. McCain stared at the grooved seat. He lowered himself into it, haunted by the familiar creaking of the wood. The thought of Marie was brief. "Miss Warwick?"

The girl in the bed hardly stirred. McCain watched her chest for movement and discerned only the slightest lift. The matron bent down across the light, her shadow falling across the white sheet as she took the patient's hand. "Miss Tulip?" she said quietly. "There is a man here to speak with you. His name is . . ." She glanced at him.

"Jasper," McCain offered. Removing his hat, he placed it on the floor next to his seat. "My name's Jasper."

Tulip's eyes opened. Her hand wandered to the nurse's arm. "May I have something to drink, please?"

"I'll ask the doctor in a minute." Juliet pulled the sheet tight and patted Tulip's hand. When she stood back out of the light, McCain saw Tulip's eyes clearly for the first time. She looked like any girl he had seen before: brown eyes; brown hair combed back from her forehead; pasty white skin; a wide, flat face and small nose that turned up just slightly at the end. All at once, McCain knew the girl would die, was already dying, the poison slowly leaching the spirit from her a little bit at a time. He fought the sadness welling up in him. It was a policeman's job to see these things, ask these questions, help her if he could.

Tulip turned her attention to McCain. "All right." Her voice had no fight in it. "What do you want to know?"

"Do you know what made you sick?" McCain put his pencil to his notebook.

"No." Tulip looked away, her eyes dulling in the shadow. "I was slimming. I hardly ate at all. Mama was terribly upset I couldn't lose weight."

"What about the chocolates in your purse?"

"I found them." Tulip shut her eyes. As he watched, McCain noted an obstinacy grow in the set of her jaw. "It doesn't matter, they couldn't have made me sick. They didn't make me sick. It must have been something else."

"Where did you find them?"

"It doesn't matter. It doesn't matter," she repeated.

"Could be there are more chocolates wherever you found these. Could be someone else will find them."

"They won't." She shut her eyes, her mouth a thin line of pain.

McCain caught Juliet's eye, and she shook her head. He had to agree. It wouldn't do to have Tulip Warwick clam up so early in the interview. Better to come back to it later. He looked down at the notebook in his hand and made a note. "Papers said there was a set-to earlier in the evening between your father and a man named John Gilmurray."

"Papa didn't understand. He thought Mama was giving Mr. Gilmurray a favor when really it was for his wife, Virginia . . ." McCain could see the pain all over her, from the sweat on her brow to her steady, flat delivery as she tried to get through the words quickly without crying out. "Mrs. Gilmurray is Mama's very good friend." There was a practiced delivery to the words that told McCain they were a lie. Despite this, Tulip's eyes moved to the matron as though she could give approval. "I always hear Mr. Gilmurray telling Mama about how they don't have much . . . There wasn't anything wrong with getting the tickets. She got one for Clover, Ivy, and me, didn't she? There was nothing wrong with that." She panted through the words. "Papa wouldn't understand that. He couldn't."

"The police who were here earlier," McCain began, "did they tell you what happened to your father?" He heard the faint click as Juliet struck her tongue against the roof of her mouth in disapproval. He went ahead. "You know everything that happened?"

Tulip searched his face for a long minute. "Yes," she said finally. The only sound in the room was her deep panting as she struggled to breathe through the pain.

"Do you know anyone who would want to hurt your father? Someone who might have been at the opera last night?"

"Papa was strict, but it was because he loved us. Wanted the best for us." The doubt in her eye made McCain feel sorry for the girl.

"Did you see your father meet anyone else, maybe have a fight with some other person?"

"He didn't sit with us," Tulip said slowly. "I don't know where he went."

"This Mr. Gilmurray, say. Were they in business together?"

"Mr. Gilmurray was Papa's lawyer. Mama introduced them at a party."

"Did she now?" McCain made a note. It made sense. Blake had just enough time to tell McCain about the money missing from Warwick's accounts. Gilmurray would need access one way or another. The wife would have been a solid first play. McCain asked, his voice even, almost disinterested, "He been his lawyer for very long?"

Tulip shook her head. "A year . . . maybe two . . ."

"Did Gilmurray and your father fight before?"

"Not that I know of." Tulip looked over to Juliet. "I know the papers said a lot of bad things about Papa, especially after the strike at the factory, but that was just business. He was a good person."

"There, there." Juliet laid her hand on Tulip's shoulder. "Don't upset yourself."

"Perhaps he fell?" Tulip lifted her voice hopefully. "Perhaps his foot slipped and he fell?"

"I'm afraid someone hurt him, Tulip," McCain said slowly. "It would be a good thing if you could help us find the man, make sure he doesn't do this to anyone else."

Her unblinking stare was unnerving. "All right," she said finally.

"Good." McCain leaned forward a bit when he said the word and added a smile. "I'm sure this will be sorted out soon. Now," he licked the tip of his pencil and set it to the paper, "we found you not too far from where we found your father. Why don't you tell us what you saw and what you did, starting from when you left the box? All right?"

The girl nodded.

Tulip proceeded, her sentences interrupted by deep breaths and pauses. She was sick twice, Juliet wiping her face and mouth with the gentleness of a nursemaid minding a baby. McCain watched the life drain from her. A strange sort of shame ate away at him as he listened, whether it was for the job or Tulip's conviction her family was loving and kind, he couldn't tell. Even without speaking to the servants, McCain already had enough evidence to lump the Warwicks into a category he normally regulated to pimps, murderers, and animal abusers.

Tulip had been beside herself with excitement during the performance. Frustrated by what Violet called her "insufferable sighs" and embarrassing "mooning about," Violet moved Tulip and Ivy to the back row next to Mrs. Gilmurray in the middle of the first act, giving the seat next to herself to Mr. Gilmurray.

Mrs. Virginia Gilmurray, McCain noted quietly, had not returned from the first intermission.

During the second intermission, Violet Warwick declared Tulip's enthusiasm for Carrera's performance insipid and banned her entirely from the box. Ivy was allowed to remain, but Tulip was forced to listen to the Barcarolle in the salon behind the box through the closed door.

McCain scratched behind his ear at that one, pausing his writing to consider breaking her monologue with a question. He had seen the antechambers for himself, tiny little rooms with a seat and a lamp. There was time enough to have the boys down at the opera house check between the cushions and in the trash for chocolates. Time enough for that and a little bit more besides. His pen returned to the page.

The arrangement was perfectly fine, Tulip insisted. She could hear Carrera from wherever she sat, her voice was that clear, that lovely. She sat quietly on her seat in the petite salon and listened through the door. Sweat beaded all over Tulip, her recitation of the events clearly taking a toll. But when she spoke of Carrera and her voice, Tulip momentarily lifted up from her pain. McCain got a glimpse of the true girl there, her face shining with the happiness that comes from a good thing, a comforting thing—something you treasure against harm. McCain placed her then, the revelation coming with stunning truth. Tulip was a girl dreaming the hours away in the library where she worked, shelving books while she slyly read them, dreaming her family into a book where everything was fine and would come to a good end. All her dreams explained the world away—her mother's temper, her father's unpleasantness—turning everything right with a delusional fairy tale. The matron was right. The girl hadn't tried to kill herself. She wouldn't have allowed herself to even consider it. Nothing had penetrated the fantasy, not even her pregnancy. Even as she lay there dying, perhaps because she was dying, Tulip wouldn't give up on the illusion that everything bad was good, everything good even better.

McCain stared at the page in his notebook without writing a word down. A creeping darkness whispered. No one put poison in chocolates without intending harm. Tulip's recitative came to a sharp halt, and McCain looked up.

Tulip shut her eyes tight, her hand gripping the sheets in a fist as she curled her shoulders up reflexively, her face a mask of pain. Coming forward, Juliet took her arm and soothed the girl, speaking softly as the spasm came and went again, leaving Tulip damp and depleted. Her hand relaxed. Juliet pulled the sheet tighter across Tulip and wiped the girl's brow with a handkerchief from her apron. "There, there, dear."

"I'm sure you are doing your best," Tulip whispered. "It really isn't your fault. But you see I have a train to catch. I must be on it." She smiled tentatively. "I really must go." She reminded McCain of a woman at a tea party asking if anyone had found a glove.

He looked up from his notes. "A train?" He turned back a few pages. "You had an unfranked ticket to Philadelphia. No departure times. It was in your purse."

"He'll be waiting for me." Tulip lay back against the pillows, her breathing difficult. "I stayed for the opera, to see Carrera. I wouldn't be able to see her otherwise. We won't have much money in the beginning, you see."

McCain did see. "Did your family know?"

"Only Ivy." Tulip tried to smile. "I had to tell her. She wouldn't have understood unless I told her myself."

"Was she happy for you?" McCain couldn't help asking, even as he guessed the answer.

Tulip's smile stayed in place. "She couldn't know what it means to get married. Not really. I told her she couldn't come until we were settled. I told her she could hold out." Tulip's smile faded as she collapsed into herself, her eyes shut tight, her mouth fixed against the pain.

"Hold out?" McCain leaned forward. "What do you

mean Ivy could hold out? From what?" He glanced at the matron, who met his glance with sharpened attention and a quick shake of the head.

"Mama—" Tulip lifted her head and let it fall back. "Mama can be hard to live with."

"She's had enough, Jasper. Tulip needs to rest." The matron wiped Tulip's face as the girl lay back against the pillow.

"I could get word to your young man." McCain stood up. "Your ticket said Philadelphia. I know a few people there. I might even know a man in the station, maybe have your young man paged."

Tulip's face brightened quickly, the color adding prettiness to her cheeks. McCain could recall his mother calling it a bloom. A blush was more like it, he thought.

"I . . ." Tulip caught his eye, the pink on her cheeks fading. "You'd tell Mama." The words were certain and afraid.

"You don't have to tell him anything you don't want to, Tulip." The matron kept her hand on Tulip's arm, her face where the girl could study it. "He's your husband, isn't he?"

"How did you know?" Tulip whispered. "I didn't tell anyone except Ivy . . ."

"The patrolman here isn't the only detective." The matron straightened the sheets across the girl's chest with a comforting busyness. "I found your ring on a chain around your neck when I undressed you."

Tulip's hand flew to her neck. "Where is it?"

"It's here." The matron opened a drawer in the small nightstand and lifted the chain. "Would you like to put it on?"

Tulip reached for the chain and brought it up to her face. "My fingers are too big. I put on weight since we—" Her words came to a stop. The girl wasn't paying attention. She was staring into the middle distance, her mouth slow. "He's gone ahead to rent an apartment. He has a job in Philadelphia, a good one." She smiled to herself. "We're going to live there on our own. Mama will be angry."

"It's your secret, child. A happy secret, isn't it?" Juliet put a hand on the girl's shoulder and smiled.

"What about your father?" McCain returned to his notebook.

Tulip focused on him. "Papa doesn't care about anything but Clover. He won't care a bit as long as I don't ask for money. And we don't need his money." She smiled with her chin out. "He has a good job." Pride radiated from her.

"Tulip," McCain leaned forward, "did you see your father at the opera house? After he argued with your mother?"

Tulip studied him. "No. He wasn't sitting with us. Mama said he had business, but he said he was there to keep an eye on her. I had to get Ivy away from them. It's not good for her."

"Why not?" McCain smiled. He was known for his friendly manner, famous for it. "She'd seen them argue before, hadn't she? Why would that worry her?"

Tulip paled, her skin so white McCain thought she might faint. "Matron . . ." She shut her eyes. "Matron . . ."

"That's enough of that." Juliet took McCain by the arm and gestured to the door. "Time for you to go wait in the hall and for me to work."

McCain stood, moved through the door. "I have to ask, Matron. There are things I need to know."

"Not now you don't." She pushed him into the hall. "Now you wait."

23

LUND KNOCKED ON THE COTTAGE door with a cold, numb hand. It was long past when he had intended to leave Piping Rock, several hours and many trains past. The train schedule in his pocket promised at least three more passenger trains before an overnight stay would have to be arranged. Two hours in the boathouse had dislodged most of Coralee's secrets. Lund knew what had driven her out in her boat on a dark night. Lund remembered the burden from his time as a police officer, that period when you know a crime has occurred but you can't point to the criminal. His body was heavy and slow from lack of sleep, yet nervous as an alert cat.

He wanted to go home to bed, and with Penelope. Not necessarily in that order.

A shape darkened the door's frosted window, blocking out the light. Lund heard the lock turn, and a man, he presumed Dale, filled the doorway and leaned forward. "You must be the man Wallace sent." He was a good deal older than Lund had expected, with deep lines etched in his face like sand had worn away the life in him.

"I am." Lund was direct. "Thom Lund."

Dale looked at his hand for barely a moment before he took it and stepped back into the shadow. "Come on in,

Thom." He added practically, "We're letting the cold in. Wanda will skin me alive." Lund noticed a strange accent and wondered where Dale had lived before moving to New York. He followed him to the back of the house where Wanda stood over a stove cooking. She watched him warily, then turned back to her skillet. The kitchen was filled with the smell of fresh fish. "Thom's here, Wanda."

She looked up. "I thought his name was Lund."

Dale leaned over the table to remove the evening paper. "I believe every man is equal, Thom. That's why I am going to call you by your proper name, and you can call me by mine."

Wanda returned to the skillet, turning her back on them both.

"I suppose you want to catch the train back to the city now." Dale dropped the paper on the floor behind the chair and sat down. "Would you mind if I had a bite to eat first? It's been a long day. You are welcome to join us." Lund glanced at Wanda for a moment. Dale said carefully, "There's plenty for all three of us. Right, Wanda?"

She nodded once. Lund said he would be happy to stay, and it was the truth. He could hardly remember breakfast. "I hope you didn't leave that house a mess," Wanda said over her shoulder.

"No, everything is as it was. You're keeping the house very neat. I will be sure to tell Mr. Peters."

"I saw you were looking in the boathouse," Dale said, openly curious. "What made you look there?"

"Your wife told me all the papers were burned. Once I looked around and realized that nothing had been left, there wasn't much else to do. I suppose I thought there might be something, receipts or the like, something I could use for the estate." He caught himself quickly, feeling he was just shy of looking like a fool.

"What is it you do exactly?"

He made a snap decision to tell the truth. "I work for New Amsterdam Bank, in the city. The bank president is good friends with Wallace Peters. He asked me to look around for anything Mrs. O'Connor might have left behind."

"I bet there's no end of work for a man like you in New York City."

"Enough to keep me busy." Lund found himself warming to Dale's comfortable way of speaking—straight and to the point.

"Ever work for the Bureau of Prohibition?"

The picture came together for him. Lund relaxed. "If I wanted to, they wouldn't have me."

Dale smiled with all his teeth. "Well now. That's a good thing to hear. A man's got to find work one way or another these days. Wanda thought you might be out here to see about what goes on during the night, you might say."

"Dale Wilcox!" Wanda gave her husband a playful swat. "Don't get him started, mister. My husband will talk your ear off." She reached over Dale to put a bowl of boiled potatoes on the table.

"Aw!" Dale reached for his wife's hand and squeezed it. "It's not that. I just want to be sure of who I'm talking to, honey. That's all." He smiled at his wife, and his face transformed. The weight of the world seemed to slide away.

"It's good to be out of the city for a while. I don't get to see trees except in Central Park. To be honest, I don't look forward to going back. I miss the water." Lund resisted the urge to look over his shoulder.

"Another sailor! I knew I liked the cut of your jib, Thom!"

"Really, Dale! You'll make the man uncomfortable."

"I'm a navy man myself, retired." Dale grinned. "I came out here for a long convalescence and never left." He nodded at his wife. "Wanda was a nurse back then."

"Did you know Coralee too?" Lund asked.

Dale glanced at Wanda, who nodded slightly. He leaned back. "Wanda introduced us, told her I knew a thing or two about sailing. Which is true. I grew up in a boatyard in North Carolina. I've forgotten more about boats than anyone ever knew. When she saw I knew what I was about, she put in a word for me with the harbormaster, got me a job there."

"She didn't keep her boat here on the water?"

Dale shook his head. "Tide gets too low. She wanted someplace that had been dredged out so she wouldn't have to worry about getting stuck."

Wanda put the fish on the table next to the boiled potatoes and then brought three glasses and a jug of water.

"Wanda was telling me that Coralee wouldn't have scuttled the *Fancy-Free*."

"I was wondering when you were going to get down to it." Dale looked at his wife, more somber than he had been before. "My wife has a sixth sense about these things. She told me you were out here about the boat. And she was right, wasn't she?" When Lund didn't answer, Dale continued. "No, Coralee wouldn't have scuttled the boat. She loved it too damn much." Dale put down his fork and looked at Lund earnestly. "Let's just stop this pussyfooting around. Why don't you tell me exactly what you're doing out here. It certainly isn't to look for receipts. All her financials would be at the bank in New York. Exactly what is it you're looking for?"

Lund trusted his instincts. "Wallace Peters hired me to find out why she killed herself. He said he and his wife need to know what happened."

"It's about damn time!" Dale slammed the table with one hand hard enough to make the glasses jump. "I can tell you what happened and save you a lot of time—murder, that's what. Coralee was murdered."

24

LUND ATE HIS FISH AND potatoes and listened. He watched the two of them tell their shared experience with Coralee as though they were confessing their sins.

"She loved that boat, Thom. Loved it! I've never seen a woman baby anything like she did that boat. And she was a good sailor who had respect for the sea. She wouldn't have done that thing, not in a million years. Okay, okay, maybe she might have hurt herself. Anyone can get low, all right? But not that boat. That would be drawing the line."

"It's what I was trying to tell you, Thom," Wanda offered. "Coralee never would have taken out those bilge plugs."

"That's right, honey. She would have removed the plug in the transom. Much faster and no going back. Once it's opened, there's no stopping the water. You're sunk."

Lund stopped eating. "I just assumed she had removed all the plugs."

"Nope, not that one. The one plug they tell you to never touch. She left it there. I'll say something else: those last few weeks, she wasn't herself. Tell him, honey." Dale took the opportunity to eat some fish while Wanda picked up the story.

"Coralee came up on the weekends every week during the summer—regular like," Wanda spoke with more animation than she had earlier, Dale encouraging her with nods. "Then one week she comes up on a Wednesday and doesn't leave the house for two weeks. Wouldn't even let me come over to clean. Finally I had to call Miss Patrice and ask her to come out, I was that worried. Patrice told me Coralee wouldn't let her come over. I just couldn't believe it! Wanda wiped her eyes with her napkin. "Miss Patrice told me she would come by later in the summer, but she never did come back."

"Who's this Patrice?"

"That's Patsy to you and me, Thom. Patsy Galton. Lives in the city," Dale answered. "There was that man she had over. I told you," he added, looking at his wife. Wanda shook her head and looked at her plate. "I saw him walking up to the house, sweet as you please. I told you, I did. The night Coralee died."

Lund was paying much closer attention. "That wasn't in the police report."

"The police? A bunch of fools, if you ask me. They gummed the works up so badly, you would hardly believe Coralee died. The biggest joke there ever was. That's why my wife thinks what she does. That's why she keeps the house so neat." Wanda went white. Dale hardly seemed to notice her as he spoke. "Going over there and cleaning every nook and cranny like it was a shrine. Waiting for Coralee to come back when she feels like she's been gone long enough."

Wanda stood up, knocking her chair over backward, and ran out of the room, slamming the bedroom door behind her.

"Well, that's done it." Dale put down his fork. "Me and my big mouth."

Lund hesitated before asking, "Could she still be alive?"

"I was the one Wallace had identify the body. Did he tell you that?" Lund shook his head. Dale took a deep breath and swallowed his food. "The police asked me to identify her before they went to the expense of sending her back to the city. So I was there, and I can tell you. It was her. Rolled on the rocks and torn up by the fish and the crabs, but still her. Coralee is dead." He added quietly, "God rest her soul."

Lund cocked his head. "Who opened the door for the man you saw? Was it Coralee?"

"Had to be her. Coralee didn't allow anyone else in the house except for the three of us: me, Wanda, and Patrice. She was wearing her boating togs, white pants, and a red shirt. She even had a hat on. Stood out a mile with the light on her from behind. I'll never forget it."

Lund shook his head. "Everyone I have met has said Coralee was friendly, outgoing. But . . ."

"But you can't figure out why she was all the way out here, can you?" Dale laughed. "You're a smart one, Thom. I'll give you that. Coralee never met a man or woman that wasn't her friend. She just liked her privacy, that's all. Don't ask me why. Wanda would show me the society pages from the *Ga-*

zette, and we could hardly believe it was the same person. Just goes to show how you never know a person."

"Did you ever see a man around before that night?"

Dale laughed. "Didn't I just tell you that she only allowed the three of us around? Me, Wanda, and Patrice? She liked her solitude." He stood up and put his plate in the sink. "If you don't mind, I'll go have a word with my wife. Then I'll take you to the station."

Lund stood when the man left the room, and began clearing the table. He heard a sound behind him and found Wanda standing in the doorway, her face streaked with tears. She seemed at a loss for what to say, then blurted out, "Do your best." Her defeated sigh sent a clear message that Lund's best would not be enough. "Just remember, she was a decent person. I knew her all my life. She was a good person."

Lund felt warmth for the woman. "Thank you for dinner, Mrs. Wilcox. I haven't eaten fish that fresh since I was a boy."

"Dale's a good fisherman," she said and blushed.

Taking his wallet from his inside pocket, Lund removed a business card and handed it to her. "Here are my numbers in the city. If you remember anyone else who might have come to the house or anything important about Patrice, give me a call. Here," Lund pulled out a ten-dollar bill and placed it on the counter, "for the call, and any other expenses that might come up."

"That's too much," she said uncomfortably. "I couldn't . . ."

"It's for what you've done keeping up the house. And anything you might have to clean up after I've gone. I tried to put it all back, but you never know." He smiled at her and returned the wallet to his pocket, walking past her to meet Dale at the door.

The afternoon was drawing in around them when Lund got in the Ford and looked back at the cottage through the trees. He was filled with an inexplicable desire to rush past the woods and go through every part of the house again until it gave up all its secrets. He looked away from the white cottage with the red trim and watched as Wanda shut the door behind herself.

"You ever hear Patrice's surname? Or anything else about her?" Lund asked when they had pulled out onto the narrow paved road.

"Just someone from the city. I thought you would have known who she was, seeing how close they were. She was out here all the time. Patrice would play the piano. Coralee would sing. During the summer, they kept the windows open when they cooked and when it was hot. Beautiful music." Dale stared at the road, his face barely visible in the dusk. Lund could feel him building to something. He stayed quiet, waiting for the man to find his moment in the dark. "It can get quiet out here, and dark. No one has any secrets when you live in the country. You can't hide them for long, in any case."

"Did you hear anything that night? The night she went out?"

Dale shook his head. "That was a hot summer. I got Wanda an electric fan for her birthday. When it's going, you can't hardly hear anything over the noise." He sighed. "I worked on that boat with Coralee side by side for weeks. You learn a lot about a person when you work together like that. She wasn't the type to do herself in." He looked at Lund meaningfully and shifted the gears.

"Maybe she ran into trouble, saw something."

"You mean like rum runners?" Dale glanced at Lund. "Put that thought out of your head there, Thom. Put it right out. You might say I have an inside line on those folks, and they didn't have anything to do with Coralee's death."

"Maybe it was an independent operator, someone who wasn't from around here."

"I see how you're thinking. But that's not how it happened. If it was a rum runner, they would have burned that boat and made it an example, not scuttled her where no one would see."

He could see Dale's grip on the steering wheel had tightened, and knew he had asked one question too many. Lund peered into the dark around the car. "What's around here?"

"Locust Valley is right over there." Dale nodded his head as they came to the main highway. He turned right where Paolo had turned left during the day. "It's the closest train station, to be honest. I'm not sure why they sent you that way except that Coralee always came that way. I can't tell you how many times I asked her why she wouldn't go on to the stop in Locust Valley. It's close enough to walk. But not in the dark."

Lights shone ahead of them off to the sides. It was so dark that Lund almost felt as though they were at sea with the water lapping up against the car all around them. When they got closer, he saw that the lights came from houses many times the size of Coralee's small cottage, their warm electric lights burning behind lushly manicured lawns and hedges.

"Locust Valley isn't as stuck up as some places," Dale said

bluntly. "But she didn't want to have anything to do with it. She told me she didn't care for those types of people and they didn't care for her. Threw me off, to tell you the truth. Until then, I had thought she was easygoing."

"Fancy-free?" Lund asked impulsively.

Dale nodded briefly. "That was her all right. To a T."

The road began to turn, dip, and curve to accommodate the gentle rolls of the valley. Houses appeared in the darkness, large, elegant country estates with cottages along the back and the occasional greenhouse. Dale slowed the car, downshifting as they went up the road that curved up and left. A parked car loomed up on the side of the road, a couple blinked in the headlights. The girl laughed and threw her drink into the road. Lund heard the tinkle of glass as it hit the passenger-side door. "Nice people," he commented.

"They're just city people. They don't know any better. Probably don't even know they're being rude. They come in for the house parties on the big estates. Must be someone's birthday. Usually don't happen so late in the year." Dale slowed the car to a crawl, and Lund noticed more and more couples in the dark corners of the hedges along the rows. He could feel Dale stiffen in the dark, embarrassed. Passing the main gates, Lund looked down the drive to see dozens of cars and a house lit up like Christmas. A band played distantly, and he saw a couple smoothly dancing across the lawn, the moon coloring them with blue and black shadows, the woman's dress a glittering bird with wings opening and closing as she moved into and out of the light. He felt a sudden pang of jealousy and wanted more than ever to be back in the city, within Penelope's reach.

"That's what I came to show you." Dale stopped on the hill and pointed across Lund. "You see that light there?" Dale pointed to a pinpoint steadily bearing out through the trees. "That's my house. If it was light out, you could see Coralee's right next to it." Lund was silent as Dale put the car back into gear. Turning a corner, he took the car down a steep embankment. "I wouldn't normally do this," he said to Lund as they bounced, "but if it helps you get a picture . . ." The man trailed off. Lund realized he had seamlessly slipped into the role of confessor.

Halting at a small landing, Dale put the brake on the car and killed the engine. "This is where she kept the boat."

Through the windshield, Lund saw the tiny house across the water and wondered if Wanda was watching them from a window. As he watched, the light went out. "What time does it get dark here in June?"

"Nine o'clock, easy," Dale said immediately. "Even after the sun drops, there's light on the water and the shore. The harbormaster told me that he saw her go out around eleven that night."

"Where does he sleep?"

Dale pointed to a small building built over the slips. "That's him."

Lund looked up and saw a man smoking a pipe, watching the harbor from a narrow bench. Rubbing his hands together, he asked, "Were there a lot of parties that night?"

"You bet there were. June is the perfect month for a party around here. Not too cold and not too hot. There must have been five, six parties that night alone."

"Anyone see her?"

Dale shook his head. "You want to talk to the old man? He'll tell you." Lund shrugged and followed Dale to the bottom of the stairs. Just before they reached the structure, Dale muttered under his breath, "That's my boss, okay? Go easy, would you?" Lund nodded uneasily. They stopped under the light cast from the open door.

Dale and the old man exchanged nods. "Dale there says you want to know about Coralee."

"If you don't mind," Lund called up.

Making no sign of inviting them up or moving, the old man said, "She came down the drive about ten thirty. It was good and dark."

"Did she drive?" Lund interrupted.

The old man was quiet for a moment and looked away. Lund had the distinct impression he had offended him. Dale said quietly, "Coralee walked. She always got a ride to anywhere she needed from Wanda and me. Mostly she just walked."

"What if she went to a party?" Lund asked Dale.

"Then she brought her own car."

Lund turned his head back to look up at the old man, who was puffing strenuously on his pipe. "I asked her if she wanted a flashlight, and Mrs. O'Connor said no." He shifted and straightened. "I asked her if she was going for a sail, and she waved."

"Was it a dark night for a night sail?"

"Dark enough." He looked out across the water. "No moon. That didn't matter—there was no stopping Coralee. She always did what she liked."

"Did she usually have a word with you before she went out?"

The old man stood there for over a minute without speaking. "Time or two she did." He said finally.

Lund thanked the man and turned back to the car. Dale hung behind and spoke a word or two with the harbormaster before returning to the truck. The door shut, and darkness fell on the small landing and the car. Lund heard running footsteps, and Dale was back in the driver's seat. "We'd better get you to the station. I didn't realize how late it is."

As they went up the steep driveway, Lund asked, "Does he have good eyesight normally? Would he have been able to see Coralee's face?"

"He said it was her. He was sure."

"But could he really see that far? On a night with no moon?"

The rest of the ride to the station was quiet. Dale parked the Ford, and Lund opened the door. Turning, he handed a card to Dale. "Those are my numbers. If you remember anything, give me a call, would you?"

"Yeah, sure thing." Dale put the card in his pocket.

"This is the last question, I promise." Lund put his hands up.

"All right," Dale laughed. "Shoot."

"Had she ever gone out at night before? Was it common?"

"Only twice that I know of. Once she and Patrice took the boat out to watch the fireworks. I drove them there and picked them up that time. Then once they went to see the harvest moon from the water." He grinned. "Crazy thing to do, if you ask me."

Lund leaned forward. "Did you pick them up that night?"

"No." Dale's smile faded. "I dropped them off all right. But they stayed out until the morning. Coralee said they got lost."

The train pulled up to the station. Lund held up a hand and said his thanks. He ran all the way to the platform and dove through the doors just before they shut. He turned to wave at Dale in the parking lot. The truck was already gone. When the conductor came by to give him his ticket, Lund counted the three letters in his wallet again, then tucked it away in his pocket. Settling his hat on his knee, he looked out the window, staring through his reflection into the dense darkness, deep in thought.

It was close to seven o'clock when Lund rang through to the Harris apartment from Pennsylvania Station. The maid was flustered, and when Penelope finally came to the telephone, she could only say, "I can't talk long. We only came back to the apartment to get something Ivy says she forgot. Then we're headed to the Warwicks. Clover still hasn't appeared, but we have to take Ivy home."

"How's the girl?"

"Tulip died." There was a pause on the line. Penelope's voice was worn, tired. "Dr. Mercer thought she might make it this morning. She didn't. I have to take Ivy home to the Warwicks. She doesn't want to go, but the police want to speak with her. I'm dreading it. Thom, would you—"

Lund didn't wait for her to finish. "I'll meet you there."

Relief reached him from the other end of the line. "Thank God," she whispered. "I can't say any more. I'll see you there."

Checking his watch as he walked, Lund made his way to the taxi stand.

25

Blake had his hand on the car door, opening it before the wheels stopped, his foot reaching for the pavement and propelling him forward as soon as it touched the cement. O'Hara came out the other side and joined him on the sidewalk as he stared up at the Warwick brownstone. Blake had already been through the wringer with surprises from this family. Roger Warwick's body was still at the morgue when it should have been released to a funeral home hours ago, because no one from the family, not even the solicitor, would claim it. The second victim—or was she the killer? Blake couldn't say, didn't know—was a different matter entirely. Roger wasn't well liked, it was true, but was so disliked someone killed him outright. Poison, on the other hand, was slow work. Painful work. Blake had a bad feeling about the matter.

Mercer hadn't been sure how long she had been taking the arsenic. He had mumbled something about checking the root of her hair, but it didn't sound very scientific. Could have been she had been making herself sick for a while. Could have been she had taken it all at once. He didn't believe McCain's nonsense about a boy. Girls didn't poison themselves if there was a husband in the wings. But still, this one made him stop, think. Death didn't hold much sway for Blake, but Tulip Warwick's had been one of the few times he had been there at the final moment. Waiting for her to say something, anything, that would move him just a hair closer. McCain said it wasn't suicide, and he was hardly ever wrong. But still, a word from the kid would have made a difference. Instead she just sat there and told them over and over how much she loved her sister, though he wasn't sure which.

O'Hara had suggested sleep, but Blake knew if he closed his eyes, he would see her staring back at him from her sickbed, whispering her final words. Tulip Warwick swore with her dying breath she hadn't poisoned herself. Some people set a certain store by deathbed declarations. Blake wasn't the type to take a person's word for gospel—he wanted to be sure.

Poison was a close thing, almost always family, but tricky. Without a witness or a confession from the poisoner, proof was always circumstantial. The motive could come down to crass meanness. Based on what he had seen at the hospital, there was plenty to go around in this bunch. "Got the warrant?" he asked O'Hara. The other policeman nodded. "Good. Show it to me." It was a simple enough document, correct and in proper order. It was time to get down to business. Blake spoke directly to O'Hara but ran his eyes over the policemen gathering on the sidewalk around them. "All right, now listen. Get the butler to show you straight to her room. Don't let anyone stop you. I want all the papers from old Warwick's office and all the ash from every grate in the house. I've met these people, and they're the works. This paper's all we need to turn this house over, and that's what I expect. Don't let nobody stop you." He handed the warrant back to O'Hara and took the front steps to the brownstone two at a time.

"Blake!" A man came shooting out of a taxi, his coat flying out behind him. A patrolman who didn't know any better tried to stop the man and made friends with the pavement instead.

"Lund! Good thing you're here." Blake met the man's eye

and saw he meant business. “Come in behind O’Hara. I want to talk to you when this is over.”

“What happened?” Lund pushed the policemen aside like they were toys. Blake laughed to himself—Penelope Harris must be inside for the man to act like that. He wondered how Lund could fool himself into thinking he wasn’t a sucker.

“Lay off my men,” Blake said from the side of his mouth and then focused on the door as O’Hara pushed the bell. Blake grimaced as Lund drew up beside him. “Chocolates. The lining of her purse was all marked up—definitely more than the two pieces we found. If she had just eaten one, maybe she would have made it. However she got it, it was a massive dose. No one would have survived it. She died this afternoon, heart failure. She kept quiet right to the end, wouldn’t tell us where she got it.” Blake felt himself shifting with the restless energy of suspicion. He looked up and down the block waiting for something to happen.

“Tough break.” Lund’s eyes searched the street. “What about the family?”

“The doctor called to tell the family it wasn’t long until the end. Mrs. Warwick thanked him.” Blake shrugged. Humanity was a bastard. “She never showed up. The coroner doesn’t know what to do with the body. Your girl, Penelope, told the coroner she’ll do something for the girl if the family doesn’t step in. Good of her . . .” Blake let the sentence drop away. “Two deaths in two days.”

“Think they’re connected?”

“They have to be.” Blake kept his voice low. “Murder is unusual enough in this crowd. Two deaths in the same family on the same day?” Blake’s silent logic rejected the idea at once. The deaths were too different from one another. Roger's death felt more impulsive, Tulip's carefully premeditated. Murder, then suicide? "It's screwy," he said finally. "Someone's killing Warwicks. Did I tell you? We haven't even found the other daughter yet. What's her name? Clover. She might be dead, too, for all we know. It's as though she evaporated."

"How did the interviews at the opera go?" Lund asked. "Anything there?"

"Not enough." Blake had seen enough of the opera for the rest of his life. "Sounded like musical chairs, if you ask me. Everybody was up and at 'em all evening long. Especially the boxes. No one kept their seat." Blake waved a hand. "The first suspect is always the wife, but she was in full view, never made a move except to put her hand in the lap of that lawyer when she thought no one was looking, and walk the promenade with the sly bastard during the intermission. She's in the clear. Although, if you ask me, she should get the chair for the way she treated her own daughter." He fought back his temper. "The killer made a mistake somewhere. We'll catch him. Ring the bell again, O'Hara."

"Poison isn't as easy as a crime of passion," Lund said after some thought. "Tulip could have had those chocolates for weeks. Someone might have given them to her, or maybe she took them from someone else. All the killer had to do was wait for her to eat them." He broke off. "It might not have even been intended for her. Could have been for her father."

"Now you're all caught up—two Warwicks dead and nothing to go on." Blake felt tired all over, as if his hands were too heavy to lift. "We have a man around back going through the trash to see if we can find the box for the chocolates, packing paper, anything. Anything that might give us a lead. O'Hara here is going to search her room. More boys on the way, but only the four of us detectives right now, including you. The patrolmen are here to make sure no one leaves the house or destroys the evidence. Got the warrant?" O'Hara nodded. "Lund, I want you to come in with me, but don't say anything. Just help me hold them all together until the rest of my men get here. O'Hara's looking for a suicide note, a diary, letters, anything like that. Maybe she killed herself after murdering her father. Maybe she lost her cool and took a swing. Then, seeing what she's done, she takes her own life. God knows it's happened before."

"Did she say anything?" Lund asked. "Before she died?"

"She said she loved her sister," Blake grumbled. "Got a little muddy at the end. She could have meant Clover or Ivy. We couldn't tell." The door to the street began to open just as Blake was losing his temper. "Here we go," he said. Pushing past Lund, Blake pointed at the butler. "You see this warrant?" The butler nodded. "We're coming in." The door was open, and O'Hara and two uniformed officers swarmed into the house and up the staircase, with the butler trying to catch up. McCain stood by the front door and nodded to Lund as they sped past him into the house.

26

BLAKE FOLLOWED THE SHOUTING, LUND close behind. They didn't have far to go before they found the source, in a large sitting room dominated by a carved marble fireplace and surrounded by modern chrome furniture. Lund scanned the room, his relief physical as soon as he saw her. Penelope was just inside the door, Eleanor beside her. Both of them were still dressed from the cab ride: hats, gloves, coats, and clutches. Penelope was lowering Ivy into a chair after what appeared to be a light faint.

Blake spoke first. "What's going on here?"

Lund caught Penelope up in his arm just as she turned. "What is it, Penelope? What's happened?" he whispered. Penelope silently gestured to the chair where Ivy sat. The dress from the night before was gone, replaced by a bright sweater with a simple but elegant dress underneath. Ivy even wore a fashionable hat, pulled close to cover her unkempt hair. The color and style suited the girl. Lund thought he saw Penelope's hand in it. Ivy looked less like a child and more like a young woman. Eleanor's face was drawn with strain. Standing at Penelope's shoulder, she kept her eyes on Violet Warwick like the woman were a poisonous krait. Violet commanded the room in a black dinner dress with expensive beading one could pay for only with a good deal of cash, her diamonds on full display on her ears and in a brooch on her shoulder. A man stood behind her, not so young but still handsome, if only just. Blake thought he could see the wear of the prohibition lifestyle that seemed to be affecting so many of the wealthy these days. His eyes were just slightly blurrier than they should have been, his cheekbones just a bit too sharp. The man smoked leisurely, watching Blake move into the room with a familiar, cold smile.

"Mrs. Harris and Miss Harris," Blake growled, "perhaps it would be better if you waited outside. This shouldn't take long." Lund felt Penelope's relief as her body relaxed against him. She left without a word, Eleanor following quietly. Lund met Penelope's eye as he shut the door behind them; her determined nod reassured him.

"Evening, Gilmurray," Blake said. "A little early for legal representation, don't you think?"

"I'm here for the family in good times and bad, Nathan. As I am for all my clients."

Without looking at him, Lund could feel Blake's irritation.

"I didn't realize you were a criminal attorney." Blake leveled a look that would have terrified a mobster. "I thought you were one of the pencil necks. Although I should tell you, that won't save you even if you are."

Lund remained between the family and the door, staying silent.

Gilmurray was undisturbed. "Estate law, yes, that's my area. I represent the family in that regard too." He posed casually on the rug, with a hand in his pocket and the other loosely holding a cigarette. He was so comfortable he looked out of place.

"I understand that you were also at the opera last night, in the Warwick box."

"I was, Nathan. My wife was there too." Gilmurray

watched him through half-lidded eyes. "You can ask anyone. She was sitting right in the box with us."

"I did ask, actually. I put a word in with your wife this morning. She couldn't talk long. She had an urgent call in to her divorce attorney."

Gilmurray sighed, allowing his eyes to roll slightly. "My wife can be quite hysterical. It is too trying."

"She seemed quite calm to me, John." Blake squared off, his feet as light as a prizefighter's. "She said you had given her the brush-off as soon as you heard Warwick was dead. Left home this morning with a suitcase full of clothes. I'd say she's lucky." He glanced at the attorney's jacket and white tie. "She's had the locksmith by, just to let you know."

"Virginia and I tried our best, and it was not enough." Gilmurray's wide smile made Lund want to kick him in the teeth. "Is that what you would like to hear? We shall be divorcing soon."

"Isn't it a little early to put your feet under the table?" Blake dropped his chin and watched Gilmurray's reaction. It passed too briefly across his face, but it had been there.

"What a distasteful comment." Gilmurray moved across him to an ashtray, where he stubbed out his cigarette with a twist of his wrist. "Mrs. Warwick and I are good friends, and I plan to help her in any way that I can through this difficult time."

"Mrs. Warwick," Blake kept his eyes trained on Gilmurray, "I understand that you were experiencing marital problems yourself. I've heard from several witnesses that you were arguing with your husband last night."

"He was somewhere he did not belong, Lieutenant." Violet Warwick spoke a little too quickly. Her eyes were just a little too wide. “It was a common problem for my husband. He didn’t seem to fit in anywhere.”

“I understand that you had consulted a divorce attorney?”

“I did. I told Roger a week ago. We were finished.” She lifted her face into the light, her nose up. The light wasn’t friendly to the tiny lines around her nose and mouth. Blake thought absently that had she realized it, they would have met in a different room.

“Were you and your husband parting amicably?”

“Since you must press me for an answer—no, we were not. My husband was a miser. There is no other word for it. He refused to give me money by which I could sustain myself and my children.”

“Did he agree to a divorce?”

She pursed her lips but held steady. “No.”

“Was your husband aware that you would be attending the opera last night with the Gilmurrays?”

Violet exhaled a short laugh. “I suppose someone hid in a stairway and heard us arguing. Yes, Lieutenant, my husband objected to my guests. He could be a very jealous man.”

“I understand that you slapped him.”

“During the interval, yes. What he said was offensive to me. I was insulted. I could hardly hurt him. Unlike him.” She lifted the sleeve of her dress and revealed a bruise on her arm.

Blake stepped closer to look at the mark. “Did Mr. Warwick give you that?”

“He did.” Violet dropped her sleeve and looked down her nose at Blake. “I didn’t kill him. But I did slap him. It was a common enough occurrence. Hardly worth notice.”

Ivy gasped. "Mama!"

"Be quiet!" Violet said sharply. Speaking as though she had been reminded of an irritating drain, she continued, "Lieutenant, I want you to arrest that Harris woman." She pointed at the door with a perfectly manicured finger.

"On what charge?"

"Kidnapping! She has been holding my child against her will!" The woman shook with righteous indignation that he was confident she did not feel. At least five credible witnesses had heard Violet Warwick disown both her daughters at the hospital the day before.

"Mama, that's not true." Ivy shook her head.

"Mama, Mama," Violet repeated in a sing-song. "You and Tulip are two of a kind, working my nerves in the worst possible ways when you know I need peace and quiet!"

"For what?" The hand hidden in Blake's coat pocket clenched. "For what do you need peace and quiet?"

A quick flash of anger illuminated Violet's face, her whole body turning toward him with her feet apart and hands free. Lund was sure she was ready to swing at Blake, or anyone who got too close.

"Lieutenant, I will have you know that my daughter is a minor. She can't possibly be expected to be responsible for her decision-making."

"You wouldn't come, Mama. Someone had to be there." Ivy looked down at the carpet, all her energy seeming to slowly drain away. Abruptly, she turned her face away. "Tu died."

"I would advise you not to speak so rashly, Ivy," Gilmurray said smoothly. "You couldn't possibly know what your mother was going through. After all, her husband had just been killed."

Violet recovered herself, turning her back to Blake. "We did love each other, once upon a time." She took the clenched handkerchief in her hand and dabbed at her eyes. "You should have thought of your family, Ivy. Before you abandoned us for strangers."

Ivy remained on the chair, her face turned away where Lund could not see.

"If we could all calm down for a moment." Blake held up his hands, and Lund felt a surge of adrenaline. Blake wasn't going to wait for the police station. He was going in for the kill here and now. "I need to ask a few questions. It is something of a formality, you understand. Mrs. Warwick, the medical examiner confirmed the presence of arsenic in Tulip's stomach. Do you have any notion of how it might have gotten there?"

"Of course there was arsenic." Violet fought against the white pallor that belied every word she spoke. "I'm not surprised." Ivy covered her face with her hands. "The dreadful girl killed my husband and then herself, of course. Isn't it obvious?"

"Violet, please!" Gilmurray remembered his priorities with sudden alacrity. "My client is grieving, Lieutenant. She doesn't know what she is saying." Gilmurray almost, but not quite, hid his shock. Lund could see it there in his eyes.

"Of course I know what I am saying. Why wouldn't I?" Violet Warwick continued, "I was her mother, after all. That terrible girl, she would have killed us all if she had half a chance!"

"I highly doubt that any suicide would go to the trouble of hiding the poison from themselves." Lund couldn't say how he did it, but Blake kept his cool. "The chocolates had been doctored quite carefully."

"Lieutenant, I hope you are not telling me that you know my daughter better than I. Tulip was a morbid child, interested only in her own problems. She spent hardly any time with us these last few months. Instead, all she wanted to do was read inappropriate books. It makes perfect sense that she would commit this act if you knew her, which you did not. Surely my opinion on the matter counts for something!"

"The lieutenant knows what side his bread is buttered on. Don't you, Nathan?" Gilmurray touched Violet's shoulder, then straightened smoothly to gaze at Blake from across the room. "The Warwicks have been upstanding members of the community for many years."

"An upstanding family that has experienced two suspicious deaths within hours of each other." Blake turned to Ivy in her chair. "Miss Warwick, we didn't have a chance to get a statement from you at the hospital. Could I ask you a few questions now?"

Looking up, Ivy wiped her face with a sleeve and nodded.

"My client is very tired, Lieutenant. Perhaps it would be better if tomorrow—"

"No, thank you, Mr. Gilmurray." Ivy's voice was small but firm. "I'd like to help. I'm ready for your questions, Lieutenant. Go ahead."

27

"CAN YOU THINK OF ANYONE who might have wanted to hurt your sister?"

Lund respected the way Blake turned directly to the subject. There were no niceties, no polite concerns. He moved in like a predator, alert and hunting.

"No." Ivy stared at Blake, her eyes opening wide as she spoke. The child was younger or older, larger or smaller. Every time Lund put his eyes on her, Ivy gave off a different impression. At the opera she had seemed larger than life. Then at the hospital, smaller. In her own home, she played a different role: an actress suffering from extreme stage fright. "Tulip wasn't against anyone. She just needed her books and she was happy. She was a good sister. We spent a good deal of time together when she wasn't at the library." Violet Warwick turned her head away and laughed as Ivy paused to take a shuddering breath. Ivy glanced around herself, disoriented, finally casting her eye on her mother, where it remained. "I don't know why anyone would have done this. It must have been a horrible accident. Couldn't it have been that? Could it have been an accident?" If Violet knew her daughter was looking at her, she hardly showed it. She turned her back on the room and the girl.

"Yes, perhaps that was what it was. Eh, Nathan?" Gilmurray gestured with a freshly lit cigarette. "An accident?"

"I told you. The arsenic was put inside the chocolate, then the holes smoothed over." Blake didn't look away from Ivy. "Seemed pretty deliberate to us."

"Of course. You are the expert." Gilmurray smiled, showing two rows of perfect teeth.

Blake returned to Ivy. "Tell me about Tulip. You said you spent a lot of time together. Did she mention anything unusual these last few weeks? Maybe she saw something, did something unusual?"

"No." Ivy's answer was emphatic. "Mama got us tickets to see Valentina Carrera. It was a special treat. Tulip loved Carrera. She saved her money from the library to buy her records. She couldn't wait to see her sing. She—" Ivy broke off and looked at her mother. "Tulip was very happy." Ivy shut her mouth, her eyes fixed on Violet.

"All right, all right." Blake put up a hand. "She had plans. What about her boyfriend? She ever mention him to you?"

"Tu didn't have a boyfriend."

"Tulip told one of my boys that she did. Said she told you about him."

Ivy looked from Blake to Violet. "I don't know what you're talking about."

"She was pretty clear about it." Blake kept himself focused on the girl. Lund let his eye wander to Violet across the room. The woman was strangely still. "All right, we'll come back to that. Did Tulip usually sneak food?"

She looked at Blake, confused. "She didn't have chocolates." She said the words carefully, emphasizing each one. "Tulip was slimming. She wasn't allowed chocolates."

"Maybe she didn't like the new diet," Blake suggested. "Some girls might carry a secret piece of candy with them that they can eat when no one is there to see. She didn't deny the chocolates were hers, wasn't surprised to see them."

"Tu didn't sneak food." Ivy's eyes were wide. Lund was sure she would bolt at the smallest sound.

Blake went on like he could stay with it for hours. "Can you remember if Tulip had received any packages lately, or if she had gone shopping?"

"We weren't allowed to go anywhere alone. Father didn't approve." The blood slowly drained from Ivy's face. "Not even shopping, not even to church."

"But you didn't go to the library with Tulip, did you? Tulip went there by herself."

"That was different," Ivy protested. "Everyone knew where she was."

"It's pretty clear that Tulip had a good deal more going on in her life than working at the library." Blake gave a short laugh. "She was going to have a child."

"I don't know anything about that," Ivy blurted out. "It must have been a mistake."

"Do you think she would have told you if she knew she was pregnant?"

"She . . . I . . ." Ivy's mouth opened and closed. She turned to look at her mother. "I haven't been home very long. Only a few weeks."

"Lieutenant," Gilmurray said, "I can't imagine what you are getting at, but your line of questioning is outrageous." He looked at the cigarette in his hand as he spoke.

"Hasn't it occurred to any of you that Tulip could have been murdered?" Blake's eyes narrowed as he stared down the lawyer.

Lund couldn't blame him. It was an odd bunch, this family. It was as though they hardly cared Roger and Tulip had died in the same day. They were hardly upset about the matter. It seemed more—Lund searched for the right word—an inconvienience.

"A good deal has been said about those chocolates," Blake continued. "What if someone knew she would fish them out and eat them? Someone could have put them in her purse. Have any of you thought of that?"

Violet put her hand to her neck. "You think one of us killed Tulip?" She laughed. "Preposterous!"

Gilmurray sighed. "My client had no idea her daughter was pregnant and is certainly not responsible for any crimes her daughter or her daughter's paramour may have committed."

"You're awfully fast to put the crime on a dead girl," Blake's fingers tightened around his pencil, his knuckles standing out white where Lund could see, "when there's absolutely no evidence to support the claim."

"Where did she go during the third act?" Gilmurray was cool. "Mrs. Warwick had to ask Tulip to leave the box, she was so agitated. I was there. I can attest to that, if you like. She must have left the salon to find her father. Maybe she wanted his blessing for the marriage and they argued. I must remind you, Lieutenant, Roger Warwick was a man with a temper. He might have struck Tulip, startled her. Then she pushed him down the stairs. When she saw what she had done, she did the only thing she could: she took her own life." Gilmurray lifted his chin. "It's the only thing that makes sense when you look at it the right way."

"That's an awfully pat story, Gilmurray. It has the air of practice. I bet you've already been to the newspaper to give that idea a trial run. What do you say to that?"

"Lieutenant," Gilmurray purred, "my client could hardly describe her heartbreak and distress at the death of her husband. But facts are facts—"

"Shut up, you. I don't want to hear another word." Blake stood his ground on the carpet, his feet apart and his chin down. Lund knew the man to be forty, but with his blood up, he wouldn't have placed any bets on age slowing his fists. The lieutenant grappled with his temper until he could speak.

"Ivy," Violet said, "look at me."

Ivy lifted her head from her hands. "Yes, Mama?"

"Tell the man what you know Tulip did. She murdered your father, then killed herself. Didn't she?"

"What? No!" Ivy leaned forward in her seat. "She didn't kill Papa. She didn't."

"Tell me, Ivy. What did your sister do?" Violet crossed the room in two strides, her heavy black dress flowing behind. "Didn't she poison herself just for some attention? It was all a game to her, wasn't it? She thought it wouldn't kill her. Tell them."

"I don't know anything about the chocolate," Ivy said, her eyes on her mother's face.

Violet moved with the speed of a striking snake. She slapped Ivy across the face hard enough to knock her to the floor. "You know something! I can tell that you do!" Violet shouted. "I'm your mother. I know when you're lying!"

Ivy froze where she fell, her eyes wide and unblinking, her fingers clutching at her sweater. Lund realized Blake couldn't keep his temper anymore. With a deep growl, the lieutenant put an arm around Violet Warwick's waist, lifting her easily and throwing her into the couch with a satisfied grunt. "That's enough of that!" he shouted, his finger pointed in her face. "Do that again, and I'll book you for assault."

"I know my children quite well, Lieutenant!" Violet shouted back. "Even better than they know themselves. It's quite clear to me that Tulip poisoned herself."

Lund lifted Ivy from the floor, settling her back in the chair. Other than her hand on her cheek, the girl showed almost no emotion at all. Her eyes remained trained on her mother, oblivious that Blake stood between them. Blake gestured to one of the patrolmen. "Get her some ice from the kitchen, would you?" He crouched down by the chair. When he was sure he had Ivy's attention, Blake said, "The chocolates in Tulip's purse had to come from somewhere. Where would she have gotten them? Would she have bought them?"

Ivy shook her head, staring her mother down like she was pleading with her. "We were never alone. Mama didn't like us to be alone. We were always together, at least two of us. I was with Tulip all of the last two weeks until tonight. She never bought chocolates. She must have gotten them from Clover. She got the chocolates from Clover!" Ivy shouted across the room, clamping both hands over her mouth as soon as the words were out.

"You!" Violet stood up. "You be quiet, you ungrateful cur!"

Blake moved between the two women. "Did Clover give Tulip the chocolates, Ivy? Did she hand them to her?"

"No! No! I didn't mean that!" Ivy's lips shook. "She would throw them away. Tulip always said it was a waste. Clover didn't eat them, you see? Tulip told me she wouldn't miss one or two." She whispered, "Clover didn't mind. She never knew."

"She took them from the garbage?" Across the room, Violet began to laugh. "How obscene of her. Now you see how it must have been. It was all an accident. Clover receives all kinds of gifts and mementos. Every time her photo is published in the paper, she gets something. Even from strangers." Violet shrugged disdainfully, and for a brief moment, Blake wondered if she was jealous of her daughter.

"Anyone in particular? Anyone who didn't like her picture?"

"Can anyone say they don't have enemies, Lieutenant?" A voice came from the door.

Lund turned.

Clover Warwick made her entrance.

28

SHE WAS BEAUTIFUL, DEVASTATINGLY SO, and no one in the room knew that fact better than Clover herself. In spite of this, there was a hardness to her, as though all her edges, from her fingernails to her teeth, were sharp. Every move, every gesture showed precisise practice to blunt that sharpness, but it still remained. Clover rolled her shoulders back and raised her chin, daring every fist in the room to take a swing at her and see what they got. Lund had no doubt the woman would gut the first one of them to try. Suddenly happy he wasn't a policeman, he observed that Blake was about to have his hands full.

As they all gave her attention, Clover expanded, her charisma falling across them in waves. Lund instinctivey took a step back. Whatever Clover was after, he didn't want any of it. When she thought they had had enough of her grand entrance, Clover rushed forward with a practiced air of stagecraft, her hands out in front, her dress swinging behind with a delicate rushing of taffeta. Lund followed her footsteps with the weary thought that things were about to get more difficult.

"Oh you poor dear." Clover slid into a kneeling position in front of Ivy, her skirt pooled out around her, legs and feet tucked up beneath her neatly. "Was it awful? Of course it was! Oh, Ivy! Did she suffer?" Ivy turned her face away and did not answer. Lund could see Blake struggle with what to do. The lieutenant stood with his feet rooted and spread like a prizefighter. Blake chewed his mustache, his eyes narrowing. It was clear he wanted answers and would get them whatever way they came to him.

"Miss Warwick," he began.

"Clover, please call me Clover." She sat down on the arm of Ivy's chair and took her sister's hand in her own.

"Miss Clover," Blake started over, "did you receive chocolates recently?"

"Don't answer that," Gilmurray said abruptly. "Nathan, I think you may find that you have exceeded your remit."

"What remit would that be, John? As far as I know, I have a badge and I'm investigating two murders." Blake held his temper, but only just.

"I wonder what the district attorney would have to say about the matter," Gilmurray drawled.

Even Lund gave the lawyer a second look. It was too early in the investigation for threats. Especially ones that couldn't be backed up. Tulip Warwick's death might have been a suicide, but Roger Warwick's was most decidedly not.

"You go ahead and ask him, Gilmurray," Blake snarled over his shoulder before turning back to Clover. "Miss Clover, Ivy tells me that you sometimes receive chocolates in the mail, from admirers. Did you receive any recently?"

"I received a box last week. I don't care for chocolates." Clover waved a loose hand.

"Who were they from?" Blake leaned forward on his feet, his little black book forgotten in his hand.

"There wasn't a card, but I know they were from Reggie." Clover's words were sweet, but the hardness behind them startled Lund. Every word she said made him like her less, although he couldn't say why that was. From the look of it, Blake didn't like her. And from his view of the room, it appeared Ivy didn't care for her sister either. Ivy pulled her fingers from Clover's grip, turning away from her once they were free.

"Would that be Reginald Galton?" Blake asked. "Isn't Galton your fiancé?"

"Yes, that's right." Clover's eyes wandered around the room as she answered. When they fell on Lund, they stopped.

"Doesn't he know you don't like chocolate?"

"Oh yes," Clover replied. "He does like to joke."

"That's a bit of money to spend on something he knows you don't like. What did you do with them?"

"I threw them away." She answered Blake but smiled at

Lund, baiting Blake like he were a lover bent on proving her infidelity.

"You didn't give them to a maid or share them with your sisters? Seems odd to just waste them."

"They were mine to do with as I wanted, weren't they?"

"What day did you receive the chocolates?"

"This past Monday. I remember because I thought it was odd to get anything from Reggie on a Monday."

"Working?" Blake asked, already knowing the answer.

"My fiancé does a great deal of weekend entertaining. He needs the time on Monday to set things to rights."

"Likes to sleep in, does he?"

"Pardon me?" Clover raised an eyebrow.

Blake saw the break in the rhythm as quickly as Lund did. He went at her by the book, doggedly continuing the same line of questioning. "Did you happen to notice the packaging the chocolates came in? Perhaps you kept the wrapping paper or a card from the shop?"

"Nothing like that." Clover spoke with increasing volume. "Why would I? I told you it was a common enough joke. I saw them. I threw them away."

"Easy enough to check the particulars with Reggie. I'm sure he remembers where they were from," Gilmurray interjected. "Really, Lieutenant, I would expect better legwork from you than this."

A little man peered around the edge of the door. "We're ready for you, sir," he said quietly, and shut the door.

"Ready for what?" Gilmurray demanded. "What goes on here, Blake?"

Blake exhaled. "I have a warrant." He cut the words off

sharply. "We're searching the house now." He was prepared for the uproar that followed, each person trying to speak over the others. All but Ivy, who sat back in her chair with her hand pressed tightly over her eyes. "Your husband's killer could have been anyone, but your daughter's killer was almost certainly closer to home."

"I told you, she did it to herself!" Violet shouted.

"You're playing a dangerous game, Lieutenant," Gilmurray said. "I want to see that warrant."

There was a knock at the door. Lund opened it, and McCain stepped through. "They're here, Lieutenant." The door shut behind him.

"What did that mean?" Gilmurray asked crisply.

"The cars are here to take you downtown." Blake smiled. "I want statements and fingerprints from everyone. I've already lost one witness. I'm not going to lose any more. I've been holding you here until I could get the paddy wagon. I've got my warrant. You're all coming with me."

29

McCain shut the door quietly behind him before he approached Lund and Blake. "They're getting their coats now, sir. That woman is a terror. She bit O'Hara. Did you know?"

Blake gave him a look that said, I do know. She almost bit me too. "Add a charge of assaulting a police officer. Tell the boys I said to. Anything from upstairs yet?"

"Just the usual." McCain rocked from his heel to his toe as he talked. "Some rat poison, hair tonic, clothing dye, and, of course, flypaper. And, this is interesting, there was some medical arsenic in Roger Warwick's bathroom."

Blake showed some interest. "Syphilis?"

"Malaria." McCain looked at his foot and put his hand in his pocket. "It was written on the label. Have to check with his doctor to make sure."

Blake grunted. "They had plenty of access to arsenic, then."

"Who doesn't? Anyone can get it anywhere." McCain caught the eye of the butler.

"Bring it all along, we'll have Mercer take a look. Any wise ideas?" Blake asked Lund suddenly.

"Those chocolates Clover says she threw away," Lund said. "I have a few thoughts about those."

"Sure." Blake looked to McCain.

"It explains one thing for me: Tulip wouldn't say where she got the chocolates. She was embarrassed she had pulled them out of the trash," Lund said quietly. "Makes sense."

"I don't know." McCain looked from Lund to Blake. "I met the girl, remember? She didn't seem like the type."

"I've seen people do some pretty extreme things when they're hungry."

"I don't mean that, Thom. She didn't seem like the type to hide it. She would have said if she got them from the trash, put a positive turn on it. Everything was positive for the girl."

Blake put his hands in his pockets and leaned back on his heels. "I'd like to lock the whole family up, but the D.A. would have my guts for garters."

"I wonder if Tulip might have doctored the chocolates herself," Lund said.

"Suicide?" McCain asked. "Not a chance."

"I wouldn't blame her with a family like hers." Blake pushed his hat back.

"Not possible." McCain shook his head.

"Explain that, McCain." The tips of Blake's ears turned pink, a sure sign his temper was grappling for a hold.

"Wouldn't have been the nice thing to do. She was like that—nice." McCain ignored Blake's infuriated stare, pulling a notebook from his pocket. "I'll ask the staff about the chocolates. Maids know everything. That's a fact."

"Poison isn't your usual murder weapon." Lund spoke slowly, working the thought out. "You have to be close to the person, know they will eat it. If you aren't near enough, you need to know exactly how to do it right. You might get it wrong—poison the wrong person."

"You think whoever it was meant to kill Clover? Not Tulip?" Blake asked. "Or someone else? Think about it that way and any one of them could have been the intended victem."

"Could be the fiancé didn't know she's been throwing them away," McCain suggested. "Or someone else, maybe? Someone who knew he sent her chocolates?"

"Or a member of the household. Someone who knew Tulip would eat the chocolates."

"You have a dark turn of mind, Thom. McCain, let's take a look at that girl's room." Blake pointed at Lund. "You and your bright ideas are coming with us."

LUND STOOD IN THE BEDROOM doorway and was startled by the almost overwhelming resistance he had to step inside. Blake and McCain went forward without him, McCain opening the wardrobe and Blake looking over the dressing table. Lund was perplexed by his aversion. He had never felt this way before. He had searched many rooms, belonging to all kinds of people. Perhaps it was because of the way she died or because Penelope had wanted her so badly to live. Or perhaps it was the echo of Coralee's neat cottage, clean and ready should she ever decide to come home. More than likely, the culprit was his lack of sleep. Gathering his thoughts, Lund looked around for a sign of who the girl had been or who she might have been if she had gotten free of her family. Except the tidiness and small size, the bedroom was the opposite of Coralee's cottage in every way he could think of. Where Coralee's home had seemed quaint and purposeful in a busy, happy way, Tulip's room seemed an austere afterthought. Lund moved to the bedside table and opened a drawer.

"There isn't anything here." Blake straightened. "How about you, Thom? Find anything?" he asked over his shoulder.

Lund cocked his head and replied, "You'd better come see for yourself." He stepped aside, moving back into the hallway so they could see the contents without obstruction. On top of the musical score for act three of *The Tales of Hoffmann* lay a small box illustrated with a drawing of a rat eating an attractive round of cheese. Above the rat were the words "Lyon's Poisoned Cheese" and below it across the bottom in red, "Poison."

"Would you look at that?" McCain said with picturesque incredulity.

"Right where we expected to find it." Blake folded his arms across his chest as he stared down at it.

"Exactly when we needed to see it," Lund added.

The three men looked at one another. Silently, McCain took a hanky from his pocket, lifted the small cardboard box from the drawer, and laid it on the bed. Using his pencil, he raised the pages of the score until they could confirm there was nothing underneath it.

"What do you suppose that music is?" Blake asked.

"It's *The Tales of Hoffmann*—the opera that was playing that night," Lund replied. "Penelope told me all three daughters are performing an aria from it at a recital later this month." Lund stepped behind the two policemen to reach the wardrobe.

"All three? Are they that good? Traveling radio family? That sort of thing?" McCain lifted his head.

"I couldn't say for sure, but I doubt it. My impression was it was for the status of the thing." Opening the door to the wardrobe, Lund asked McCain, "Did you check these boxes?"

"Just shoes," McCain answered.

"You mind if I have a look?" The other man shrugged, and Lund returned to the wardrobe. He was thinking of all the bookish women he had known, his own mother included, and how odd it was that Tulip did not have a single book in her room. She had worked in the library, hadn't she? And yet the score seemed to be the only reading material. Three shoeboxes lined the top of the closet. He lifted them one at a time, weighing each in his hand. The second seemed heavier than the others, so he tried it first. Removing the lid with his handkerchief, he found a pair of heavy winter boots. The second box contained a pair of carefully dyed black dancing shoes. When he removed the lid from the third box, he found a pair of everyday shoes, the heels scuffed but the toes dutifully polished. Lifting them out of the box, he checked the inside of the first and then the second shoe. His fingers found a small diary, no bigger than his palm, wedged in the toe. He lifted it into the light, where McCain gingerly folded it into his handkerchief.

"Now what made you look there?" Blake asked as he looked down at the little book in McCain's hand.

"She wouldn't have had any privacy in a room like this." Lund looked around at the empty walls. "If Tulip had a diary, the only way she could have kept it private would be to carry it with her wherever she went. She wouldn't have been able to take it to the opera. So she left it behind where she didn't think anyone would think to look."

"What about the score?" Blake asked as he wrapped the diary up and put it in his pocket.

"What about it?" Lund glanced at the manuscript on the chair.

McCain looked down at the first page. "She wrote all over it. Might mean something."

"And how would I know anything about that?" Lund chuckled.

The two policemen stared at Lund. "You have a pretty thick skull, don't you, Thom?" Blake picked up the manuscript and held it out to him. "Take it to your girl and see what she can make of it, but I want it back."

"I'm not so sure I want Penelope in the middle of this," Lund protested.

"Thom," Blake leaned in, "she saw the girl die. We know it was murder. So does she. You think she doesn't want to help find the killer?" Blake held out the manuscript. "Ask her."

Lund nodded once. He took the score. "There's something else. About Roger Warwick—he was down at the bank Friday morning screaming to high heaven about an overdrawn account. Our accountant showed him everything was in order, but it was a bit of shock to him. You'll want the accountant's statement."

"What about your statement?" Blake focused. "Why don't you tell us here?"

"The other bank detective, his name's William Bird, he knew the accounts better than I did. Knew Warwick too. Ran around a little bit with Clover." Lund chose his words carefully.

"Bowing out, are you, Lund? Can't take the heat?"

"Not my circus. Not my monkeys," Lund replied blandly.

"Not to mention, you and your girlfriend made headlines just a month ago." Blake leered. "All right. I'll let you go on this one. McCain, get yourself down to the bank when you're done here. See what you can find out."

30

It was always that much easier when the old man went back to the precinct, McCain thought. Everyone had a breath of air and relaxed. Nothing like the sudden absence of a policeman to make a person happy to be alive. Everyone from the cook to the footman would suddenly find their voice and sing a song of relief—"Thank God it wasn't me" being the usual chorus. The Warwick house was another matter entirely. A suffocating stillness held everyone to single syllables. The butler spoke of Roger Warwick with warmth but did not stray from the same stilted statements. The cook belligerently refused to speak anything but Italian. Very bad Italian, at that! When McCain responded with the correct grammar, she had stopped speaking entirely. Neither of the two maids—one upstairs, one downstairs—had much to share about the household. Each refused to speak without the other present, filling in sentences and blanks for each other and watching the other's face as though for her to break first. He was the last police officer in the house, O'Hara having left hours before with boxes of household arsenic, along with correspondence and papers from Roger's office.

In the odd quiet, McCain took the careful notes Blake demanded of everyone he worked with and then went outside to speak with the chauffeur. The butler shut the door behind him and made a point of turning the lock.

"He knows what side his bread is buttered on," a man called up to McCain from the street. "I bet they didn't give you an inch, did they?" McCain didn't reply, took one step at a time as he wrote his notes in his little black notebook.

Heavyset and soft, the chauffeur leaned against the car and looked up at the townhome, smoking a hand-rolled cigarette. "You made a mistake coming so early," he called out. "You should have waited until after the will is read. They all think they're going to get something."

"You don't?" McCain made a show of putting his notebook away in his pocket. He took a place next to the man and leaned on the car to look up at the townhome as well.

The man spat on the ground. "Nope. Either they don't know me well enough or they know me too well."

"Strikes me that could be a man's problem no matter where he went."

The chauffeur laughed outright. "That's my predicament, sure enough."

McCain put his hands in his pants pockets and crossed his feet. "You don't strike me much like a chauffeur," he said sedately.

"Don't I?" The man laughed. "Well, maybe that's because I wasn't a chauffeur before. Probably won't be again."

"What are you then, P.I.? Ex-cop maybe?"

"You got the sight, officer! You and my granny!" The man wheezed, laughed, and wiped his eyes before taking a draw from his cigarette. McCain looked back to the house and contemplated it, watching the lights turn off one by one. After a moment, the front door opened and the butler came out. "Mooney, I told you to get on with picking up Mrs. Warwick. Get on with your work, man!"

"Or you'll what?" Mooney stood up, and McCain noted that he wasn't all soft, not yet.

The butler shook his head and shut the door, locking it from the inside.

"Now that the old man's gone, I got no chance. Mrs. Warwick told me today. This is my last week." He leaned back on the car and leveled a watery eye at McCain. "Guess I'm not in the will then, huh?" He laughed.

"Why aren't you on the force anymore, Mooney?"

Mooney's laugh slowed to a wet cough. He threw the stub of his cigarette into the gutter and fell back against the car. "It was the booze. It got me."

McCain nodded and returned to looking at the front of the house. He said, "When I walked up to this house, I said to myself, I bet that house is bigger on the inside than it looks from the outside." He shifted. "Lots of houses are like that. I've seen them myself. But not that house." McCain took on an uncharacteristic hardness. "That house is just as small as it appears to be." Mooney got his coughing under control and sighed beside him. "I've been here two hours," McCain shared a knowing look with the chauffeur, "interviewing the staff. And I haven't learned anything that I didn't already get from the first moment I saw this house. Small and narrow. Makes you wonder what they did with all their money."

"They spent it," Mooney said definitively. "Don't let nobody tell you any different. They spent every cent."

"Warwick wasn't loaded?"

"With a wife like that? And three daughters? There's never enough." Mooney pulled a tobacco pouch from his pocket and began the long process of rolling a cigarette. "There would have been more money if he wasn't so bad at making it. He should have sold while the market was good."

"Sounds like you've known him for a while."

"I was private security at the factory," Mooney grinned, showing a missing bicuspid and a broken molar, "helping him out of a very sticky situation."

McCain thought about it for a moment. "Wasn't there a strike in '27? Picket line broke . . . There was a riot, wasn't there?"

"Wire hangers," Mooney laughed. "Who knew they could be so much trouble?"

"When did you come on here?"

"'Bout a year ago. Warwick wanted someone who could look after his daughters. Wasn't too bad at first. Mostly I was just driving around Clover, keeping her out of trouble."

"What kind of trouble?"

"Listen, brother, you don't know what kind of trouble a female could get up to until you met Clover Warwick. I didn't know, and I used to work vice!"

"You're pulling my leg! A society girl like that? Sings opera, I heard."

"That ain't opera she's singing when she's looking for a bit of rough, if you know what I mean." Mooney laughed into his hand, shuddering as the laugh devolved into a cough.

"I don't believe it," McCain said flatly.

"Suit yourself." Mooney shrugged and returned to his cigarette. "I'm going to miss that girl. I never knew what to expect, and that's a fact."

"What about the other two? Tulip and Ivy?"

"Pathetic examples of womanhood standing next to their sister, if you ask me." He licked the edge of the paper and fitted it in the corner of his mouth. "Dull as dishwater."

"I talked to Tulip before she died. She wouldn't tell me a thing."

"Well, she wouldn't, would she? They were sisters, see? In a house like that they learned how to keep a secret."

"You think she did it herself?"

"All I ever did was drive the girl to the library. She hadn't ever done a bad thing in her life. There wasn't a reason in the world to kill that girl. I'd swear to it. Now, if we're talking about suicide, that's another matter. Have you met her mother?" Mooney chuckled as he took a lighter from his pocket and lit his cigarette. McCain stayed Mooney's hand when he tried to return the lighter to his pocket.

"That's a nice thing," McCain said thoughtfully as he looked at the lighter in Mooney's hand.

Mooney handed it to him. "Go ahead. Clover gave it to me. Tell me now you don't believe me."

"'For good times. C,'" McCain read aloud. Handing it back to Mooney, he commented, "Pretty bold gift for a nice girl who stays home nights."

"Yeah, well," Mooney put the lighter into his pocket and paused to smoke, "it was something in the order of a parting gift. She had another mister, poor bastard."

"You mean her fiancé?"

Mooney burst out with another volley of laughter. The street seemed to fill with it. Mooney laughed until a light went on in the house. The front door opened, and the butler took several steps forward. "Mr. Mooney, I must warn you. If you do not leave immediately . . ."

"Hell," Mooney complained. "Come on and get in. I figure we're going to the same place anyway." He slid behind the wheel as McCain joined him in the front seat. The car pulled away from the curb like it were floating on air. McCain leaned back in the seat and enjoyed the moment. "Take off your hat," Mooney said suddenly. "I don't want no one to think I'm riding around with a policeman."

McCain silently removed his hat. "So if it wasn't her fiancé, who was it?"

"Some poor sap, if I know Clover as well as I think I do. Probably just like me but younger, see?" Mooney looked tired in the light of the streetlamps. McCain adjusted his age to fifty. "She had a type. Wow," he exclaimed, "what a girl!"

"And the fiancé?"

"What is it with you and the fiancé? Old Reggie was just a front for her father. There wasn't anything there at all. Just a couple of kids out for a good time."

"So they weren't going to get married?"

"Well, why wouldn't they if they liked each other? I've seen worse starts for marriage." Catching the look of disgust on McCain's face, Mooney continued, "See here, she used to tell me that they had an understanding. She said there wasn't anyone in the world who knew her like Reggie did. That sort of put my hat back, if you see what I mean. Being that I knew the woman pretty well myself."

McCain nodded. "That's the precinct house up there."

Mooney pulled the car over and killed the engine. Opening the door, he stood up in the street and stretched. "Well, that's it for me then. Time to find another job. Here, you can tell them where to find the keys. God knows they won't believe me. I'm not going back there for love or money." Mooney threw the keys into the air for McCain to catch. "So long, officer."

"Mooney," McCain called after him, "where do you drink? I'd like to buy you one sometime." The lie came easily to McCain as he watched the big man laugh in the moonlight.

"Stretch's place, down on the docks."

"Hell's Kitchen?"

"That's the one." Mooney turned and staggered into the night, disappearing in the shadow of a building. McCain thought he heard a whistle start—"I wanna be loved by you," if he was any guess. McCain looked down at the hat in his hand and the car at the curb. He went into the precinct.

31

ELEANOR AND PENELOPE SAT TOGETHER in the cozy living room, Eleanor with her feet curled up in her favorite chair, Penelope in a corner of the couch. They both watched the fire in the small grate, their thoughts a mash of exhaustion and grief. "I wish I had known her better," Penelope said after a long silence.

"I know," Eleanor said softly.

Tulip's face flashed across Penelope's mind, the lobby of the Metropolitan Opera House rising up around her. Out of a sense of self-defense, she thought of a list of things to keep her mind from Tulip—opera, Carrera, her lovely dress, then, finally, Lund. She glanced up at the clock again; it was ten after nine. Perhaps Lund forgot. "I forgot to tell you, Mother. Lund was at the opera last night. We sat together."

"I wondered why he turned up at the hospital." Eleanor leaned her head on her hand, her face soft in the dim light. Penelope could hardly bring herself to look at her mother, watching her from her perifery instead. Eleanor lifted her head with interest. "If you were with Thom, who did Mary sit with?"

"A friend of Helen's." Penelope was struck by a sudden pang of guilt. She hadn't seen Mary after the first interval and hadn't had time to ring her.

"I hope you didn't leave your cousin to a stranger, Penelope." Eleanor returned her head to her hand.

"Of course not!" She should have called Mary first thing. Penelope had gotten herself mixed up in someone else's business again, happy to be there for everyone but the people who needed her. Mary had given up her ticket to a man she found irritating and embarrassing just so Penelope could be with Lund, and what had Penelope done about it? Nothing. Not one word of thanks or even a call to the house to make sure Mary had arrived safely. Penelope promised herself she would make it up to her as soon as she could. She looked at the clock again. Where was Lund? Perhaps she could call Mary now. The butler would know even if Mary was already asleep. Penelope began to stand. "I should have called her this morning. I'll do it now." She froze as she caught Eleanor's face. The tears weren't visible, but the wet trail across her cheeks were.

"Oh, Mother!" Penelope crossed the room in a flash, her arms around her mother's neck. "What on earth is wrong?"

"I'm not crying for you, silly girl." Eleanor stroked Penelope's hair. "Or maybe I am. I was thinking about that horrible woman—Violet Warwick—and I wondered what it would be like to live with a person like that, day after day. Then I remembered that you had. You lived with Kinkaid." Eleanor exhaled and put her hand on Penelope's cheek, keeping it there. "I think I must have convinced myself that night we saw you in the hospital was the first time. Now that I've seen it . . . I don't know what you must have gone through." Eleanor reached her hand into her pocket for a tissue. "The doctors didn't want me to see you, said it wasn't an image fit for a lady. I told them, 'My daughter is a lady, and if she can take it, then so can I.' I thought that must have been the worst part of living with a man like that," Eleanor whispered. "Now that I've seen Ivy, I know I was wrong."

"Mother," Penelope pulled away and looked everywhere but at Eleanor, "you've got it all wrong. Kinkaid didn't beat me."

"Penelope." Eleanor took her by the hand, pulling her close. Her fingers were warm, her voice soft. "I hear you tell that lie, and I know why you tell it, but you don't have to repeat it to me. I know what happened. I've known since I saw you lying there, Thom sleeping upright in a chair at the foot of your bed."

"Thom told you." Penelope sat back on her heels, the shock numbing her. She studied the carpet; the familiar pattern of the Axminster provided temporary relief from the memory.

"No, you foolish girl." Eleanor sounded like she was about to laugh, or sob. "You told me. Told me, told your father, told Lund."

Penelope gasped, and Eleanor put both hands on her face.

"The only people you wouldn't say a word to were the doctors and the other policemen. Everyone else you'd tell outright. You said, 'I shot the bastard.' Your father didn't care for the language, but we both agreed it was an appropriate usage. I recall David saying he wished he had been the one to pull the trigger. We all agreed, all of us, to keep the secret."

Penelope laid her head on her mother's lap, her eyes strangely dry. They had known? All this time?

"I didn't know whether or not to tell you I knew." Eleanor had a faint smile. "This century is a bit overwhelming to a daughter of Victorians. Your generation shares every little thing about your lives. Some days I thought you remembered you told me. Other days I knew you did not." Eleanor leaned her head in her hand, laying the other on Penelope's head in her lap. "Then today, watching Voilet Warwick with her daughter, I knew it hadn't been one violent moment just before the end with Kinkaid. I knew he had treated you like that woman treated her own daughter—like a dog with a rag. I know why you wanted to help that poor girl." Eleanor settled in her chair, turning so she could give Penelope her full attention. "I understand what happened. I do. There's only one thing I don't understand. Where on earth did all the money come from?"

"The money?" Penelope's mouth went dry all at once. She tried to smile and found she couldn't. "What ever could you mean?" She sat up, looked away.

Eleanor expelled a wry laugh. "What a good actress you are! If I hadn't seen it for myself, I would believe your every word. My dear, I mean the money in the locked suitcase at the back of your wardrobe. Thirty thousand dollars, more or less, if my counting is correct. Is it your money? Or someone else's?"

"It's mine." Penelope kept her eyes on the grate.

"Well, I don't know where it could be from. Your father's estate was large enough to see us settled here with a small income for me, but there wasn't anything else. Certainly not thirty thousand dollars. And your casino burned to the ground while you were in the hospital." Eleanor added darkly, "Your partners made sure of that. There was nothing left. James handled your matters while you were in the hospital, and he would have told me about that amount of cash."

Penelope stared hard at the fire. Her mouth moving without a word coming free. "Who knows? Does James know?" she asked.

"I didn't think it was any of his business. Isn't any of mine, either, if you take my point." Eleanor laughed. "I've no right to know. It's none of my business. I'm only curious. I think you suffer from the same affliction. I can't seem to help myself."

"I'd rather forget about it, if you don't mind." Penelope stood up and poured herself a whiskey neat. She hardly recollected how she made it across the carpet. She was suddenly there, with the bottle in her hand.

"Get one for me while your at it." Eleanor settled her hands in her lap. "I know I don't have a right to know. You don't have to tell me anything, but forgetting about thirty thousand dollars in cash is hard to do. Have you spent any of it?"

Penelope drank the liquor in one pull. "I gave some money to Uncle Harry. Otherwise, I haven't spent a penny." She poured her mother's whiskey, trying hard not to meet her eye when she handed it to her.

"Were things that bad, then?"

Someone knocked at the door.

"There he is. That's Lund. No one else would have the nerve." Eleanor nodded. "We are going to talk about this again. I want to know what you're hiding from. It's not Kinkaid. He's dead. And it isn't James and I, because we already know. There's something else eating away at you, Penelope Harris. I'm your mother. I want to know what it is. And put on your robe before you answer the door or you'll give the poor man a heart attack."

Penelope blushed, unable to think any single thought clearly except that she must not think of the suitcase or Tulip or the money or Kinkaid, continuing on like this until she was overwhelmed by everything she must not think about. She stopped in the bathroom on the way to the front of the apartment, pulling a heavy robe from the hook beside the sink. Tying it tightly around her waist, Penelope ran her fingers through her hair and hoped she didn't look as though she had been crying.

She opened the door to Lund. He must have been exhausted, dead on his feet, but his eyes were still sharp, his hair still combed neatly back, his suit clean and correct. "You look lovely," he blurted out and then blushed.

"Come in. Mother and I have been waiting for you." She smiled, her happiness shy.

Lund followed her into the living room, where Eleanor was curled into a chair, her plaid dressing gown cinched tight, her face thoughtful as she looked into the fire. "Thom." She showed no indication that they had been discussing how Penelope had killed her husband just a moment before.

"Don't get up," Thom said lightly as he stepped forward. "I can't imagine asking someone who looks so comfortable to move a muscle."

Eleanor shook her head and laughed. Putting her feet on the floor, she slid them into her slippers.

"I understand from Blake it's been grim," Lund said. "I think you've earned your time in front of the fire."

Penelope studied her mother. The lines in Eleanor's face were deep, the circles under her eyes heavy in the darkness. She wondered why she hadn't noticed it before.

"Grim?" Eleanor's face paled. "Tulip! That poor girl! I don't know if I shall ever forget it."

"Thom, it was terrible." Penelope pulled him down beside her on the couch. "In the end, they tried to . . . to . . . pump it out of her."

"I know all about it. Blake told me." Lund took her hand, his skin warm and dry against her palm. It anchored her, kept her mind on the present. Memories of her past melted into the shadows of the evening, where they could be ignored.

"She gave a statement. Have you seen it?" Penelope watched him, distantly aware that he had not let go of her hand. When he shook his head, she continued, "It took the most extraordinary effort. Tulip was so weak. She didn't poison herself, Thom. She just didn't."

"Tulip was running away from home that night," Eleanor

added from her chair. “She had every reason to believe that things were looking up.”

“Running away? Blake didn’t tell me that.”

“It sounds so ordinary.” Eleanor smiled ruefully. “There was a young man. She married him. She wouldn’t tell anyone what his name was, even at the end. Tulip had everything to look forward to. She certainly wasn’t about to kill herself.” Eleanor’s face creased in the firelight. “She never said his name. Judging by how her mother behaved, he might be the only person who really cared about her.” Eleanor caught Lund’s eye. “Thom . . .”

“The police will find him, Eleanor. Don’t worry about that. A couple of detectives will make quick work of it. Trust me.”

“What do you have there?” Penelope pulled the papers rolled up in his hand.

“We found this in her room. It was one of the only personal effects she had.” Lund let her take them.

“It’s the score to *Hoffmann.*”

“Blake asked me to bring it to you. He thought there might be something in her notes.”

“You mean like a secret message?” Penelope stared at the pages. “How sad.”

Lund’s eyes grew heavy as he leaned back into the couch. Penelope stood and carried the score to a lamp. She began to turn the pages slowly. Each page was covered with loops of writing, musical observations that were obvious repetitions of something Tulip had heard but not understood. Penelope sighed.

“Anything interesting?” Eleanor prompted.

“Only that she seemed to be guessing about a good deal.

Tulip wanted very much to do a good job." Shaking her head, she waved her hand at the script. "It's as though she was doing what she thought was right by marking it up. Most of this is nonsense." Reaching the last page, she turned back to the front. Her eyes lifted to the top of the page. Penelope was perfectly still.

"What is it, darling?" Eleanor stood up, coming toward the lamp with her hand out for the manuscript.

"This is Clover's name on the score. Tulip's is marked out."

Eleanor looked over Penelope's arm. "Is that unusual? You said Clover was looking forward to singing."

Penelope looked up. "This whole opera is very odd. I can't get it out of my mind. What in the world was the society thinking to cast three sisters who can hardly sing and whom no one seems to like or know very well to play all three of the major soprano roles? Yesterday Violet Warwick argued with the chairwoman, said Clover could sing Ivy's part. Now this has Clover's name on it too."

"Maybe she's trying for a hat trick," Lund mumbled from the couch.

Penelope smiled. "Ivy is still singing Olympia. Clover wouldn't have all three roles, just the two."

"Eleanor rubbed the bridge of her nose. "I think you should leave it to Lund, Penelope. He's the professional."

"But this has nothing to do with an investigation," Penelope protested. "This is about opera."

"If you feel you must, then you must. But I'd rather you left it alone. You'll be happier," Eleanor smiled to herself, "and I'll start getting to bed at a reasonable hour."

"Thom, what do you think?" Penelope turned to the couch, where Lund had slumped over, overcome by sleep.

"Leave the poor man alone. There's time enough tomorrow." Eleanor reached over to turn off the lamp. You can bring him a blanket and a pillow after you put me to bed."

"You act like you're an old woman, Mother, when you are anything but."

"Days like today make me feel old, Penelope." Eleanor put her hand on Penelope's cheek. "I worry about you. There's been so much unhappiness. I wish you hadn't seen that today. I wish . . ." Eleanor broke off.

"Mother . . ." Penelope was at a loss as Eleanor pulled a handkerchief from her pocket and wiped her eyes. "You don't have to worry about me. We're together. We are all together, and we are safe."

"Mothers worry, Penelope. It's our constant state of being. Just promise me you will leave this alone. When we were in that hospital room today watching that young girl die, all I could think was her only family was that child Ivy."

"We couldn't leave Ivy alone."

"I realize that. We couldn't. But think about how it must have been for that dying girl—surrounded by people she didn't know, only one sister at her side, knowing that her father was dead and the rest of her family wouldn't come. And us, just standing by, watching."

Penelope shuddered. "You're giving me chills."

"It's my mother's Scottish blood, that's what it is." Eleanor took a breath. "It makes me cold to think about the mother who could leave her dying child. I'm afraid that woman has brought terrible judgment on herself."

"That's quite enough of that." Penelope reached over and turned on the hall light. "I won't be able to sleep with the lights off for a week."

"I'll be up reading if you want company." Eleanor opened her door and turned on the light.

"Good night, Mother." Penelope turned back into the living room and watched Lund on the couch, his breathing deep and steady. She remembered a blanket and a pillow in the hall closet. By the time she had found them and returned to the room, she found Lund had lifted his feet to the sofa and claimed a throw pillow as his own. Penelope finished the job, untying his shoes and putting the blanket over him before scraping the grate to kill the fire. Then, after turning out all the lights, she kissed his cheek, her hand lingering on his warm neck as she watched him breathe. A moment before, the room had been filled with the memory of Kinkaid. Now, here was Lund breaking the spell with a gentle snore. She stood and pulled the blinds so the morning light would not wake him.

Penelope stopped dead in her tracks in the open door of her room. Mrs. Reynolds had been about straightening before she left. The bedside lamp gave off a cozy glow in the room, and Penelope's bed was made, the sheet peeking out a clue that the cook had changed the sheets after Ivy had left. On another day, Penelope would have blessed the woman and tucked herself in between the clean sheets, which would smell faintly of bleach. Instead, she was transfixed by Ivy's dress, clean and pressed, across the foot of the bed. Mrs. Reynolds must have taken a hand, done her best. The stains from Ivy's time at the hospital were completely gone, as though the day had never happened. Turning out the light and shutting the door to her room, Penelope walked back to her mother's bedroom, where she found Eleanor reading a book. Eleanor watched her, then lifted back the cover on the opposite side of the bed. Penelope climbed in without a word, falling asleep as soon as her head touched the pillow.

32

"I THINK MRS. REYNOLDS LIKES YOU, THOM." Penelope considered the food on the table. A plate of eggs, toast, bacon, and biscuits were laid out like a buffet directly in front of Lund. "She made you bacon. Mother, I thought Mrs. Reynolds only came Saturdays."

"Ivy ate all the bacon. In addition to not being able to tolerate your brother's complaining, I couldn't stand waiting for another week." Eleanor sniffed. "And anyway, Mrs. Reynolds said she was worried about us, wanted to make sure we were all right."

The memory of Ivy at the breakfast table gave Penelope pause. Ivy hadn't said a word to either Penelope or her mother the whole breakfast, just ate and drank and stared straight ahead. When she wanted something, she had gotten up to get it herself, sometimes reaching over Penelope to get to it. When Mrs. Reynolds had asked Ivy if she had slept well, the girl turned her face to the wall and wouldn't say a word.

Penelope gave a start when Lund put his coffee down.

"Where is James?" Lund reached for the toast as he asked, offering her the plate before he took some himself.

"He left for a hospital downtown before you got up." Eleanor spread butter on her toast with a graceful wave of her knife. "He works in a surgery there. None of the doctors work on Sundays, so someone with his experience is always appreciated as an extra set of hands."

"Tulip made the front page again," Penelope said. "Yesterday it was Helen's byline on the front page. Today it's someone else. It should have been her scoop about Warwick. It seems unfair, when you think about it."

"That reminds me." Lund looked at his watch. "I need to call Helen, ask if she can give me an inside line on a society person."

"She'll pump you if you call her at the paper. And if she doesn't, her editor will," Penelope reminded him. "Is it about Tulip?"

"No, it's for something else I'm working on." Lund shook his head and returned to his eggs. He went on, almost as though he was talking to himself, "Blake won't like me talking to the papers about it. There's no time to get to the bank and call her from there. I'll just have to risk it. I have to get going. I should have had that score back to Blake last night." He focused on Penelope. "Was there anything in the notes? Anything worth mentioning to the lieutenant?"

"Only that Tulip was an eager student. Perhaps a little overeager. None of the notes made sense."

"Oh well. It was worth a try." Lund shrugged as he stood up, a cup of coffee in one hand and a piece of toast in the other.

Penelope was caught off guard, the cozy breakfast interrupted. She couldn't help but try to think of a reason he might stay. "There was one thing I thought was interesting," she blurted out. "Tulip's name had been marked out and Clover's name added. I don't know what relation it might have, but I thought it might help. All three sisters were set to be in the recital. Clover wanted to sing all three roles. Now she can."

"Penelope, really! What are you suggesting? That Clover killed her own sister for her part?" Eleanor let her fork drop with a clatter. "How horrible! As if the family hasn't been through enough!"

"You met them, Mother. You saw what Violet is like! You can't imagine that one of them might commit a crime to get what she wants?"

"Yes, a crime. But murder?" Eleanor shook her head. "I can't imagine it."

"I don't know." Lund put the cup on the table and removed his jacket from the back of his chair. "Normally I would agree with you. But after what I witnessed last night, I must admit anything is possible with the Warwicks. I'll tell Blake. It's his case. He gets to decide what's important."

"I'll get the manuscript." Penelope pushed back her chair and left for the living room. When she returned, Lund was slipping on his coat and reaching for his hat, Eleanor beside him buttoning up her coat.

"Are you sure it's all right?" Eleanor asked Lund. "Normally I wouldn't take a cab, but I'm afraid I'll be late." Glancing at Penelope, she added, "I have to see Harry this morning. He's had a letter from China about your father's business interests, and he's in a bit of a flurry about it. I keep telling him there's nothing left, but he won't listen to me." She adjusted her hat with a firm hand. "Better to tell him in person."

Penelope felt an unfamiliar pinch of discomfort. She did not want to be alone in the apartment, not with Ivy's dress at the foot of the bed. She wanted very much to go with them, just so long as she was away from it.

Eleanor kissed her daughter's cheek. "Are you all right? You look a little peaked."

"Shall I come with you? I could be helpful. See Mary." Penelope reached past Eleanor for her coat. "Keep you company."

"Oh, yes, I forgot to tell you." Eleanor dug into her purse. "I made an appointment for you to speak with someone from the opera, about teaching. Here." She handed Penelope a small card with an address and a time written on it. "His name is there." Eleanor smiled and patted Penelope's hand.

"On a Sunday?"

"It's the only time he had, and I wasn't about to argue. Be on time, Penelope."

They were gone in a flash, the door shutting behind them with a click that seemed louder than it actually was. Penelope looked at the card in her hand as she walked back to the table, where the cook was already cleaning up. "Here, Mrs. Reynolds. Let me help," Penelope said with industry.

"Oh, no, my dear. I have it." The cook waved a hand. "Would you like anything else before I go?"

"No, thank you, Mrs. Reynolds."

Penelope studied the card in her hand. She could just read her mother's handwriting. It read: M. F. Mackey 2 pm.

Penelope had an idea. She searched through her purse

until she found the card she wanted. Going to the hallway, she dialed the number.

"Patsy, so glad I caught you. May I come by? I would like to talk to you about opera."

33

Blake dropped the third act of *The Tales of Hoffmann* on his desk and sat on the edge, his feet spread wide to support his weight. He crossed his arms and narrowed his eyes. "I thought I asked you to have it back last night," he said abruptly.

"Sorry about that. I fell asleep while Penelope was looking it over." Lund sat down in the chair opposite Blake and crossed his legs.

"Sleep is for amateurs," Blake replied.

"As I am no longer a policeman," Lund smiled, "I can confirm that statement is entirely accurate."

Blake huffed and paced behind his desk, where he sat, pulled out a drawer, and put his feet on it, pushing his chair back at an angle. "She find anything?"

"Only that Tulip was a novice. Perhaps she had talent, perhaps she didn't." Lund thought about Penelope's observation regarding the roles. There could be something in it if you looked at it from the right angle. Jealousy, maybe? If Clover really was out of control, that could be enough motive. Lund made up his mind. "Also, Tulip's aria in the society recital might have been reassigned to Clover." Lund indicated the top of the page.

"So they moved it, or she wanted it moved." Blake narrowed his eyes in thought. "What are you thinking? She wanted it badly enough to kill her sister?"

"Maybe she thought the arsenic would put Tulip out of commission for the recital. Maybe she didn't know it would kill her." Lund hung his hat on his knee. "Penelope told me about Tulip's plan to move to Philadelphia. Any joy there?"

"Just bank balances, Philadelphia phone numbers, and addresses." Blake ran down the list with the usual police zest for detail. "I have one of the sergeants going through it now. If she was running away to Philly, that knocks out suicide."

"Depends on the point of view." Lund made himself comfortable. "Have you ever been to Philadelphia?"

Nathan Blake's laugh was a rough bark that startled the desk sergeant.

"Look, Nathan, it can't be that much different here in the States. In Shanghai we had a suicide in the British zone that was almost certainly muder, but the family got to the newspapers first. Made it play out in the press until the court case was a shambles." Lund shrugged. "If the Warwicks are determined that suicide is less shocking than murder, then there won't be any convincing them otherwise. The whole thing will play out in the press and destroy the D.A.'s case before it ever comes to trial."

"Not my problem, thank God. The district attorney gets to handle that hot potato, and I couldn't be happier about it." Blake ran his hand over his face and sighed. "I was rooting for the Warwick girl. We all were. The doc told me there wasn't anything we could have done, but I can't help feeling if we had found her sooner, maybe she would have lived." Blake looked down at the score. "My gut is telling me they're hiding something, but what it is I couldn't say. Something worse than murder and suicide? What the hell could be worse than that?" Blake gathered up the pages and put them to the side of his desk. He ran his hand over his bald head. "None of the staff will talk. McCain has the idea that they are all on the take, but I don't see it. He's following a few things up, but so far the household is in the clear. He had a chat with the chauffeur that pointed him toward Clover, but it isn't nearly enough."

"The story about the maid is enough to put her in with the rest of the suspects."

"She's wild." Blake was clipped. "But we already knew that. So, maybe she's a bit more wild than we thought. Doesn't make it matter any more or any less." He looked at Lund. "But she says she's got an alibi. One way or another, we'll find where she fits in."

"Any news about the rat poison we found?"

Blake smiled wryly. "Which one? The house was practically swimming in the stuff. Plus, the box we found in her drawer had everyone's fingerprints on it. Everyone's but the victim's." Blake stroked his mustache absentmindedly. "My money's on the mother putting it there herself." He muttered to himself. "Finding it there would fit with the murder-suicide angle. She might have thought it would get us off her back."

"Makes you wonder, seeing a mother act like that."

Blake snorted, then said flatly, "You've met her. Maybe it's for the best. These high-society people don't like making the papers. The D.A. may say he wants a thorough investigation, but what he really wants is for this to go away. Already called me twice this morning to ask for a progress report."

"Gets to everyone after awhile."

"Maybe so." Blake blinked and sat up.

"Listen, Nathan. I wonder if you might let me ask a couple of questions around the station about a case I'm working. Wallace Peters asked me to look into his sister-in-law's suicide. I've got the report the family had, but I wondered if there was—"

"Wallace Peters," Blake interrupted him. "You're looking into Coralee O'Connor's death." Blake's words might have been flat, but his eyes were sharp. The lieutenant had stopped moving. It seemed as though every living cell in the officer's body had turned its attention to Lund. "And what does ol' Wallace hope to get out of an investigation?"

"He wants to know why she did it."

"Oh, is that all?" Blake lifted his eyebrows and stared into Lund's face. "I never would have thought he had it in him. Especially since his wife was the one hushing it all up."

"Did she?" Lund sat forward. "Cover it up?"

"He didn't tell you that, did he? Or maybe he didn't know. Could be the old boy has dropped you right in the middle of a marital argument. Wallace struck me as one of those people who isn't dealing with a full deck, if you know what I mean. He was pretty broken up when Coralee died. Guess he wasn't paying attention to all the moves his wife was making to ensure it was buttoned up nice and neat." Blake exhaled. "No, it had all the signs of a suspicious death to me, but the D.A. didn't agree. I don't know." Blake stood up. "Maybe I was seeing ghosts where there weren't any. As far as we could tell, the woman had no bad habits, no illegitimate children, no history, no enemies. She had her benefacting societies, and that was about the size of her life. Coralee didn't like parties, didn't dabble in high society, and didn't make a ripple the entire length of her short life. I suppose you want to talk to whichever poor bastard did the looking into. That would be me, but I'm sure you guessed that already."

Lund rose from the chair. "I did take a guess it would be you."

"Wasn't that lucky." Blake put a hand on the door to his office and stopped. "I'm sorry, Lund. Suicide never made much sense to me, or maybe I see murder everywhere I look. It's a professional hazard. As far as I could tell, Coralee was an upstanding citizen who never did anyone any harm at all."

"I was at her cottage yesterday at Piping Rock." Lund put on his hat. "Seemed like a man had lived there."

"No man that we found. Everything was gone by the time we were there—no clothes, no personal effects, didn't even have a bar of soap, if I recall correctly. Weeks had passed since she had died. Her sister had been around, tidying." Blake remained by the door without moving.

"I spoke to some people who live up there. They said there were some suspicious circumstances."

"Why? What did they say?"

Lund couldn't see the reason why Blake was so guarded. He proceeded carefully. "I spoke to a man out there who saw her before she went out on the boat that night. He said it was around ten thirty and she waved at him."

"We got that too." Blake nodded.

"He said she was wearing a hat, a great big one."

Blake squinted. "At night? Was he sure?"

"He was." Lund paused. "The caretaker thought there were a few other odd things that night. She said a man came to visit."

"Maybe if her family had reported her missing before her body was found, we would have had a better chance at it." The old policeman grunted. "The sister had gotten a note in the mail. It was all she needed to be convinced."

"In the mail?"

"It was a new one for me too. It was Coralee's handwriting all right, in French. I'll let you see it. Let you see the whole file if you like, but I want something in return."

"What is it?"

Blake took his hand from the door, rubbed his chin. "The Warwick maid—the one who lost an eye. I hear she's living somewhere in Queens. I'd like to ask her some questions, but it's just a hunch and I can't spare the manpower for a shot in the dark. Plus there's the D.A. Not sure he would take kindly to us looking under the rug when he's working so hard to roll up the case." He grimaced. "I need someone to go out there and ask her a few questions."

"That sounds serious."

"I'm on a deadline. Just like a damn newspaper," Blake grumbled.

Lund shrugged. "I'm happy to do it if it helps."

Blake was already writing an address down on a piece of paper. "Take this to the desk sergeant downstairs. He knows the girl's uncle and can give you the address. He can also point out a cabbie who won't rob you blind to run you out there." He handed the paper to Lund and sighed. "Coralee O'Connor . . . I never thought that case would ever get reopened."

"Don't get ahead of me, Nathan. It isn't reopened yet."

"You got the locals to talk to you. That's further than I ever got." Blake stretched as he opened the door. "Don't forget the desk sergeant. I want to hear back from you tonight. I've got a bad feeling about this. Like I missed something. I don't like it."

Lund nodded and made his way to the desk sergeant.

34

Penelope was out of breath by the time she knocked on Patsy's apartment door. The elevator was out, and climbing the five flights up had been hot work. She had gotten all the way uptown to the townhouse where she and Mary had attended the tea party only to learn that Patsy had borrowed the house from her brother for the tea and lived on the opposite side of the park. Penelope raced across the city in a taxi, then took the stairs at a fast clip when she found an out-of-order sign on the elevator. She was just getting her breath back when the door opened to Patsy herself, with no maid in sight. Penelope thrust her hand forward, "Hullo, Patsy. So good of you to have me over." As was usual when she was nervous, Penelope found her mouth running away with her. "The cab driver wasn't really sure what to do about the address, so we had to make do, and—oh, what a lovely kimono you're wearing! Then the manager downstairs said I had better walk, and here I am! Five flights of stairs. Phew!"

Patsy looked at Penelope's lopsided hat and rumpled suit and said, "Looks like you got here just in time." She leaned forward. "Did they catch you?" Penelope blushed, although given how red her face already was, she doubted Patsy could see. "Let's hang up your coat so you can cool off. I'll make you some tea. Sounds like you had some trouble finding the place."

"I went all the way to your house uptown. When I told the cab driver I wanted to come all the way back, he was a little put out." Patsy helped Penelope out of her coat. "I just didn't think to check your card. Silly, really. I live one block down from you and didn't even know it!"

"Then you ran all the way here?" Patsy had an air of austerity. Penelope couldn't tell if she was being teased.

"No, the cab brought me back. The elevator was broken, so I had to take the stairs."

"It irks me how the management in this building lets that elevator go. You would think that they would fix the damn thing once and for all!"

Penelope was hardly shocked by the casual manner of the other woman's swearing. Managing a casino, she'd heard a great deal of street language and sharp talk. Penelope didn't mind it at all. In fact, she felt more comfortable because of it. But her attention was drawn to the fact that Patsy didn't care what Penelope thought about it. Penelope stopped to take notice, wondering if there would be more surprises.

Patsy gestured to a couch for Penelope and chose a soft

leather chair for herself, promptly falling back comfortably into the thick cushions. Under the beautiful orange-and-red kimono, she wore pants and worn flat leather slippers.

Penelope tried hard not to stare. It wasn't the shock of the moment that captured her but the curiosity of how Patsy had done it. Penelope had heard that certain Parisian tailors might make a pair if the price was right. Trousers on women weren't just frowned upon. Paris had already seen the arrest of a number of women who dared to wear pants on the street. Penelope wasn't sure, but she hadn't seen a single woman in a pair of pants since they had arrived in New York three months before. Could the U.S. be the same? She couldn't get the thoughts straight in her head—she had too many questions. Did Patsy have the trousers made? Did she buy them at a store? Was there somewhere you could buy pants for women? Did they have pockets? Were they lovely big pockets? She was overcome by questions she couldn't ask. The closest she had come to a suit for herself was a pair of formal pajamas, which were hardly practical. She stared at the pants like a starving child stares at chocolate cake. How had Patsy done it? Were things so different in New York?

Patsy sat quietly while Penelope gaped. "You mentioned that you wanted to talk about opera?" she prompted gently. Penelope was startled by the sudden change in Patsy's mood. The steady discomfort she had witnessed at the party was entirely gone, along with the jewelry and the corset. Although, Penelope had to admit, doing away with a corset could do that for a woman. Without the jewelry and the stiff curls, Patsy had the look of an adventuress relaxing in the shadow of her plane.

"Oh yes, quite." Penelope put her purse beside her on the

couch and began removing her gloves and hat. "I wanted to thank you for your tickets. It was a lovely thought, very kind."

"I didn't see you in the seat." Patsy spoke in a slow, relaxing drawl, unlike her clipped, tense words at the party. "I thought your cousin brought Gibert Richie with her."

"You know Gil?" Penelope blurted without thinking. "That was an accident, to be honest. I met a friend in the lobby, and he had an empty seat on the floor. Gil sat next to Mary so she wouldn't be alone."

"I couldn't believe she got Gil to sit so quietly." Patsy laughed. "You will have to tell me how she did it." Leaning her head on her hand, she said, "Seems like that rehearsal was a thousand years ago, doesn't it?"

"Yes." Penelope was fascinated by Patsy's transformation. Her eye traveled from the cuff of the tailored pants to a trim leather belt and a button-down shirt free at the collar. Patsy had rolled the cuffs up to mid-elbow so they just appeared through the arms of the kimono. "What will you do about the recital? Will it be canceled?"

Patsy crossed her legs. "You would think it was obvious it must be canceled, wouldn't you? Valentina's manager has called to give her regrets, which I expected. She can't be associated with a scandal, even if it is only tangential to the society. Her appearance as the diva would have been a special treat for the society members. It cost the earth, but it would have been worth it." Patsy shrugged loosely. "I couldn't care less. I don't even care if Valentina keeps the money I paid her." Patsy was so relaxed, Penelope believed every word.

"Of course." Penelope nodded absently. "I'm sure everyone will understand."

"Are you?" Patsy laughed quietly. "I've heard from members all morning about what we should do next. Not everyone agrees the recital should be canceled. Others think I should resign. Can you imagine? As if the murder of that odious man was my fault! I suppose the board has forgotten that just yesterday they ordered me to give all three parts to Clover."

"All three? But what about Ivy? Isn't she well enough to sing?"

"Of course she is." Patsy studied Penelope. "And she sings quite well too. Most days she sings better than Clover. Better than you heard the other day, that's for sure. Clover wants the roles so she can command the stage. She won't sing all three, because she can't. Her voice isn't strong enough. It would give out halfway through Olympia's aria. She'd let her voice slide down into a flat note and never get it free again."

"But Ivy wants to sing. She told me so. Can't you do something? You're a founding member!" Penelope objected.

Patsy laughed. "You're more upset than I am. I don't care what the board decides. It might have been good fun once, but it isn't anymore," she observed dryly. "Too many members like the Warwicks turning it into their personal vanity project. It's theirs now. I have an idea Clover will find a way to lower the range and talk through the hardest parts rather than sing. I expect she'll wear her tap shoes for Olympia's aria. I'm done with it all." She laughed again. "She rang me just this morning to insist that rehearsals continue. That was after I told her Carrera had pulled out."

Penelope's skin turned cold. "Doesn't she have any shame at all?" She blurted the words out. Even Patsy seemed shocked, her face void of movement, her eyes watching Penelope closely. Penelope looked down at her hands and gathered herself. "It has been very difficult these past few days."

"Yes." Patsy leaned her head on her hand again. "I couldn't believe it when Clover told me what happened. She's a vapid, shallow girl, but it must have been hell sitting next to Tulip until the end."

"Clover told you that?"

"Yes, she said that it was a very painful end but that she and Ivy had stayed with her. Are you all right?"

If Penelope's hands had not gripped one another, they would have trembled. She was furious, and her heart sped away with her until her breath caught in her throat and made her choke.

"Do you need some brandy?" Patsy seemed to come clear of her stupor and leaned forward to touch Penelope's hand. "You're as cold as a stone!" She stood up and crossed the room in three long strides. "There's no brandy. Can you drink whiskey? Whiskey will have to do! Here!" She sat beside Penelope on the couch and forced the glass into her hand.

Penelope drank. Putting a hand to her head, she closed her eyes for a moment and tried to control the tremble that shook her. Her voice tattered by her rapid heart and the whiskey, she whispered in a single breath, "I don't know if I should tell you this or not—if my mother were here, she would stop me—but I have to tell someone." Her voice rising, Penelope lifted her face, took Patsy by the hand, and said, "Clover never entered that sickroom once, never came to the hospital. Not once. Tulip was there by herself, not a single member of the family beside her. Ivy sat in the hall and wouldn't come inside. My mother and I . . ." Her breath caught in her throat, and she walked her breath back, lowering her volume until it was almost normal. "My mother and I did what little we could for her. It wasn't enough. Clover never came. Violet never came. Ivy sat with her at first, but in the end she left her to sit in a chair in the hall." She released Patsy's hand and drank the rest of the whiskey in one gulp. "Clover is the perfect Guillietta! I can see her ransoming men's souls just for a joke."

Patsy replied somberly, "I thought it was quite the joke to cast the daughters as the doll, the dutiful daughter, and the courtesan. I thought it would bring me some satisfaction. You see, Violet only knows what Clover tells her about the opera. She'd never get the joke, not until the whole society was laughing at her. Violet was beginning to catch on yesterday when she saw Ivy sing."

"A hat trick," Penelope replied flatly. "That's what Thom calls it."

"Three successes? If I had succeeded, perhaps. I wanted to humiliate them. All of them." Patsy took a drink as she thought. "You're the first person with the nerve to even bring it up to me—to my face, at any rate. You're a very interesting person, Miss Penelope Harris. Very interesting indeed. I suppose you know the rest of it. You should. You look like a woman of the world to these old eyes. Tell me, what do you see?"

Penelope took in the masculine leather slippers, the crisply tailored grey pants, the fitted men's shirt with the sleeves rolled up to mid-arm, no jewelry, no rings, and short hair falling in curls around her ears. She saw the sensual mouth that had looked so out of place with lipstick but was perfectly balanced without the jarring makeup. Patsy sat back into the leather seat and took a long drink of whiskey before she crossed her legs and looked at Penelope as an entirely new person. Her eyes held a story Penelope had known before from a woman in Shanghai, a wealthy woman with plenty to keep herself far away from her family, where the newspapers would never see. Shanghai, not Hong Kong, because Shanghai was a place where she might be happy if no one cared to look too closely or ask too many questions. A spinster, a widow, a lonely old woman—any disguise was good enough as long as it kept the curious at bay. The woman would come to the Jade Tiger and gamble late into the night, happy to be somewhere she could wear a tuxedo, smoke cigarettes, and not be harassed. Kinkaid allowed anyone a turn at roulette in any attire they cared to wear, as long as they had money to put on the table. The woman was still there, as far as Penelope knew, frittering away her days attending high teas in uncomfortable dresses, spending her nights in a tailcoat, betting on black at the roulette table.

"You're being blackmailed?" Penelope asked, the answer coming to her as a fact long before Patsy nodded. She had the sudden urge to confess her whole past to Patsy, tell her everything about her own blackmailer, Renee Strong. The relief of meeting someone who was also an outcast overwhelmed her. "Because—because of who you are?"

Penelope could feel Patsy, whose eyes narrowed, taking measure of her. "You mean because I'm a homosexual? Go ahead. I can see it doesn't shock you." Patsy laughed, her eyes twinkling. "They all know—high society, I mean. They know everything about me and have known it all my life. I'm fifty-three years old, Penelope. I've learned how to survive. Five decades of observing my fellows practice deceit and corruption, gathering evidence against them all the while. I built myself an empire of reciprocal dependency. Rat on me and watch your troubles play out across the front page." She laughed again. "It kept my secret safe until the Warwicks. I don't see how anyone could be safe from them. They fell on high society like a plague of locusts. When Clover learned my secrets, she was determined to make a grab for whatever she could. I was lucky I could slow her down with cash. But when she asked for all three roles, I couldn't give them to her. I had to find a way to stop her. Casting her sisters was all I could do to slow her down. It pleased me to frustrate all her careful plans. And of course, it was easy to manipulate Violet to come along."

Penelope leaned back against the couch, the whiskey going to her head. She suddenly saw Clover on the outside looking in, no matter what she did or how much she spent. No wonder Tulip had tried to get away.

Patsy continued, "As soon Clover got herself engaged to my nephew, I knew she would blackmail me. Reggie doesn't know how to keep a secret." She shook her head, her smile bitter. "Until Clover realized I had something she wanted, I was free. I tried to run away. I went to Europe for a year. When I came back, she found me as soon as I stepped off the boat. The Warwicks are all devils, if you ask me. How did you get involved? You couldn't have possibly known Ivy. She only just came back from abroad."

Penelope sighed. "We met at the operatic society tea party. Then Ivy saw me at the opera and begged me to come with her to the hospital. I think she knew Violet wouldn't go.

I rode in the cab with her all the way. Tulip was . . . very ill. Violet did come later, but when she saw us she made a scene and left." Penelope broke off. "I couldn't leave Ivy there by herself."

"What do the police think happened?"

"Tulip was poisoned."

"Poison? That can't be possible." Patsy sat forward, all her attention on Penelope. "I thought she was attacked, like her father. The way Clover talked . . ." She trailed off.

"Arsenic. There's no way Clover or Violet can change that fact—Tulip was poisoned with arsenic." Penelope fumed. "I should have known! Of course, none of them want to admit what happened. Even if Tulip was murdered, they wouldn't care."

Patsy leaned back in her seat, hooking one leg over the chair arm. "One way or another, time after time, people like the Warwicks fall into a trap of their own making. Whenever they see a chance to go right, they go left. It never fails."

"I keep thinking about Tulip," Penelope said quietly. "No one deserves to die like that."

Patsy refilled their glasses.

35

SHE WAS LATE. M. F. Mackey—or was it Monsieur F. Mackey?—well, whoever he was, he would have to cope. Penelope watched the traffic lights pass without much doubt that her mother was sending her on another fool's errand. Some children's choir director needed an extra hand or a secratary or worse—a babysitter. It happened Penelope agreed with her mother. It was important to stay busy, to work if possible, but to always stay busy. But she did not agree that any employment proximal to singing was worth the effort. Penelope did not want to spend the rest of her life listening to other students get the chance she had missed. Teaching privately was much more dignified and held fewer confrontations with regret.

Despite her feelings, when the taxi stopped, Penelope moved with a whiskey-fueled determination to fill with aplomb whatever obligation her mother had assigned her, and tripped on the first stair up to the building door. Straightening up, she started again, only to be overwhelmed by exiting French dancers replete with bags that hit her uncomfortably in the knees. Stepping back, she looked at the address again. A male dancer paused to look over her shoulder at the paper.

"You are at the wrong door, Mademoiselle," he said in French. "It is the basement you are looking for." He pointed over her shoulder at the arched street-level windows.

Penelope thanked him and approached the stairs cautiously. Even if this was one of her mother's wild goose chases, Penelope was determined not to start the interview flat on her back.

The small flight of steps ended at a door containing a second flight of steps that led down to a narrow room facing the arched windows. It wasn't the usual basement, she thought. It was quite dry and well lit. The street-level windows let in more light than she had expected. Two wooden chairs sat against the brick wall. One was empty; the other contained a man reading a paper. Whoever he was, he did not look up from the paper. Street traffic made the light in the room flutter. One thing about the room was certainly typical of a basement—it was cold.

How late was she? Penelope glanced at her wristwatch to discover she wasn't late at all. Had her mother gotten the day wrong? Penelope stepped closer to the door. Gold lettering spelled out M. F. Mackey against the frosted glass. The room behind was dark.

Penelope advanced, her footsteps making her self-conscious. She knocked on the darkened door and received no reply.

The man in the chair folded his paper and dropped it on the floor next to him. "You like peaches?" He held a can of peaches in one hand, a can opener in the other. He began working the can opener around the lid, the rasp of the metal cover echoing in the cold room.

As it happened, she did. Penelope nodded.

"Well, have a seat. This will just take a minute."

Not knowing what else to do, Penelope sat down on the empty chair. The opener clipping through the tin lid was the only sound in the room.

It was a strange kind of cold. Heat radiated from the creaking pipes above Penelope's head, but around her ankles, she felt a chilling draft. She watched the feet running past the windows and thought that it might have been colder inside the building than it was outside. She pulled her scarf closer to her neck and wished she had traded it for a fur collar. She had left the apartment in such a rush, she hadn't thought of it.

When she had told Patsy about the appointment with M. F. Mackey, the woman's eyes had grown wide and she had insisted on attempting to sober Penelope up. When she asked why on earth she should be sober for an appointment regarding teaching children how to sing, Patsy was shocked into laughter. "If that's what you want to call it, that's fine with me."

Now, sitting in the wooden chair, Penelope wondered what Patsy had meant. There were certainly no children to be seen and no music anywhere. The man handed her a piece of peach at the end of a penknife. Removing her glove, she took it from the end. He seemed friendly enough. She risked it. "Do you know Monsieur Mackey?" she asked.

"You mean him?" He hooked a thumb at the door. "I sure do."

"Who is he?"

"Well, you're here at his office. Don't you know who he is?" The man held out another piece of peach.

"No, my mother sent me. Thanks."

"You look a little old and a little alone to be hanging on to the apron strings, aren't you?"

He was laughing at her, but Penelope didn't mind. The canned peach was delicious, sweet and crisp. She pushed the peach to the inside of her cheek and covered her mouth as she spoke. "It's not like that. My mother is always finding work for me to do. I don't mind." Penelope thought of a career as a musical babysitter and corrected herself. "Sometimes I don't mind. We understand each other. For the most part."

The man followed along with her, nodding as she spoke.

"You think you're here for a job interview?" he asked, somewhat perplexed. "What kind of job?"

"Teaching children to sing, of course. Mother said that I was here to speak to someone about teaching. I . . ." Teaching, from the opera. Her mother had said she was to speak to someone from the opera about teaching. Penelope caught her breath. She stood up and looked down the hall at the name. She sat down and looked at the card in her hand. She looked at the man. "Is Monsieur Mackey with the opera?"

"Monsieur? You mean Mackey? Yes, in a way. I—"

"Oh no." She stood up. "Which one? No, don't tell me!" Penelope paced to the windows, looking up at them like one might be an escape hatch. "Oh no." She walked back and sat down again. She turned to the man, who was holding out another piece of peach. Penelope took it and put it in her mouth, thinking it might be a good remedy for alcoholism. "Let me guess. Monsieur Mackey instructs operatic singers."

"Something like that." The man kept his chair and his smile.

"Have you seen any—" She broke off, unsure of how to put it to the man. "Is there anyone in there with a camera? You know, a newspaper type?"

He gave her a strange look. "Why would there be?"

Penelope stood up, thought better of it, and sat down. Turning back to the man, she blurted out, "She's sent me on an audition and I didn't even know. Oh no." She looked at her watch. "Oh no."

"Stop saying that. Mackey isn't the devil."

"You don't understand! I've been drinking. On an empty

stomach." Penelope began searching her pockets for a mint she knew wasn't there.

"This early in the day?" She felt the man was looking at her in a little less friendly way.

"It was an accident! I don't drink. I was making a friend, and we got to talking . . ."

"Drinking with a stranger, on an empty stomach?" The man smiled and offered her another peach. Penelope took it and popped it into her mouth.

"See here," she said as she chewed, "I'm going to try that door down there. If it's open, I'm going to go in and find a piano."

"Are you sure he has a piano?"

"He's sure to have a piano!" Penelope's sobriety was gaining on her. "I'm going to find a piano, and I am going to warm up my voice. I have to, you see. I must."

"If it's that serious, I can loan you my key." The man stood up leisurely. She stood up with him. "Here, hold this." He handed her the can of peaches.

Taking the penknife and the can, Penelope speared another peach and ate it. "Do you really have the keys?" He held a key up in his hand and bowed. "Oh, bless you! What's your name?"

"Fred."

"Bless you, Fred! Come on now. We don't have long." Penelope put her clutch under her arm and confronted the door in what she hoped was not a drunken stagger.

"Well, he's already late. Maybe he's not coming."

The man was teasing her, but somehow she didn't care. "Or he could be here anytime."

Fred nodded and put the key in the lock, true enough. "Look, it was open after all."

"Don't tell me he's in there dead! Just don't tell me that!"

Fred looked askance at her. "Why would you say that?"

"You just don't know the month I've had. That's all."

She walked past him into the room. The first thing she noticed was the warmth. "Here." She handed the peaches and the knife back to Fred. "I need to make tea. Where is the tea?" Penelope took off her hat and coat and threw them across a chair.

Fred stood in the middle of the room and looked around. "Check on the bookcase over there. That's a usual suspect." He put the can of peaches on a small table and returned the penknife to his jacket. Taking off his jacket revealed a thick sweater underneath. He sat down at a baby grand piano in the corner of the large room and began to warm up his hands on the keys.

Penelope stood from her position next to the small camp stove when she heard the music. "You should have told me you played for Monsieur Mackey!"

"All the time," he replied happily. "Look, I'll help you warm up. Then when he comes, you'll be all set."

Penelope looked at him from across the room. "Well," she said cautiously, "I suppose so . . ."

"Don't get cold feet now, sister." He stopped playing. "We're both on the hook for breaking and entering."

Penelope was opening her mouth with a quick retort when the tea kettle blew its whistle.

"Bring me a cup too," he shouted across the room. She returned with the two cups, pausing briefly to shut the door with her foot. "Why'd you do that?"

"It was getting cold." She warmed her hands on the cup and stared at him from the other side of the baby grand. "Why is this room so big?

"Rehearsal space in the Metropolitan is a little tight, so we use this place." Fred gestured to the room with a full sweep. You'd be surprised how many people fit in here. All right," he played a fanfare, "shall we begin?"

Penelope took a deep dreath, exhaling just as deeply. Fred began the usual exercises. Penelope met them easily, feeling her throat warm to the music. She wasn't sure why, but the room was suited for sound. She could hear herself singing more clearly than she had since China.

Fred stopped abruptly and looked at his watch. "You think he's still coming?"

"He is late, isn't he?" Time had passed too quickly. Penelope felt a keen disappointment.

"You sound let down."

"I don't get to practice very often. Now that I am warmed up, it seems like a waste."

Fred understood immediately. "Of course. What would you like to practice?"

"What music do you have?" Penelope looked around the large room, looking for the sheet music.

Fred shrugged. "I don't need music. Never have. I see it once, play through it twice, and it's all up here." He tapped his forehead.

"But I . . ."

"Look, these arias you sopranos sing. You rely too much on the music. You don't feel it. Start singing. You'll remember." Fred nodded to himself. If Penelope was surprised to hear him begin to play her favorite Rossini, she wouldn't show it. She planted her feet and thought of the lyrics, singing Rosina's words from the heart. Just as she was about to shut her eyes and give her full breath to the floral notes, Fred cleared his throat.

"Don't show off, girlie. You don't have to do that here." He kept playing.

She laughed through the notes and felt herself give way to Rosina's good humor. When Fred had played the final fanfare, he stood and took a bow. Feeling herself blush like a girl, she curtsied deeply. "Thank you, Maestro."

Fred stood up and leaned on the piano with one hand. "You have something there. Who did you say your instructor was? This woman who taught you the pretzel stuff?"

"Maria Eileen Calhoun."

"Well, that figures."

"Did you know her?"

"I don't know her, which explains why you have so many bad habits."

"Bad habits?" Penelope felt a flush begin at the base of her neck.

"You may understand what you're saying, but your diction is rough. You're singing too high for your range, and your breath—"

"My breath is perfectly fine!"

"My dear," he put a hand on her shoulder, "your breath is stupendous, but you don't use it to its full potential. Your phrasing should be much more controlled. See here—" Fred stopped and looked behind her.

"What?" Penelope said absently. "Is Mackey coming? Is he here? I'm not ready."

Fred gave her a sharp glance. "Wait here." He started toward the door, making it about halfway before it opened. The figure in the doorframe managed to catch just the right light, even in the limited resources of the basement. Whoever she was, she knew how to make a good entrance.

"Get out some glasses, darling." There was something in her profile. The high bone of her cheek. Something familiar about her. Penelope couldn't place it. She came through the door with a flourish, her fur coat draped over her shoulders, a bottle of champagne in each hand. She crossed the distance to Fred in three steps, throwing her arms around his neck. "Michael, darling, I've missed you so much! Your switchboard is a disaster—I've been calling for days! Haven't you gotten my messages?"

Penelope drew closer. Michael? She wanted to be closer, get a better look at the woman's eyes. She knew she had seen her before, somewhere . . . it couldn't be . . .

The woman tilted her head up and tried to reach the pianist's mouth with her own even as he was reaching up to remove her arms from his neck. "Get out some glasses, darling. I have news! I would have called you earlier, but I couldn't get free from the police. They're such a dreadful nuisance. I can't wait to get away from all of this."

Penelope didn't need to see any more. It couldn't have been anyone but the third Warwick daughter.

36

THE SWEET HAPPINESS OF THE Rossini dissolved in the wake of Penelope's anger. She looked around the room, found where she had thrown her jacket and clutch.

"Clover, this is not the time. I'm with a student." Fred put his hands on her forearms and removed her, pushing her back a couple of steps.

Too right, it wasn't the right time, Penelope fumed. With Clover's father and sister in the city morgue, here she comes with champagne? Penelope's hands closed into fists as she fought her temper back. It wasn't the time, she told herself, not with Monsieur Mackey scheduled to appear at any moment. It would be just her luck if he appeared right as she gave Clover the thrashing of her life.

With a champagne bottle still in each hand, Clover lost some of her practiced poise. She wrinkled her nose and said with a playful pout that struck Penelope as out of character, "That can't possibly be true, Michael dear. You aren't taking any more students. Remember?"

"Well, that was true for then. Now it's not."

"You don't take students," she said again. "You said if you did take students, you would take me on. That's what you—"

"Clover, please. This is not the time or place."

"Is she here? Is she still here? I want to see her. I want to know who this student—" Clover broke off as Penelope allowed her hand to drop from the piano and turned. The two women faced each other across the width of the room.

"It would have to be you," Clover said after a moment of surprised silence. "Of course it would."

"Clover!" Fred's voice was sharp. "She doesn't even know who I am! Her mother tricked her into coming down here. Listen—" Fred stepped in front of Clover. "It's been over for weeks now. You know it as well as I do. We had our fun, but neither of us wanted to make anything more of it. Admit it, Clover. You don't even want to sing, not really. You want to be in the movies. Hollywood has what you want, not me." He met her eyes and stepped back suddenly as though he had touched a hot stove.

Clover took one step to the side and began a leisurely walk toward Penelope. Her voice was sickly sweet with steel at the heart of it. "Is that black for my sister Tulip? I assure you it's unnecessary. She killed my father, or didn't you know? I don't mourn murderers."

Penelope stood her ground. "Nothing could melt your mercenary heart. Not even the death of your own sister. What's the champagne for? Is it because you get to sing her solo?"

Clover turned to look at Fred and said, "Watch your fingers, Michael. Did you know that Miss Penelope Harris was once a Mrs. Kinkaid Ambrose? That didn't end well. Did it, my dear? Didn't your first husband end up dead?"

Penelope lifted an eyebrow. "Choose a better mark, Clover. You can't push me that easily. You're not half as good as the last liar who threatened me."

"Wasn't that Renee Strong? Didn't she end up dead too?" Clover smiled and looked over her shoulder at Fred. When she returned her eyes to Penelope, the smile faded. "Everyone knows you want to break into the opera. Too bad you're a hack."

"Clover, that's enough." Fred took a step forward.

"It's bad enough that you tried to steal my sister's part so you could be the doll in *Hoffmann*. Now you try to take my lover." Clover put a hand on her hip. "Well, I won't let you, Mrs. Ambrose. Michael and I have something special. Nothing you can do will take that away."

"That's enough." Fred, although Penelope was genuinely beginning to wonder what his real name was, grabbed Clover by the arm. "I invited Miss Harris here. She's my guest."

Penelope had heard enough. "I'll be happy to leave. I never stoop to take up someone else's seconds. No matter who they are. But if I did, I wouldn't worry about what someone like you could do about it." She leaned forward and whispered, "I hope you've kept your nerve. You'll need it all when word gets around you weren't at the hospital when your sister died. That she died surrounded by strangers. Poisoned. While you were," Penelope cast her eye down to the bottles of champagne, "living it up on the high life?"

"I'll kill you," Clover breathed. "I'll kill you for this!" Dropping one bottle, Clover swung the other at Penelope and missed. Fred caught her by the waist and pulled her away.

"And you!" Penelope turned on Fred. "You must think this was a pretty good joke. Monsieur Mackey, I presume?"

"Michael Mackey, Michael Frederick Mackey, as it happens."

"Oh, I suppose that makes it so you didn't lie to me? Was it for a story you'd like to spread around? How you cornered Mrs. Ambrose in your studio and tricked her into singing?"

Penelope had not realized how angry she was until she called herself Mrs. Ambrose. A slip of the tongue to stop her from calling herself the Jade Tiger. "I shouldn't have come. I won't be back."

Fred pushed Clover away from him and moved toward Penelope. "I want you as a student. You must say yes. A voice like that should be on the stage. You must say yes. You must."

"Why? So you can convince me to become your lover, like Clover? I'm no fool." Penelope angled her head. "Or perhaps you think I have money. It seems everyone thinks I do. It would be for the opera, of course. Wouldn't it? Or the publicity? Need a little bit of that? Seems headlines are like cocktails for some people; they just can't get enough of them."

"I think you may have misunderstood, Clover and I—"

"I understand very well, Mr. Mackey. Really, I do. Good day." Penelope scooped up her coat and hat and left the room, her hands still clenched into fists.

Clover shouted after her, "I'll see to it you're ruined, Penelope Harris. You'll never take the stage in New York after I'm done with you! Never!"

As Penelope walked away, the words broke through to her. Clover couldn't take the dream away from her when it was already gone. She would never take the stage. The fragments of her hope fell around her like broken glass.

37

"WHAT YOU NEED IS A strong cup of tea." Mary bustled around the Harrises' living room while Penelope lay on the couch, a cold compress over her eyes.

"I was drunk in front of Fred Mackey!" Penelope said from behind the cold compress. "Mary, what do I do?"

"I'd say he's probably used to idiosyncrasy—his parents being who they are—but that didn't make you feel better the first three times I said it." Mary cleared a spot on the coffee table for the tea tray. "Penelope, pull yourself together!" Mary swatted at Penelope's feet so she could sit on the couch. She poured tea as she spoke. "Did you sing? What did he say?"

"I can barely think of it! Don't ask!" Penelope held the compress tighter to her face.

"All right then," Mary said primly. "You can pour out your own tea if you feel that way." She picked up a cup and took a sip.

"I'm sorry, Mary. I'm a baby, aren't I?" Penelope sat up, immediately clutching at the armrest for support.

"You are, but we all have a right to be a baby once in a while. After all, he is the Metropolitan's newest and youngest director."

"This one should do me up until Easter at least."

"Maybe even next Christmas." Mary opened her eyes wide and tried her best to look innocent. "What was God's gift to opera doing there, if I might ask? And I mean Clover, not Mackey." She gave Penelope a devilish wink. "Give me all the dirt, and I might let you have a small fit before Valentine's."

"Oh!" Penelope stood up suddenly, stamped her foot, went white, then said in a much smaller voice, "Oh . . ." and sat back down.

"Here, have some tea. It will help." Mary handed Penelope a cup and saucer.

"Mary, I swear to you that if I ever see Clover in a dark alley and I am armed with a gun, I might just shoot her right in her Chanel pumps!"

"I hope you're joking," Mary took a cookie from the tray, "because you would be the number-one suspect if that were to actually happen. No one has the guts to stand up to Clover, except for maybe you. What did you tell her?" She took a dainty bite out of the cookie.

Penelope took a sip of her tea. "She knows about Kinkaid."

"No! Surely not!" Mary took another bite of the cookie. "This is delightful. My bridge club will be so pleased."

"At least that we were married. Maybe not the rest, but that was enough to get me going. I believe I called her mercenary. And I think I accused her of murder . . . It gets a little fuzzy after that. Patsy's whiskey was really too good. It had a kind of slow-acting effect, if you know what I mean."

"Murder? Penelope! What were you thinking?"

"She made me so angry! Telling those lies about Tulip and Ivy. Do you know she told Patsy that she was there when Tulip died and that it was suicide?"

"You mean it wasn't?"

"Of course it wasn't, Mary. No one kills themselves with arsenic!"

"Well, why not?" Mary asked practically. "It's everywhere, and everyone knows it will kill rats."

"It's a horrific death!"

"Does everyone know that?" Mary took a sip of tea. "I mean to say, everyone would have to know that in order to not kill themselves with it. It's not as though they actually see it kill the rats they put it out for, do they?"

"What a fool I am. I thought that I would be able to start over, leave Kinkaid behind me." Penelope sighed and put her head in her hands.

"Well, you have. What's so wrong about them knowing you were married? Or that he's dead, for that matter? Or that he was a very bad man? You aren't any of those things." Mary counted her fingers. "You are unmarried, alive, and most definitely not a bad man."

"What do you mean?" Penelope focused a blurry eye on her cousin.

"New York isn't a small town, Penelope. Not everyone knows everyone else in this city. They have to have something to go on in order to know who to invite to what and how to make out the invitations. It was quite a fuss trying to sort out whether to call you Mrs. Ambrose or Miss Harris." She took another bite. Pushing it to her cheek, she added quickly, "Of course, going back to your maiden name was a good idea. Made it much easier for everyone."

"Do they even know he's dead?"

"High society? They don't care whether he is or isn't, my dear. The story is what counts, and you are giving them such a good one right now that no one wants to break the spell and ask." Mary leaned forward and said confidentially, "You're better than a movie serial. Don't doubt it for a second. And every second you get that kind of spotlight just kills Clover Warwick dead. Bullets and fisticuffs are unnecessary, take it from me. Success is going to be your best revenge in that quarter."

Penelope sat up and stared into her tea thoughtfully. "You're such a good friend." She added suddenly, "What did I do to deserve a cousin like you?"

"We're related," Mary pointed out practically. "It's a special treat that we like each other."

Penelope laughed and took a tea cake.

Brushing her hands, Mary picked up her teacup and leaned back, smoothly crossing one leg over the other. "What did Patsy have to say for herself?"

"That the recital is probably off. There was something about Clover insisting the performance continue. But why?"

"Why indeed?" Mary massaged the words, which was as good an indication as any that she had already looked into the matter. "Mimi Wasserman was spreading it around Violet called every board member insisting it go forward." Mary put down her empty teacup. "Can I be frank, Penelope?"

"Of course."

"From Violet's perspective, the cancelation is a disaster. Tulip was the most respectable of her daughters. Now that she's dead, the board will never let the other two sing. And from Clover's perspective, if you consider that her father was broke and her mother is a spendthrift, this may be Clover's last chance to get noticed. I don't doubt that she's been haunting Mackey and maybe even taking advantage of him a little bit to try to advance herself. Clover must be desperate to get out of New York."

"Where does she want to go? Why can't she just go there?"

"Clover wouldn't go to the land of make believe unless she had a sure thing lined up." Mary nodded her head as reinforcement.

"What are you talking about?"

"The one and only, my dear—Hollywood. Clover has already faced up to it. She isn't an opera singer, and she knows it. Until you showed up at that nightmare of a party and sang the Habanera, high society was willing to play along with her. She sang everywhere, trying to get the attention of a Broadway producer. It took everything she had, and you ripped it away in three and a half minutes. Now all she can hope is the magic lasts long enough to have a producer or two come out from California to look her over. God help her if you stand on a couch and sing opera at that party too. I've heard more than a few rumors that she's set her cap at a particular man who's only here to recruit girls with fair voices and long legs. The recital was her last roll of the dice. Now that it's gone, she must be desperate."

"You can't be serious. Why on earth would she want to be a movie star?"

"Clover may have been her father's favorite, but that didn't make her impractical. Between her mother's expensive taste and her father's terrible business sense, she knows there isn't enough money left for much of a life. She has to find work. And you and I both know a woman like Clover will never work the perfume counter at Bloomingdale's. Even Reggie can't give her the life she wants. He's broke. Gets all his money from Patsy." Mary squeezed Penelope's hand. "Society life is very dull, Penelope. Half of us have nothing to do, and the other half are only pretending to do something important. We pretend to be something we aren't, and we work like dogs to make sure no one ever finds out. It's an acute case of poisonous self-awareness. Don't be fooled. We all suffer from it: you, me, Patsy, and especially Clover. Clover knows she's a fraud, and she's hell bent on getting out before society makes her out to be the latest joke. I bet she went to Mackey's because she knew the recital was sunk. He was her last shot at keeping it going. What does she find? You standing at the piano singing like a bird and making Fred Mackey fall a little bit in love." Mary nodded wisely. "You've sunk her, Penelope. There's no need to meet her in a dark alley. Not now, not ever. You've already shot her dead. It's over."

Penelope thought of all her failed auditions and all the insubstantial dreams that slowly slipped through her fingers. "I feel a little sorry for her now." She stared past Mary into the middle distance.

"Don't feel sorry for her," Mary chirped. "Or do, actually, because for Clover that just makes it worse. Penelope, everything you have she has to work hard for, and something tells me she will always have to work hard for it."

"I should talk to her. Maybe I can do something. Help her."

Mary sighed. "Don't fight yourself. Just be who you are. Not all of us can be ourselves, you know. If you can be yourself, maybe the rest of us have hope."

"That's the second time you've said that to me." Penelope looked at her cousin. "Why are you so sad?"

"I'm not sad. I'm realistic. With Papa staring financial ruin in the face and my dear brother unemployable, I've had to think about what I'm really good for. It's isn't much. Then Gil told me—"

"Gil!" Penelope struck her forehead with her hand and immediately regretted it. "I completely forgot! Was he as good as he promised to be for Carrera? Or did you have an usher throw him out?"

It was difficult to tell with so many spots in front of her eyes, but Penelope was sure she saw Mary blush. "He was a gentleman, to be honest. Except—" Mary covered her mouth with her hand.

"Except for what? Mary Staughton, are you laughing?"

"Well, Deirdre Cummings saw me in the mezzanine and came all the way from her box to say something nasty about Charles."

"What did she say?"

"That she had heard Charles had gone to Vermont to dry out, when she knows very well he went there to ski."

"And to dry out . . ."

"Well, yes, but she didn't have to say it out loud. She's . . . she's . . ." Mary's face turned pink with effort. "She's a dog! That's what she is!"

Penelope was certain that was not the word Mary meant. "Don't keep me in suspense. What did Gil do?"

"I don't know how he did it, I really don't. But as she was walking away, he made it sound like she . . . like she . . ." Mary looked around, at a loss for words. "Like she passed air!" she said finally.

"No!" Penelope sat up.

"Yes!" Mary replied, sitting up a little straighter. "And right in front of Montgomery Brooks. I've told you about him.

He's the one who throws all the parties and keeps a little book of everyone he invites and doesn't invite. Well, he gave her such a look! And then he took out his little book and wrote her name down and drew a line through it right there while she was watching!"

"She just stood there?"

"She was like a hypnotized buffalo, Penelope. She couldn't look away!"

"Who knew Gilbert Richie would redeem himself for two broken piano strings by making it look like Deirdre Cummings had passed air?" Penelope giggled.

"Well, certainly not me," Mary replied primly. "And the next day, he sent a note. Thanking me."

"Gil Richie sent a thank-you note? What did it say?"

"That he had a lovely evening passing the time with me." A furrow appeared above Mary's eyebrows. "The note was oddly reserved. After all, the man is known for being rude."

"And your piano strings! Mary, don't forget about your strings!"

"About that." Mary's blush deepened. "Gil came by yesterday afternoon."

"After his note?"

"And he fixed them."

"Gilbert Richie can string a piano?"

"I was surprised too. He said that it was typical of the wealthy to not know how to do anything for themselves. That's what got me thinking. Penelope, I want a job."

"Gil convinced you of this?"

"No, this is just me. He didn't talk much."

Penelope's eyebrows went up.

"He just played the piano."

"And what did you do during all this piano playing?"

"I wrote a letter to Charles, and read. He's coming back tomorrow."

"Charles?"

"No," Mary looked puzzled, "Gil. He says he doesn't have anyplace quiet to practice."

"Mary—"

"Why would you think I meant Charles?"

"This sounds a bit like you're being wooed."

"Charles isn't coming back until Christmas." Mary looked up sharply. "What was that about being wooed?"

The doorbell rang. Penelope swore and stood up. "Give me a minute. It's probably just a delivery that came to the wrong door." She walked to the door in her stocking feet and opened it wide.

"My dear!" Helen Mayfield entered in a flurry of fresh scent and fox furs. "You must tell me what Lund is on about! Don't keep me in suspense! Is he here yet?" She looked around with vivid excitement.

"No—should he be? But come in. Mary and I are having tea." Penelope showed Helen through to the living room, where Mary stood up. Penelope couldn't help noticing Mary's blush.

"Mary!" Helen reached for her and gave her a kiss on the cheek. "Thank you for taking Gil off my hands. It was a good thing I made it to my editors when I did. I was able to scoop everyone, and when word came through the old man was dead, he kept me on with the city desk to make sure they had all the names and times right. I owe you."

"No," Penelope thought Mary might have said the word just a little too quickly, "you don't owe me anything."

"All the same, I'm going to take you for a drink in my favorite speak one of these days. Anyway, I have to talk fast. I have an appointment at a debutante ball in an hour and a half. How about I just tell you and Mary what Lund wanted to know, and you can tell him."

Penelope couldn't resist the quiver of curiosity Helen brought with her wherever she went. "Do tell, Helen darling!"

"Yes," Mary held out a cup of tea, "do tell!"

Helen laughed. "You got it, doll! Show me where you dames keep the good liquor."

38

"WELL, MY DEARS, IT GOES like this." Helen spread out the photos on the coffee table. "The summer home of the Milton-Fraziers, June 1927. Easily the wildest party of the season. I had managed to get an invitation from a maid. Technically I was crashing. But so many people were there, who could tell?" She stood up to turn on the light.

"Are those the Astors?" Mary asked.

"Right you are. Everyone was there. For a while, it was just your regular garden party with the usual frocks from Paris, handmade shoes, and large avant-garde sun hats. But as soon as the sun went down," Helen bit her lip, "things got a little wild. Gave me enough material for my column until October. What a party!"

Penelope took off her shoes and slid down to the floor. She picked up the pictures, looking at each one carefully. Mary was soon beside her, the two of them trading photos back and forth, remarking on the goings-on. Helen leaned across the table and pointed to a photo of a fully dressed woman being pulled into the sea by a young man in swim trunks. Next to her, another woman dove into the water cleanly, her shoes and dress and stockings left on the beach. "My God," Mary said as she pointed. "That's Marjory Lindsey. She just got married last week—and not to anyone in that picture."

"If you think that's racy, you should have seen what happened after it got dark. There were fireworks and a band and dancing. The entire house was open that night, with all the lights on." Helen shrugged. "Didn't matter one jot. None of that light made it past the lawn. Oh, my dears, there were some shotgun weddings in September, let me tell you. I don't know what happened, but a lot of the photos are gone. I had to track down the photographer I took with me to see if he had any. He made these up for me. If he hadn't, I would have just had the one or two photos that ran in the paper. I guess newspaper publishers have bills to pay too." She sighed.

"Look here, Penelope. This looks like Ivy." Mary passed the photo across the table. "I don't know who she's with. Helen, do you know? I don't recognize her."

"That's funny. That's what Lund asked me to find out." Helen turned the photo around, handing it back with a flourish. "Ladies, this is Coralee O'Connor. She was a quiet type, but as I said, everyone was there, even the wallflowers."

Penelope stared at the photograph of the woman standing next to Ivy. She was older than Penelope had expected. There was a strain in the lines of her mouth, a tightness in her eyes. "Has Thom seen these yet?"

"Not yet. I told you, I had to track them down." Helen picked up a photograph. "I didn't realize Coralee was at the party until after Lund had hung up. I don't suppose anyone else remembered either. He asked me to look up her husband, Daniel O'Connor, to see if he was still alive."

"And is he?"

Helen sat up straight. "Ladies, that's the story! There is no Daniel O'Connor! I called the War Department, made them look everywhere. No soldier named Daniel O'Connor who died in the war—at least not in the place and regiment Coralee told everyone. She must have been laughing up her sleeve every Armistice Day. She would sing every year without fail. I can't wait to hear what Lund's dug up. Whatever it is, it can't be better than that, can it?"

"Coralee could sing?" Penelope's interest was piqued.

Mary picked up the photo. "Coralee was one of the founders of the Hudson Valley Operatic Society, Penelope. Along with Patsy. Didn't I tell you?"

Penelope stared at the photo, Ivy's sullen countenance slowly blending into the background as she stared at Coralee. Leaning toward Ivy so the brim of her large sun hat almost touched Ivy's shoulder, Coralee faced the camera, almost pulling off the façade of the perfect guest. Real or imagined, Penelope thought she saw dark smudges under Coralee's eyes, and her smile didn't quite reach her eyes. She was tired, worn—a different kind of discomfort. Patsy wore her unhappiness like a ship sailing into a tsunami with all flags flying, valiant and futile. Penelope wondered if Coralee had lacked that measure of strength or if she was looking for something that wasn't there at all. Opera must have been the source of much happiness for two such uncomfortable people.

"Here's another one," Mary said with concentration. Penelope moved to look over Mary's shoulder. This photo was taken at midday with four women sitting in lounge chairs smiling into the camera. Three women wore hats. Two had their hands near their brims in an affectation of surprise. Coralee made up the third. She practically hid under her hat as she leaned on the arm of the chair with her hand at her mouth. Penelope couldn't see her eyes clearly, only her hands and her mouth.

"She looks like she's going to be sick," Penelope said absently. "Look at her."

"She does," Mary agreed. "Isn't that Clover?" She pointed to the fourth woman in the photograph.

Clover wore no hat. It would have hidden her beautiful hair. Of the four women, she was the most glamorous and the most at ease with the camera. Her bold sunglasses and lipstick set her apart from the others, even in the black-and-white of the photo. "She doesn't need a hat."

Mary cocked her head to one side. "Not sure I've ever seen her in one, to be honest. She's always showing off her lovely hair."

Penelope looked up from the photograph like a person coming up for air. "Is Patsy in any of these?"

"Patsy doesn't go to parties," Helen said as she flipped through the photographic evidence of excess. "She hasn't for as long as I've known her, at any rate. She wasn't at this one, I can tell you that. Coralee was on her own." Helen put down the photograph and looked at them both directly. "You know, she was pretty broken up after Coralee died. Came to the paper and wanted to speak with Mrs. Anthony Stone directly. Of course, I couldn't tell her she already was."

"You're Mrs. Anthony Stone?" Mary's jaw dropped.

"In the flesh, dah-ling!" Helen gave them both a wink. "Hopefully not for much longer." She picked up the photo of Coralee and Ivy.

"Sorry I didn't tell you, Mary." Penelope explained, "I went to the paper after your party to ask Mrs. Stone what she had on Charles's fiancée. Turns out she was an actress. This is the real Mrs. Anthony Stone. She swore me to secrecy."

"Ta-da!" Helen framed her face with her hands and widened her eyes like a Kewpie doll.

"Helen, what did Patsy want?" Penelope pressed.

"The scoop, my dears. She wanted it all. She asked for the photographs, but the editor wouldn't hand them over. Then she asked for the notes from the party—who was there, when they were there. When she didn't get what she wanted, she kicked up quite a fuss."

"I wonder what she was after." Mary looked at the table of photographs. "This wasn't her type of party at all."

Helen sighed. "It's a kick to remember a fun party, but most of the time it's girdles and shrimp salad. Time for a retirement party for Old Mrs. Stone."

"Not really?" Penelope looked up from the photographs.

"My heart isn't in it. I have the feeling if I stay with this kind of work, I won't have any scruples left to gamble with."

Helen sighed and picked up another photo. "Maybe I'm just getting older, or maybe it's because Gil works so hard. But, I look back on these, and I wonder why I thought it was fun." She laughed ruefully. "Listen to me, being a sad sack. Do you know someone stole the Milton-Fraziers' Daimler?"

"No," Mary cried out, "I never heard that one! Roddy loves that car."

"Yes, he does. It was missing so long he offered a reward." A crease appeared in Helen's forehead. "It seems unnatural to love a car that much. He went around quizzing everyone after they found it was missing. Someone must have taken it on a joyride. Whoever they were, they got sick all over the back seat. He was quite upset."

"Why steal a car when you have more money than you know what to do with?" Penelope leaned up against the couch.

"Tell me about it! Someone stole a motorboat too, same night. They found it tied up in a cove one town over. God knows why I can't remember any stars. There must have been some though. Everyone was out on the water. There must have been something in the air. That was the night Coralee took her sailboat out and scuttled it."

"I remember that." Mary put a hand on Penelope's arm. "Coralee killed herself, left a note and everything."

Penelope felt the same jolt she felt when an operatic chorus and the orchestra played in unison: a hundred people, dozens of musical strands and instruments meeting together on the same note. She proceeded, careful not to disturb the growing musical thought. "Helen," she asked, "who were the other founders? For the operatic society, I mean. Did they carry on after Coralee died?"

"It was just the two of them to start with." Mary tilted her head. "Coralee was just twenty when she and Patsy founded the society. To begin with, it was just a way to perform. Coralee had a good voice, always took care of it. They would find little recital halls and pianists and put something on. It just came about naturally."

"It was a way to fit in," Penelope said to herself.

"I wonder what makes you say that," Helen said, curious. "Coralee was quiet, but you're right. She fit in. Patsy was the awkward one. They made quite the pair at the meetings. Patsy was good at getting things done, and Coralee was good at keeping everyone agreeable. Why do you ask? What's on your mind?"

Penelope shook her head. "It's probably nothing. Only, I saw Patsy earlier today, and she didn't mention it. I wonder why."

"That's odd." Marry furrowed her brow.

"It sure is," Helen added. "Patsy was broken up when Coralee went missing. She practically tore up the city looking for her. Even accused the family of doing something awful."

"It was very uncomfortable." Mary nodded in agreement. "But the worst was when she canceled the winter recital."

"Yes, she said it was too much to go on after a founder had died. Not everyone agreed. Being a founder, the bylaws made it possible for her to cancel the recital. There was an uproar."

"And now she doesn't have the control to stop the recital?"

"That board is made up of every type of prima donna you can imagine. Nobody liked having Patsy curtail their private moment of glory. They changed the bylaws while she was in Europe. Quite a catty little coup, if you ask me." Helen leaned on her hand. "Let's face it, girls, if they go without a recital two years in a row, that's the end of them. No more Hudson Valley Operatic Society."

Penelope picked up the photo of Ivy and handed it to Helen. "What was she doing there? Did she know Coralee?"

"Sure she did. Coralee led vocal lessons for some of the younger girls. She took all of them under her wing, so to speak. I bet that's how she knew Ivy." Helen shuddered and laid the photo on the table facedown. "That girl gives me the creeps." Glancing at her watch, Helen gasped and rose from the floor. "Well, ladies, I have a debutante birthday at the Ritz. There's just enough time to get dressed and sneak in the back entrance."

"Wait a moment, Helen," Mary said. "Penelope and I have a disagreement you can settle. Society suicides—what's the going method?"

"Why, my dear, you interest me! What a coldhearted question!" Helen put a finger to her chin and thought. "Barbiturates," she said with confidence. "Sleeping tablets. Anything else would be too messy."

"Not arsenic?"

"Arsenic? Can you imagine someone from high society killing themselves with rat poison? Think of how that would read in the paper! And what if they lived? They'd never live it down. Their friends would be calling them 'Ratty' all the way to the bitter end!"

Penelope walked Helen to the door. When she came back into the living room, she found Mary leaning over the table with the photo of Ivy in her hand. "I'm trying to remember when I met Ivy before. I knew of her, of course. I've heard all about her. But I can't place when I met her." Mary paused for a moment. "You know, Penelope, I don't think I ever have. Not until Friday. Isn't that odd? It's as though she suddenly appeared out of nowhere."

"YOU GIRLS ARE GOING TO ruin your stockings if you sit around the house with your shoes off." Eleanor shook off her coat and put it away in the hall closet. "Has Thom come by yet?" she called out as she fixed her hair in the mirror.

"Was he planning on coming by?" Penelope was slipping on her shoes as her mother walked briskly into the room, turning on lights.

"What's all this?" Eleanor gestured to the coffee table full of photographs. Picking up the photo of skinny-dippers, she sniffed. "Scandalous." She found the poker and the wood and began to make a fire. "Cold as blazes out there. Feels like snow."

"I must go home." Mary roused herself from the couch.

"Sit down, Mary. Mother, did you hear me ask if Thom was coming by?"

"Don't be peevish, Penelope. Yes, I heard you. I left a message with his landlady to drop by if he could. The front desk had a package for him, anyway. A Dale Wilcox came by this afternoon. Said he had to deliver a photo by hand because he didn't trust the post. Apparently, he almost didn't trust the concierge either. He said Thom called him this morning and asked if he had a photo of a person named Patrice."

"Well, let's see it then," Mary said and waved a hand above the table. "We've already seen all of these. It can't be worse than seeing Major Sullivan skinny-dipping. The man must be forty if he's a day!"

"I don't know if that's such a good idea," Eleanor began as Penelope stood and walked to the hallway, returning with a small brown package tied with string.

"Mother, how bad could it be? After all that?" Penelope nodded to the table with her head as the paper came off in one hand and the framed photograph came cleanly into the light.

"Penelope, what is it?"

"It's . . ." Penelope looked down at the photo in her hand. Two people at perfect ease with one another, each looking at the other with the happiness that comes from years of comfort, years of love. "It's a photo of Coralee," she said, "with Patsy."

The orchestra came together with a crash that left her ears ringing. She looked down at the table where the photos were scrambled together. Ivy was with Coralee the day she died. Clover was at the same party. The opera. The Hudson Valley Operatic Society. The canceled recital. Handing the framed photo to her mother, Penelope ran to her bedroom, still as neat and trim as Mrs. Reynolds left it. The only change: Ivy's dress was gone, sent on to the Warwick address via the Excelsior concierge. Penelope threw open the doors to the wardrobe and reached for the velvet purse she had taken to the opera. She could tell before she tore it open. The weight was different.

The gun was gone.

39

As he turned the corner, McCain straightened the front of his uniform and put his left hand in his pocket. It was late. Blake had kept him at the precinct longer than he expected, filling out forms and chasing down leads. There were at least three hundred witnesses left to interview from the opera alone. Some of them were showing up to the precinct in their best clothes demanding an interview. All of them wanted to be seen, none of them had anything new to share. McCain was tired. Wealth and influence could wear on a man.

There was one last stop to make at New Amsterdam Bank. If he hurried, he'd have time to read the paper before the super's wife put dinner on the table. If luck was with him, the night watchman might have a moment for a cup of coffee and a chat. It was getting the feel for the place McCain was after, not an interrogation. Yes, a cup of coffee and a chat might give him just what he needed to know about the setup, so to speak. McCain was curious, and letting his curiosity get the better of him was a prospect he looked forward to almost as much as Mrs. Anthony Stone's society column.

McCain stopped in the street, allowing himself a good look at the New Amsterdam's stone façade. He stared for a long moment, then alighted on the thought: Plain for a bank, wasn't it? Where was all the marble? He climbed the steps to the door and gave the handle a perfunctory rattle while peering in through the window. He could see a marble floor (there it was), and a series of wooden cages where the tellers would stand counting money. Well back behind that were offices. All dark. The only light came from a door propped open, a staircase going up just behind it. McCain rattled the door again, then rapped on the glass inset.

He imagined the sound traveling across the lobby to the stairs, where natural acoustics would bring the knock to the night watchman's attention. Probably some seasoned ex-policeman putting his feet up near a radio and a cup of hot coffee, one ear listening to the shows, another listening for a rap at the door. It would take the watchman a good piece of time to hear the rapping and come and see. Four, five minutes, maybe. McCain had begun to pivot on his feet so he could keep his eye on the empty, dark street when there was a flutter in the light on the stair. That was quick. Generally speaking, McCain's instincts were already honed to the fine point of suspicious paranoia, but he had the habit of holding himself back from conclusions. It was a good habit, kept him sharp when other policemen had been forced to retire. But even he had to admit it was too quick. The watchman had been listening for something, waiting.

He came into view, and McCain could see right away he was right. Old but fit, the man had the look of former police service. It was unmistakable once you knew what to look for. He practically ran across the lobby, his keys in his hand. McCain took him in, from his bare head to his suspenders, and his thoughts turned to the worst. The man hadn't just been waiting for someone. He'd been badly shaken up. It was the only explanation for why he left his hat and jacket behind. McCain's curiosity stirred again when the watchman dropped his keys twice.

"I told you lot to use the side entrance!" he exclaimed when he had the door open. "I don't know what he'll do now!"

"Where is he?" McCain took his hands from his pockets, looking past the watchman to the stairs.

"Third floor," the man gasped. "He's got a gun."

"You call the precinct?" McCain started from the front door, his stride lengthening as he made for the back stairs.

"You mean they didn't send you?" The watchman's face was white in the moonlight. "No wonder you came right up to the front door!"

"Wait here." McCain made for the stairs.

TWENTY YEARS OF TAKING THE stairs to his fifth-story apartment two at a time every Monday, Wednesday, and Thursday paid off. McCain approached the challenge of three stories with hardly a broken breath, despite his age. On top of that, he had the advantage of being a small man, which helped him keep his feet light and noiseless.

He looked down the stairs at the watchman, who stared up the well of the curving stair. McCain nodded once. The watchman nodded back silently, inclining his chin toward the door to McCain's left. Then he was gone, probably to the side entrance. McCain took a breath and opened the heavy door, wincing only a little when the hinges creaked.

The dark room he came upon was filled with desks of varying sizes, each with ledgers and papers stacked neatly at the corners. On the other side of the room, a series of doors faced the desks. Only one stood open, yellow light spilling out onto the floor and nearest desk. McCain started around the periphery of the room, keeping well out of the light. He was about halfway when a figure stood in the doorway and looked straight at him. McCain was as still as he could be, hoping the difference in the light and the dark would blind the man. He wasn't that lucky.

"You'd better come in." A revolver dangled from the man's right hand. McCain looked at it cautiously, then stepped away from the wall.

"You got the watchman a little nervous." McCain's voice traveled across the desks with surprising clarity.

"Old Bill?" There was a moment of surprise. "He's got nothing to worry about. You'd better come in." The man turned back into the room, his face coming into the light, where McCain could see the grief drawing down on him. The skin around his eyes and mouth was slack and grey, his blue eyes muddy with exhaustion. He had been crying, that much was clear to McCain right away.

McCain picked up his feet and followed the man, his thoughts strangely clear. "Are you William Bird?" It was a strike in the dark, a risky one at that. But he took it anyway. He had the sense of the thing before the man nodded his head. "Thom told me I might find you here. Came to see you."

"Came to arrest me?" Bird smiled, a half-hearted grin that looked out of place on his haggard face. When the policeman didn't answer, Bird gestured to the tables behind him. "It's all there. You can tell Lund I didn't leave anything undocumented. It's all there." Bird met McCain's eye and looked away. "I thought he might be the one to come along and root me out." Disappointment tinged his words. Bird walked to the corner of the room, keeping the tables between himself and McCain. He repeated, "It's all there," and gestured to the books with the hand that held the gun.

McCain took a moment to look around the room. They were surrounded by shelf after shelf of books, ledgers of all kinds, filing cabinets, and baskets of paper. In the middle of the room, tables had been set in two long lines where a dozen clerks could sit and take all the necessary room to review a ledger the width of the table. Across the table nearest the stacks, six ledgers were open and laid out alongside each other, so close their covers touched. McCain's eye followed the handwriting at the top of the page. He couldn't follow the numbers, but the name was clear enough: "Warwick, Roger."

"It took me all day." Bird's words were ragged in the silence. "At least they'll know I wasn't a thief."

"Just a murderer?" McCain glanced at the young man from under his cap.

Bird faltered, his face screwing up into confusion. "Murder?" He hiccupped, at first affronted, then began to cry. "I never meant to hurt anyone. Murder takes that, doesn't it? Don't you have to mean to hurt someone?"

"Tell that to Roger Warwick."

"Warwicks!" Bird spat the word out. "I wish I'd never seen them! All I was after was a little fun, and look what it brought me. Bloodsuckers." He gestured to the ledgers with the gun. "I tried to tell Mr. Warwick what happened, told him where the money went. He wouldn't believe me. He told me to meet him at the opera, said he didn't have time to meet me anywhere else." Bird looked down at the ledgers. He sniffed. "It's all there."

"Did you meet him?"

"Yes." Bird stared down at the ledgers on the table between them, his mouth slack. "I got a ticket for standing room only from a girl I knew in the chorus. It cost me my last dollar. I thought I could talk him out of filing charges, but I don't have that kind of luck. I've been having a run of bad luck like you wouldn't believe. I should've known what would happen."

"What did happen?" McCain's ears picked up on a sound. It was too far away to tell for sure, but it could have been a foot on the stair.

"I met him where he said, near the boxes on the second floor." Bird sagged, his head hanging with such misery that McCain almost felt sorry for him. "Warwick asked me if it was his wife or Gilmurray who had robbed him. I told him the truth, but he didn't believe me."

"What happened?"

"It doesn't matter." Bird shrugged. "Either way, he's dead."

"You have to tell someone," McCain insisted, his eyes on the revolver. "Why did you do it?"

"But don't you see?" Bird laughed, a mordent, heavy laugh wet with desperation. McCain knew as soon as he heard it, Bird wouldn't come without a fight. "I didn't kill him. I told him who was stealing from him, and he took a swing at me. Shouted his bleeding head off. When I tried to run, he grabbed me by my coat. I did what anyone would have done. I didn't kill him. I just defended myself. He fell. I didn't kill him. I didn't."

McCain could feel a movement of air that could have come only from an open door on the floor. He kept his eyes trained on Bird, holding his attention. "If you weren't doing it, then who was? Who had bled Roger Warwick dry?"

"That's the joke." Bird swayed. "It was Clover. She—"

Some elephant in a police uniform ran into a desk in the room behind him. McCain swore under his breath and went straight for the hand that held the revolver. Table or no table, McCain had to keep the gun turned away. Bird was quick but hadn't counted on McCain's concentration on the gun. McCain latched onto it like a bulldog with a rope, all his questions holding his determination in place. He hadn't asked about Tulip yet, and he had to know. He had been there at the end with her, a young child like that with her life ahead of her. It was hard to let go. McCain found his feet and threw his shoulder into Bird's chest, bouncing the man into a metal shelf from leverage alone. Had Bird been Tulip's man at the library? Had Bird made promises he couldn't keep until he had to cut himself free? It made sense that Clover had caught wind of it, made him hand over access to her father's accounts. McCain kept his fingers so tight on the man's wrist and hand that he hardly felt the quick punch to his kidneys. McCain thought of Clover on one side and Tulip on the other, and Bird, weak willed and ready to break, caught between them. Bird hadn't gone to the opera to meet Roger Warwick. He had been there for Tulip. It wasn't the first time a young, impressionable woman was taken advantage of. Not many killed for it, though. Could it be the chocolates were intended for Tulip all along? McCain's feet found purchase on the floor, and he pushed his shoulder into Bird's chest again, lifting

Bird's feet from the ground and throwing him back into the ledgers. The shelving gave way, and Bird fell, McCain's fingers finally prying the gun loose.

There was a shout as the others came into the room, pushing the tables aside like matchsticks, piling up on McCain and Bird so they were held up and pushed back. Warm hands reached around McCain, grabbing every part of Bird their blind fingers could find, pulling the man up like he were a rag doll, only to punch him back down to the ground.

"Wait a minute, boys!" McCain found his feet, pulled a patrolman off Bird by his collar. "Hold it a minute!" He found Bird at the bottom of the pile, his hands loose and defenseless, blood from a broken nose covering his mouth and chin. Pulling Bird up by the lapels, McCain shook him. "I want to know why!" He shook Bird until his eyes opened. "Why'd you kill Tulip?"

Bird's unfocused eyes found McCain, the shouting around them subsiding as a dozen men leaned down to hear the answer.

"Why'd you kill her, Bird?" McCain turned Bird's face to his. "Was it because she loved you? Because she wanted to marry you? Was it because she was pregnant? She died without saying your name once, you bastard. Did you know that? She wouldn't give you up—not even at the end!" McCain slapped Bird across the face with an open hand. Bird's glassy eyes rolled, spreading their view across the sea of hard faces until McCain wrenched his chin back. "Why'd you kill Tulip?"

Blood bubbled. Bird coughed. "Who's Tulip?"

40

Lund looked behind him at the car at the curb. The cabbie sat quietly behind the wheel, his eyes on the *Sentinel*'s sports page. The houses around him were quiet, their dry lawns stretching to the curb like rough carpet in the deepening afternoon light. He felt oddly exposed and realized that there weren't any trees. Each street rolled out with nothing but grass and a sidewalk to break the monotony. Lifting the latch on the screen, Lund knocked on the window of the interior door and stepped back to wait. A girl answered, no more than ten years old, her brown hair in braids to her waist. "What do you want, mister?" Bright blue eyes squinted at the sun and watched him warily. With suspicion, she appraised him frankly. The screen door remained shut.

"My name's Thom Lund. I'm looking for Eileen Fahey. Sergeant Fahey said he would call ahead."

"Uncle Mitt sent you?" The girl stared at him for a long moment and shut the door. He could hear her shout, "Ellie, the police are here!"

Putting his hands in his pockets to keep them warm, Lund turned away from the face of the house and looked around at the surrounding homes. None of them looked like they were insulated for the cold, and all but the boardinghouses appeared to be empty. He watched the door for the house across the street open inward to reveal an elderly man looking out at him. Then Lund heard the door behind him open.

The young woman in the doorway shared enough of a resemblance to the girl with the braids to allow the presumption of family. Brown hair in one braid draped over her shoulder, a worn green sweater wrapped tightly against the cold. She said, "Who are you? Why aren't you in a uniform?"

"I'm not the police. My name's Lund. Are you Eileen Fahey?" Lund smiled. "Lieutenant Blake told me to drop by. Sergeant Fahey said it would be all right if he sent me instead of a patrol car. Did he call ahead?"

"The phone's out." She stood there watching him for a long minute. Lund waited, trying not to spend too much time staring into her eyes. One of them had to be glass, but whichever it was, the craftsman had gotten it exactly right. The street was tranquil. From behind him, Lund could hear a quavering voice call out, "Everything all right, Ellie?" Lund turned to look. The old man across the street had opened his front door and come out onto the porch.

The girl suppressed her irritation. She called out, "Yes, Mr. Espisito. Nothing to worry about." Opening the screen door, she jerked her head toward the interior of the house. "You had better come in, Mr. Lund. Better not give the neighbors too much to talk about."

He found himself in a warm cottage with waxed floors and braided rag rugs. Lund took off his hat and ducked, worried that he would brush against the low ceilings. The furnishings were worn but carefully cleaned. He could hear voices in the kitchen talking, the smell of stew or some other soup drifting comfortably through the front of the house. "I'm sorry to bother you, Miss Fahey. Lietenant Blake thought you might be able to help him with an investigation into the Warwicks. He didn't have a man free, so he sent me along instead. It's routine, really."

There was a footstep on the stairs. A broadly built man was coming down, buttoning up his waistcoat, a jacket over his arm. White hair sprang in curls around his head, and thick white eyebrows drew together in paternal concern. "Going to take my shift now, Eileen. Who's this?" The man leaned on the banister three steps from the bottom and looked Lund over from his head to his shoes.

"Uncle Mitt sent him from the city, Da. Says he has some questions." She said to Lund, "This is my father, Duncan Fahey."

"The city? Warwicks, is it?" Duncan Fahey ran a hand through his white hair and considered Lund. "Thought that was all settled. What more do they want?" The man filled the doorway to the stairs, his strong forearms bulging where his sleeves were rolled up. "Well?"

Lund began slowly. "I'd like to ask you a few questions about the Warwicks."

"What are you looking for, an alibi?" Duncan Fahey snorted. "I'd say you've told the police enough." He put his hand on Eileen's shoulder.

"No, nothing like that." Lund took off his hat. "It's more a matter of background. We can't get a straight answer out of the current house staff. How things are set up, who does what tasks. That kind of thing."

The man came down the last step, put his hands on his hips. Lund had to take a step back to give him room. Close up, the man was a mountain. He had a good three inches on Lund. "All right, then," Duncan said cautiously. "But not too many questions. Been aid enough to the police for the Warwicks. And what good has it done us? Cost my girl an eye, that's what." He gave Lund a last weary look. "Come on, then."

Eileen led them into a small sitting room. Thom sat down on the couch and hung his hat on his knee. "Miss Fahey, can you tell me how many members of staff there are in the house?"

"They wouldn't even give you that much?" Duncan interrupted. "What kind of trouble did they get themselves into this time?"

"They both died, Da. Don't you read the papers?" Eileen kept her back straight and her eye on Lund.

"I know they did. I want him to tell me." The man's eyes narrowed as he leaned forward. "Why don't you say it, bub?"

"They were both killed," Lund said. "Roger Warwick was murdered. Tulip may have taken her own life. They were both at the opera."

Duncan laughed. "Fat chance of finding us there!"

"Miss Tulip? Take her own life?" Eileen looked at Lund as though he were a stain in the middle of the clean carpet. "She wouldn't ever do anything like that. You've got the wrong line, Mr. Lund. You can tell them that from me."

"Why do you say that?"

"Just isn't the type. She coped. Always kept her chin up. She was the nicest of the lot of them. Kill herself? You'd have to know her to understand. It's not possible."

"The police have to follow the line of inquiry." Duncan patted his daughter on the shoulder with a hand the size of a small ham. "You know that as well as the next person."

Lund tried to smile. "If you could tell me what the household looked like a year ago, might be helpful to us." He took a small notebook from his pocket.

Eileen took a deep breath. "There were us three upstairs maids, a cook, a butler, and a chauffeur."

"Was there a gardener or someone who might have looked after the garden, kept things up?"

"Garden? What garden?" Her words were sharp. "Mr. Warwick said that he wouldn't have nothing to do with keeping up the outside. It was everything he could do to maintain the inside, he said. He was a close one," she added. "Tight, if you know what I mean."

"Anyone else? Footman, porter, errand boy—anyone else? Nanny?"

"Nanny?" Eileen was puzzled. "Tulip didn't need a nanny for years before I went to work there."

Lund shook his head. "I meant Ivy's nanny, Miss Fahey. Ivy's only fourteen, isn't she?"

Even if the girl had been a gifted actress, she couldn't have hidden her surprise. She looked from Lund to her father and said, "Ivy is the oldest, Mr. Lund. She's twenty-six. Tulip was the youngest. She's . . . she was barely twenty."

"Are you quite certain?" Lund stopped writing, lifted his pencil from the notebook.

"Ivy? She was only just going on twenty-five when I left last year. She and Mrs. Warwick didn't get on a bit. They'd go at it like a hammer and tongs." Eileen shook her head. "Wasn't right. I've never seen two people who hated each other like they did."

"What did they fight about?"

"What does that have to do with anything?" Duncan leaned forward in his chair, making the wooden legs scream for mercy. "I thought you were here to ask about the help around the house?"

Lund glanced at his notebook and thought fast. He considered the nosy neighbor across the street. "Just cuirous. We can't make sense of what we know so far. I thought I would ask. If it's important, Lieutenant Blake can send out a patrolman."

"I thought you said this was a friendly conversation," Fahey growled.

"Could be that way." Lund was noncommittal.

Fahey frowned, sat back. "Tell the man, Eileen. What did they fight about?"

"Ivy was . . . awkward, never acted the way Mrs. Warwick wanted. Mr. Warwick thought all the girls were a waste of his time. All of them except Clover." Eileen met Lund's eye. "They were cruel people. Whenever Mrs. Warwick could, she sent Ivy away. Finishing school, she called it. Just about the only one of them who could get what she wanted was Clover." Eileen stopped suddenly, glanced at her father, and pinned her mouth shut.

"Now you know what they fought about," Duncan was absolute. "Ask your other questions."

Lund felt the familiar focus that came from instinct. "Did she give a statement after Clover attacked you? Ivy, I mean. I looked around for one and couldn't find it."

"There weren't any statements." Duncan raised his voice enough to attract attention. A woman appeared briefly in the doorway to the kitchen, wiped her hands on her apron, and turned back inside. "My brother Mitt made sure the police knew what really happened. If I hadn't had a brother on the force, those people would have slurred our good name. They were already trying it, even after Ellie lost her eye. They told the investigating sergeant Ellie was a drinker, that she stole things. Can you imagine that?"

Eileen stiffened in her chair and stared at a spot on the floor.

"But you dropped the charges?"

"You tell me what you would have done going up against that kind of money?" Duncan sat forward. "Even with my brother helping, people like us, we don't have a chance."

"Did they offer you money?"

"You're damn right they did." Duncan's voice filled the dark sitting room. Sounds from the kitchen stopped. Lund had the sense the whole house had paused to listen. "The only condition was we move out of the city. Well, that wasn't a problem with me! We took that money, and I bought a little ice cream stand we run for Playland during the summer. The girls went back to school, even Eileen here. Got her diploma. Now she does the books for a lumberyard in Queens." Lund looked back at the young woman, who was sitting straight-backed, staring at her hands in her lap. Fahey continued with a kind of pride. "I work nights in the winter to keep the money going. And all three of my girls have an education, and they work good jobs." He reached over and put one hand over his daughter's. "Ellie lost an eye, but we made the best from it. When I think how that girl could have killed her . . . I can't tell you how mad I get." Duncan released his daughter's hand and sat back quickly. "None of this has anything to do with us, Mr. Lund. Ask your questions. I don't like to be late to work."

"Can you tell me if the house had any problems? Leaks, plumbing issues, rats?" Lund watched the girl.

"That's why you asked about the gardener. The rats." Eileen nodded. "Clover carried on about them something awful. Told her father she could hear them in the walls. There weren't any rats. I tried to tell them."

"What do you mean?"

"I never saw any rats in that house, and I was up and down and all over enough to know." Eileen's eyes weren't on her father, but Lund could see her reservations in her body language. "It was Miss Ivy scratching at the walls to scare Clover. But I never could convince Jefferson. He was the butler then." She shook her head with a frown. "There was so much poison out that Miss Clover's dog ate some and died." Eileen shuddered.

"How do you know it was Ivy scratching at the walls?"

"Caught her at it, didn't I?"

"Now, that's enough of that, Eileen," Duncan said. "I can't see what that would have to do with Tulip."

Eileen sat back in her chair.

"Go on." Duncan gestured to Lund. There was a warning tone in his words.

"Eileen," Lund began, "why won't the staff talk to the police? The sergeant on the case tells me he's never seen a staff more clammed up."

"I can tell you, Mr. Lund." Duncan leaned forward. "It's because they haven't been paid yet. I can't tell you how many times Ellie would come home and say there wasn't no pay that week. Docked this and that until there were pennies left. Ask them after Friday. You'll see."

"Maybe you're right." Lund put the notebook in his pocket and stood. "I won't take any more of your time. If the police want anything else, they'll send someone."

Duncan sat forward. "I'd rather they didn't, Mr. Lund. This is a quiet neighborhood. Even if my brother is a cop, nobody likes to have the cars around too often. I'm going to have trouble enough explaining why there's a cab pulled up to my front lawn." Lund nodded, and they shook hands. It was like putting his hand into a meat grinder. "Eileen, see him out, would you?" Sounds of life returned in the kitchen. The smell of a meal filled the small living room. Duncan Fahey made his way into the kitchen and to the promise of soup.

Eileen led Lund to the door, her arms crossed over her chest, her head down.

Lund put on his hat. "For what it's worth, I'm not here to spoil whatever deal you have going with the Warwicks." He looked over his shoulder toward the bright kitchen. The doorway was still empty, the sound of plates and silverware coming through. "You don't have to tell me a thing, and there's nothing I can testify to in court. I'm not a police officer. We're just two people talking." Lund met her eye. He gambled. "What was it that set Clover off that day she hit you? You don't have to tell me if you don't want to."

Eileen looked over her shoulder at the kitchen and put her hand on the front doorknob. "It's such a small thing," she whispered, looking back at Lund. "I was unpacking Clover's weekend bag, and I found some wet clothes and a hat all rolled up. The hat was almost ruined, shoved in the bag like that. I unrolled it and asked her if she wanted me to reshape it." Eileen looked over her shoulder again. "She just came at me."

"Over a hat?" Lund shook his head. He had heard it all now. He was sure of it.

"You don't know the Warwicks very well, do you, Mr. Lund?"

"I suppose not." Lund stepped past the door and was surprised to see Eileen following alongside. She pulled the door behind her, open enough to see the kitchen door, closed enough so their voices wouldn't carry.

"Mr. Lund, is it true that Tulip killed herself?"

"The police don't seem to think so. They believe someone poisoned her with some chocolates."

"Was that why you was asking about the rats?"

"You know I can't tell you that, Eileen."

"I know it." Eileen's hands gripped each other, her knuckles turning pink in the cold. "Tulip was always good to us. Good to me, I mean. Was anyone with her, at . . . at the end?"

"Ivy was there. Along with someone she met that day, a woman from the opera." Lund's mind flashed to Penelope in her gold dress, her hand in his, her breath on his ear. He almost didn't notice that Eileen had flinched. Almost, but not quite. He couldn't put his finger on what had surprised the girl.

Eileen looked behind herself at the house. Sure that no one was coming, she pulled the door shut and stepped forward, her words an urgent whisper. "Was Ivy ever alone with her? Was she, Mr. Lund? I have to know!"

"I don't think so, but she might have been. Why would it matter?"

Eileen bit her lip as she made up her mind. Finally certain of herself, she nodded once and said, "Because Clover isn't the Warwick I'm afraid of, and you shouldn't be either. She didn't attack me. It was Ivy."

41

LUND TOOK THE STEPS TO the precinct house two at a time, his legs stretching to a deeper step than everyone around him. If there was a complaint from the line when he cut through to the desk sergeant, he didn't hear it. He was too focused on getting to the bullpen and Blake. Pushing past the uniformed policemen moving through their shift change, Lund walked with a singular purpose. A familiar energy met him at the door of the bullpen. Something had happened. Lund could feel it.

"Thom!" McCain called his name from across the room, gesturing with his hand. "Over here!" McCain started talking before Lund reached him, his voice rising above the din. It was loud, louder than usual, with plainclothesmen and uniforms everywhere, all watching a bank of windowless doors. "Thom," McCain began, "I want to be the one to tell you, before anyone else says—"

The door behind McCain opened. As it swung out, a silence grew, starting with McCain and moving out. Blake appeared, scanning the crowd around the doors. "Get back to work," he growled. Gradually, the men dispersed; only a few remained standing around the desks. Blake pushed past the men by McCain. "You tell him yet?"

The few men left in the room turned to hear what the lieutenant would say next, all of them standing on the balls of their feet—ready to move, ready to fight.

"Tell me what?" Lund met Blake's eye. "I just got here."

"From the island?" Blake nodded once. "Find out anything?"

"You have something you want to tell me first?" Lund looked around at the stone-faced policemen hanging on their every word.

"You tell me what you found out. Then we'll talk about the other thing." Blake was solemn. "Go ahead."

"I met with Eileen Fahey. She told me something that wasn't in the case notes. Clover wasn't the sister who attacked her."

Blake's expression focused, his blue eyes tightening on Lund. "Go on."

"Ivy was the one who went after her. Clover had to pull her off. Clover took the blame so Ivy wouldn't have charges pressed against her. Clover gave Eileen money—*personally* gave her money—to keep her mouth shut. She's been sending it on this whole year. Only stopped last month."

"On top of what she got from the Warwicks?" McCain asked. Lund nodded. McCain whistled. "That's a lot of dough."

Blake kept his eyes on Lund. "Anything else?"

"Yes," Lund met Blake's eye, "the arsenic around the house—that was Ivy too. She'd rigged the walls to make it sound like rats. Did it to scare her sisters. Miss Fahey said there was so much around the house that Clover's dog ate it and died. Only she's not sure the dog ate it on its own. Could have been poisoned."

"She was practicing," McCain said to Blake, "to be sure she had it right."

"Why?" Blake's voice traveled across the bullpen.

"Ivy was always fighting with her mother or her father or the servants. The way Eileen described it, well, it must have been hell to work there. Things seemed to happen after one of the sisters got her name in the paper. Staff would get sick. Things would break in the middle of the night. The dog was killed after Clover got engaged."

McCain winced. "And they were close? Even after that?"

"She said there wasn't anything that could come between the three of them. Not men, not their parents, not anything." Lund glanced from Blake to McCain.

"What about the hospital?" McCain asked. "Clover never stepped foot in the place the whole time Tulip was there."

"Fahey said Clover must not have known or been told." Lund shook his head. "They protected each other. Kept each other's secrets. Tulip and Clover never had a bad word to say about Ivy, even when she was at her worst. Now, what is it you have to tell me?"

McCain faced Blake, who nodded once. McCain said, "Your friend William Bird, he's confessed to killing Roger Warwick. Says it was an accident. He says Clover Warwick has been blackmailing him for a year over something that happened at a party last summer. We can't get a straight story out of him. And none of it makes sense. At least it didn't make sense until—"

"Until just this moment," Blake finished. "We need to find Clover and Ivy Warwick."

ELEANOR PICKED UP THE PHONE on the second ring. "Thom, oh thank goodness it's you! I've been worried sick."

"Eleanor, is Penelope there? I need to speak with her urgently. It's about Ivy Warwick."

"No!" Lund couldn't tell if Eleanor's voice was shaking or if the line was breaking up. "Thom, I must ask you something."

"Just a moment."

Lund watched McCain hang up a receiver on the other side of the room and shake his head. "The Warwicks' butler says they both left an hour ago, in a hurry. Ivy and Clover were together. Clover was driving."

Blake pointed to the phone. "Get back on the horn and put out a bulletin to the squad cars to be on the lookout." Blake returned to Lund. "Any luck?"

Lund shook his head and said into the phone, "I need to find her, Eleanor. I've called every place I can think of. Mary isn't home either."

"Mary is here with me." He was certain now. Eleanor's voice was shaking. "Thom, Penelope has lost something. She tried to call you, but your landlady told her she wouldn't take a message."

"I don't have time for this, Eleanor. I'm sorry, but I must go. Call me at the precinct if you hear from Penelope. I need to speak with her urgently."

"But, Thom!" Eleanor's voice resonated through the line. "She needs to speak with you! That's what I'm trying to tell you. She's missing something, and she has to find it right away!"

"All right, what has she lost?"

"Her gun. She's lost the .22. Ivy was here. Penelope has gone to Patsy Galton's house to see if she can help her find Ivy."

"The gun?" Lund swore quietly in Danish. "I'll find her, Eleanor. Give me Patsy's last name again. Galton . . . all right, I have it." Lund put the phone down.

"Did I hear that right?" Blake leaned both hands on his desk. "Your girlfriend is missing her gun?"

Lund straightened. "It was a gift from her father, Nathan. She keeps it locked away. It was perfectly safe."

"Except it's missing now. Where did she go? Who does she think has it?"

"Ivy Warwick went home with Penelope after the opera. She loaned the girl some clothes and took her back to the hospital." Lund could feel his heart beating hard. "Penelope might be at Patsy Galton's—"

"Patsy Galton." McCain said. "Nathan, do you remember her?"

Blake ran a hand over his eyes. "Of course I do, Jasper. How could I forget? She showed up at the precinct every day for weeks, asking what we were doing to find Coralee O'Connor. I had to threaten her with arrest to get her to leave me alone. What the hell does that have to do with anything?"

McCain crossed the room, throwing the office door open. "Nichols, have you finished with Bird's statement? Good, bring it here."

"What's this about?" Blake's hands were on his hips, his face red with anger.

McCain went through the typed pages quickly, his fingers following the lines of type. "Here it is. Listen to this." McCain read from the sheet, "'I met Clover Warwick at a party in June 1927. She witnessed me drinking alcohol and other illicit activities that would have ended my career.' Then he goes on about the blackmail. But the party. Nathan, the party! Coralee O'Connor disappeared from a party in June of '27." McCain scanned the rest of the statement. "Here it is. Says here Locust Valley."

"Could be the last night Coralee was seen alive," Lund offered. "I have the date in my notes." Lund reached into his interior pocket. "I looked around the house and spoke to the neighbors. They took me around to see where she launched the boat that night. Here it is. Look at this." Lund took the note he had found in the boathouse from his wallet. "Someone was blackmailing her about something. Maybe even this Patsy person."

A uniformed policeman stuck his head just inside the door. "Pardon me, Lieutenant." Blake looked up from the note in his hand. "There's a woman on the phone. Says she has an urgent message for you or Mr. Lund."

"Send it in." Blake reached for the phone when it rang. "Listen, Thom, you mean well, but this doesn't mean anything. Coralee had money, didn't she? Seems like all we get these days are criminals with black books. Blackmailers are a dime a dozen. It doesn't mean the two things are connected." He spoke into the receiver. "Yeah, what is it?" He paused for a moment and straightened. "Jasper, get the boys ready. Two cars."

McCain pivoted through the door, adjusting his hat and giving up a shout. The thunder of a dozen men standing up came through the door to where Lund stood.

"What is it?" Lund felt as if the ground were going out from underneath him. Dread whispered that he had waited too long, spent too long puzzling it out. "Who is that on the phone?"

Blake picked up a pencil from his desk. "What's the address? Got it. Stay where you are. We'll call you." Slamming the receiver down with one hand, Blake picked up his hat with the other. "Mrs. Harris just got a call from her daughter. Penelope told her, cool as a cucumber, that she found what she was looking for at Patsy's apartment and is having a nice chat with the Warwicks. No one has a nice chat with that family," Blake growled. "If Ivy and Clover are both there, chances are one of them has her gun." Blake put his hat on. "Let's go."

Lund was already through the door.

42

PENELOPE PUT THE PHONE BACK in the cradle and clenched her fist to hide the tremor in her hand. "How lovely you look, Ivy." She clung to polite conversation. "Isn't that the dress you wore at the opera?" The awkward fit remained, although Mrs. Reynolds's excellent laundering had made the neckline and waist crisp. The dress had been revived, even if the girl within it had not. Ivy's face was drawn and pale, and her hair could have used a good brush.

"What are you doing here?" Ivy studied her without expression. She kept her hands at her sides, hidden within the folds of the gown.

"I told you. I need to speak with Patsy. I need to use her phone."

"I suppose you want to come in, then." Ivy didn't try to hide her irritation. She turned to walk ahead of Penelope, leading her down the hall to the room with the long bank of windows. With the night sky and inky darkness of the surrounding buildings, the view felt more like the backdrop on a stage.

As she walked through the door, Penelope had to search for the two women she knew were there. The room was so quiet, she wondered wildly if Ivy had already put her gun to use. Two lamps on either side of the room provided the only light. Patsy and Clover blurred into the dark shadows, only their profiles sharp in the gloom.

Clover stood with her back to the windows, a cigarette smoldering in her trembling hand. She sagged when she saw Penelope. She looked younger than she had at Mackey's, or perhaps it was just that now she wore no makeup. Penelope could see freckles scattered across the bridge of her nose. Without the artifice of her makeup, Clover was more beautiful. It hardly seemed possible. "It would have to be you," Clover said in exasperation. "Do you ever know when to mind your own business?"

Penelope relied on nervous energy to get her across the room. "Thank you for letting me just drop in on you like this, Patsy. I had to call my mother, and I just thought of it as I passed. I thought you wouldn't mind if I used your phone." Penelope was sure her inanity was clear to everyone. She hardly cared.

"You climbed five flights of stairs to borrow Patsy's phone," Clover stated with flat disbelief. "And I suppose you always go out in the cold without a coat?"

"Nothing like a good hike in the cold to get the blood moving." The lies were coming fast now.

"I don't believe it," Clover spat. "You can't leave me alone for one minute. You even followed me here."

Penelope scanned until she found Patsy seated in her comfortable leather chair on the other side of the room, one leg crossed over the other, a glass of whiskey in her hand. Patsy showed absolutely no sign that she had seen or heard Penelope, who blurted out, "Patsy, are you all right?"

"Of course I'm all right. Why wouldn't I be?" Patsy said finally, keeping her eyes on Clover. "Miss Warwick was just telling me how I've ruined her career. Although I can't say what career she meant, since she can't sing."

Clover spoke to Patsy with the petulance of a child. "You know you have. You canceled the concert knowing a producer came all the way from Hollywood just to see me." Clover pointed at Patsy with the hand that held the cigarette. "It's a good thing I can think on my feet. Otherwise I'd make you pay for that. As it is, I won't ruin you. I just need what it takes to start over somewhere new. Somewhere I can earn a living."

"Earn a living?" Patsy gestured with her glass. "I suppose you could call what you do with the opera 'work.' I would agree if you did. It is hard work listening to a hack like you."

Ivy stirred, shifting from one leg to the other.

"Patsy," Penelope began, her eyes following Ivy nervously as the girl drifted across the room to stand next to the window, "perhaps you should wait a day or two before making up your mind."

"Clover's right about one thing," Patsy replied with disinterest. "You don't know when to keep your nose out of other people's business."

Penelope's attention snapped back to Patsy, Ivy's pale dress disappearing into shadows of her peripheral vision. How to get them to understand? She could barely think straight. She was sure Ivy had the gun there with her. It was loaded. A bullet in the chamber.

"I'm sorry to interrupt. But since I'm here, Ivy, I think you have something of mine." Penelope focused on the girl. The purse Ivy held was clearly too heavy, the shape distorted by something bulky.

"No, I don't." Ivy looked down into the street. She added casually, "Liar."

"You can't just barge into a person's apartment and accuse them of stealing." Clover seized at the opening, lifting her cigarette chest high, her face relaxing. "It won't read well in the press."

"Try it." Penelope focused on Clover. "Try it and see what you get."

Patsy sighed. "What a child you are, Clover. I would have you remember this is my apartment, and I can have who I like in it. Penelope may stay. You can go."

Ivy moved slightly, drawing Penelope's attention. She could see the purse where it now hung loosely from the girl's wrist. The fabric of the purse was too slack. She could tell from across the room it was now empty. Stepping around the couch, Penelope kept her eyes on Ivy, willing her to move her other hand where she could see.

"I don't care about your stupid society. I never did. I have more talent in my little finger than you ever will, Patsy Galton! I can do it myself!" Clover tapped the ash from her cigarette onto the carpet. "I already have my train ticket. I'll go to California and break into films on my own. I always had to do everything on my own anyway. What I need is money. You'd hardly miss a couple thousand for me to start over someplace new. That's what you've wanted all along, isn't it? To get rid of me? You've been jealous because of Coralee. You should admit it. It'll make you feel better."

Ivy stirred, her concentration on Patsy slowly shifting to Clover. A bright pink appeared on her cheeks, and as she stared at her sister, her lips parted as though she was about to speak.

"Jealous of you?" Patsy watched Clover over the rim of her glass as she drank. "She came back to me in the end. Whatever fun she had with you, she came back to *me*. I'm not giving you any more money. You've had enough from me. You can tell whoever's left in the operatic society whatever you want. They're finished anyway. And frankly, I don't care what they think of me. I'm finished too. I'm leaving for Europe as soon as I can get a ticket. Leave all of this behind."

"No you're not. Not until I have my money. I've got to have it!"

"You think you're good enough?" Patsy laughed.

"Good enough for Hollywood?" Clover stood up straighter. Her arm dropped, and she looked down at Patsy with half-closed lids. "I've already had a screen test. A producer offered me a contract."

"That's what you meant at Mackey's—you were celebrating," Penelope realized aloud.

"Yes, celebrating getting the hell out of here. And if you

hadn't stuck your nose in, Michael might be going with me! I got my ticket this afternoon. I'm leaving town as fast as I can."

"You aren't going to California. You aren't going anywhere." Patsy sat back in her chair and laughed. "I knew you'd claw and fight to get those parts. God knows why you felt like you had to kill your sister for the solo, but the police will find you out soon enough. I'd save my money if I were you. You'll need it to buy them off."

The light shifted. Penelope looked up to see that Ivy had moved forward, her right hand hidden in the deep folds of her dress.

"Hollywood." Ivy gave the word a strange emphasis, as though it were a foreign language she was sounding out. "I want to see the ticket. The one you said you had." She stepped toward Clover.

Clover didn't seem to hear her. She stared down at Patsy in her chair, her words coldly furious. "How ridiculous! You think anyone will listen to you and your stories? I'll sue you for slander—and I'll win! I'm going to Hollywood on my own merit. You'll see. You'll all see!"

Ivy shivered, her right hand finally coming into view.

"Ivy!" Penelope pitched her voice above Clover's easily. "Ivy, give me the gun."

43

IVY LIFTED THE GUN, HOLDING it with both hands. It looked quite large. Disproportionately so. Ivy's hands didn't shake a bit as she held it though, her index finger on the trigger. Penelope wondered if the gun looked as large and inappropriate in her own hand. She had never thought so, but here in the dark room with the city looking in through the windows, her perspective shifted. The gun was a ridiculous metal thing, as out of place as a drop of blood on a white linen tablecloth.

"Ivy," Penelope said quietly, stepping forward between Patsy and Clover toward Ivy. "May I have my gun back, please?"

"No." The girl spoke without looking away from Clover. "Are you going to Hollywood, Clover?"

Clover tried to smile, the curve of her mouth uncertain. "You'll love California. We'll be together—"

"That's what Tulip said. She said she was going to Philadelphia, that I would like it." Ivy made a face. "But she didn't ask me what I wanted to do. I didn't want to go to Philadelphia. I didn't want her to get married. I don't want to go to Hollywood. I don't want you to be an actress."

"Point that gun away from your sister, Ivy," Patsy said crisply. "Do you want to kill her?"

The gun went off.

At first, Penelope wasn't sure what direction it had been pointed. She turned to Patsy, who was still upright in her chair, her face frozen with the blood slowly draining away. But when Patsy stood, Penelope could see it was shock and not a wound that caused the sudden blanche of color. There was a thud against the carpet. Penelope looked down to see Clover had fallen to one knee, one hand on her abdomen, the other grabbing Penelope by the sleeve of her dress.

"Stop!" Ivy's voice was imperious. Clear and loud. The cigarette fell from Clover's hand as she slid to her hip.

"Clover . . ." Penelope reached for her.

"Don't touch her."

"Ivy, let me help her," Penelope pleaded.

"No." Ivy's face was without expression. "Don't help her." She held the gun level with Patsy's head as she considered her sister. "Tulip told me about the movie producers. She said we should let you do it because you had star quality. She always had your side. She told me you wanted to sing 'The Doll Song' because the costume would show off your legs better. You can't even sing 'The Doll Song'! I knew you were going to leave me with Mama. You both were. Tulip told me it would only be a little while, but that was a lie. You would have forgotten about me like you always did when I went away." Ivy smiled, reaching forward with the toe of her shoe to touch the blood pooling on the floor. She pulled her foot back, smearing blood across the wood. She continued conversationally, "Tulip was going to leave that night, after the opera. She only stayed to hear Valentina Carrera sing. I left some chocolates out in my room. I knew she wouldn't be able to resist. I didn't know it would take so long. It didn't before . . ." Ivy frowned.

"I won't leave you, Ivy. I've got tickets for both of us." Clover gasped for each breath, the pain pinching her face. "Call a doctor. Please, Ivy."

"What a liar you are!" Ivy exhaled in a sharp laugh. "You

could have been a great actress. But I'm a better one." She lowered her chin, still pointing the gun at Patsy.

"Ivy," Penelope began.

"Don't patronize me. I can shoot you too." The gun jolted forward toward Penelope's chest. "Do you know what Mama called the sanitorium? She called it 'finishing.' Like I was a cake that needed icing. She told me it would be a lovely rest with other girls. It wasn't like that at all. I wrote letters. I told Tulip and Clover. I was sure they would come. But Mama said they wouldn't, and they didn't. I only made one friend. It wasn't much, but it was what I had." Ivy slid her eyes, and the muzzle, to Clover on the floor. "You had to ruin that too."

Clover looked up at Ivy from the floor, her skin an ashy white. "I didn't know, Ivy."

"Liar. You knew plenty. Do you know what she did?" Ivy looked at Penelope, keeping the gun trained on Clover. "When Clover found out I had a friend who might help her become a star, she buttoned her up for her own. She seduced her. Took her away from me when she knew how I felt. Then she blackmailed her so she could have better singing roles—"

"Coralee . . ." Patsy's voice shook. "You're talking about Coralee."

Ivy rolled her eyes. "Don't act like you didn't know. You must have suspected."

"Ivy," Clover's voice was growing weaker by the moment, "I didn't do it to hurt you. I have to get away, don't you see? I did it so we could both get away."

"Coralee avoided me for months until you took me to that party. Then there she was, sitting on the lawn in that ridiculous hat. All I had to do was sit down next to her and wait her out. She could barely look at me. Then, when you were flirting with that man from the bank, she told me about the two of you. She begged me. Can you imagine? She begged me to ask you to stop blackmailing her. That's when I knew you didn't even love her. I had thought about killing you first, but I changed my plan." Ivy licked her lips, leaned forward. "I put poison in her lemon squash. But you already knew that. You caught me at it, didn't you? I was sure they'd blame you once they knew what you had done. But you managed to cover it up. You made it look like suicide." Patsy gasped. Ivy blinked slowly and looked at her, drawn by the sound, then continued to speak. "When she got sick, I took Coralee to the bathroom. Then I went and found Clover and told her what I had done. Clover took care of it. I thought for sure she would get caught with the body. But she managed it. God knows how." She gestured with the gun and spoke to Penelope. "Hand me that purse." When Penelope did not reply, Ivy pointed the gun at her. "Hand me Clover's purse."

Penelope picked it up by a corner and held it out.

"On second thought," Ivy's eyes narrowed, "you open it up. Tell me if Clover really has a ticket to California."

Penelope lifted the clutch flap, her mind moving quickly through scenarios. She had to get her gun. Her fingers found the paper ticket flat against a small mirror. She lifted her hand from the clutch carefully. Slowly. "There's two."

"What?" Ivy covered the ground between them in one step. "Let me see." Her right hand fell, her left snatching the clutch from Penelope's hands. This was her moment. Penelope grabbed for the gun. It went off.

Lund hadn't felt this sort of fatigue since the war, when the trenches held every horror. Nothing had prepared him for the quiet of the carpeted apartment hallway, hearing the women speaking to one another through the door, he and the cops being unable to knock or speak.

"If she's got a gun," McCain whispered, "we don't want to spook her."

They made their way to the kitchen entrance, a narrow door barely wide enough for a single man. Toomey picked the lock, and they went through one at a time. McCain first, Toomey last. Each man soft on his feet.

"There's a person on the ground in there," McCain whispered. "I can see them through the crack at the bottom of the door."

Lund's feet felt heavy and his vest and jacket constricting as he willed himself to remain still.

McCain gingerly pushed open the swing door of the kitchen, his movements painfully slow. He met Lund's eye and mouthed, "Not her." He let the door slowly close. Rising from his position, he added, "There are three of them in there, all standing close together."

Blake unholstered his gun. "I'm the best shot. I'll go first. If I can get off a shot, I'll do it."

"Nathan," Lund began.

"You stay here." Blake pointed stiffly at the kitchen floor.

Lund stood to his full height. "Lieutenant—"

The retort of the shot vibrated through the kitchen. McCain was first through the swinging door, Lund close behind him.

Penelope stood shoulder to shoulder with Ivy, her hand grasping the gun and pointing it away from the kitchen door. On the floor beside them, Patsy struggled to get up. Blood discolored the grey wool of her slacks as she clutched hard at the wound. Yet he thought only of Penelope, of getting her away from the gun. McCain reached them first, hooking an arm around the Warwick girl's neck and pulling her back as he kicked her knees out from under her. Lund collected Penelope roughly into his arms, lifting her feet from the floor and carrying her away from the center of the room as a rush of policemen pushed through the apartment door.

Ivy fought like an alley cat, her dress making it harder for the officers to keep a grip on her as she raged. She kicked wildly, losing both shoes. Two patrolmen had her by the arms, and she still managed to kick a plainclothes policeman into one of the large windows overlooking the city, shattering the glass. The sounds of the street five flights below came through with the cold. Lund could hear distant shouting as people looked up to see where the glass had come from. A patrolman lost his grip on her, and the next moment Ivy was loose and looking back at them from the sill of the broken window, one bare foot on the edge, a hand holding her balance as she pulled her second foot through. Ivy glanced at them over her shoulder, her hair blowing around her head by the updraft, her eyes wild. For a moment, it seemed to Lund the world spun a little more slowly. He looked at Penelope.

When he looked back to the window, Ivy was already gone. Only then did Penelope look away. The emptiness stretched out around them.

It began to snow.

44

PENELOPE SAT ON THE COUCH and felt exhaustion begin at her feet and work its way up. Clover was on her way to the hospital. She might live. Penelope asked Lund to phone Mrs. Warwick and prepare her. Why, she wasn't sure. No, that was wrong. She knew why. Because it was her gun Ivy had shot Clover with, and that made her responsible. The effort had come to nothing anyway. Violet had hung up on Lund. If Violet Warwick wouldn't appear for a child who was dying by poison, Penelope couldn't imagine her doing much for a wounded child under arrest for accessory to murder, even if Clover was her favorite. In three days, she had lost a husband and two daughters, with the third under arrest. Lund touched Penelope's shoulder and she laid her cheek against his hand.

"They're gone," he said quietly. "It's just us." Pulling the curtains across the windows, he stepped on a piece of glass that had fallen into the room. Patsy lifted her head at the noise. He pulled the curtain the rest of the way, the window now boarded up half-heartedly by the building superintendent. "How's your leg?" Lund indicated Patsy's leg.

"It aches. I'm guessing the quack's painkiller is wearing off." Patsy pointed to Penelope. "Get the decanter, would you? Let's have a drink."

Penelope retrieved glasses and the decanter. She poured three neat and handed them around.

"You know how to pour," Patsy observed with a damp sniff.

"I used to own a nightclub." The admission was easy and unexpected. When she handed Lund his glass, he raised an eyebrow. "Not many people know that about me." Only everyone who reads the newspaper, she added silently.

"And how do you figure in?" Patsy directed her question to Lund.

"I'm the policeman she seduced."

Penelope gave Lund a playful slap before she settled in beside him on the sofa. "Patsy, Ivy shot you with my gun."

Beside her Lund swore in Danish, adding, "Penelope, for God's sake."

"She'd find out one way or another." Penelope watched Patsy. "Wouldn't you?"

"More than likely, yes. One way or another, if there's something I want to know, I find out." She took a long drink. "I wanted to know what happened to Coralee. And now I do. Whether I like it or not." Patsy grimaced. "I just knew Clover was hiding something. I thought if I gave her the part, I could get closer to her, find out what really happened. It meant I had to give all three of them a role. None of them did anything consequential without the others."

"Did you know about Coralee and Ivy?" Lund asked.

"No matter what Ivy says, their relationship was a friendship, nothing more. Coralee didn't lie about things like that." Patsy sat with her elbows on her knees, both hands holding the whiskey. "Coralee liked Ivy. She thought she just needed someone to care about her. Really care about her, not send her away to a sanitorium. You've met Violet Warwick. You can imagine what she would do to a child who didn't fit in. Coralee wanted to be a friend to the girl, someone Ivy could rely on. She wouldn't have taken advantage of her."

"You're Coralee's friend Patrice," Lund said. "Dale mentioned you when I was at the cottage yesterday."

Patsy turned the whiskey glass in her hand so the crystal facets sparkled. "I knew Coralee was helping Clover with her career and that Clover was pressuring her. That's all I knew. Coralee was with someone new, but it didn't matter to me, so long as she was happy. Then one day, it was over. I never knew who it was, didn't care to ask. Didn't want to know. I never guessed it was Clover. I'm glad I didn't know. I can't imagine what I would have said." Patsy leaned her glass against her temple and concentrated on Lund. "How did you know to come here?"

"Thom has been looking into Coralee's death for Wallace Peters." Penelope took a small sip of whiskey.

Patsy nodded. "Wallace never did understand why Coralee wouldn't marry him. He married her sister, Lora, instead. Lora never would let up about her marrying. Coralee had to fabricate a marriage just to have a peace. Lora knew it wasn't real but was happy to have an explanation for her society friends." Patsy wiped her eyes with the heel of her hand and emptied her glass in one swallow.

"You must have been close to making the connection this

afternoon, Thom, or you wouldn't have shown up with the police." Penelope took Lund's hand in hers. "You were just in time. "

"Astonishing woman, how did *you* know?" Lund twined his fingers between hers.

Penelope proceeded carefully. "Helen brought *Sentinel* photos from a party. I noticed Clover first. Then I saw Ivy sitting right next to Coralee. She looked so uncomfortable—Coralee, I mean. And, having experienced Ivy's peculiar way of attaching herself to a person, I realized Ivy had formed an attachment to Coralee." Penelope shook her head as she continued. "Forgive me, Patsy, but Ivy's dislike of you . . . I couldn't help but wonder if it was jealousy."

Patsy exhaled. "Hand me the whiskey, would you?

Penelope passed the decanter. "I remembered some of what Ivy said while we were together. And of course, my gun was missing. She was the only one who could have taken it. I think Tulip knew Ivy had poisoned her. If we hadn't insisted that Ivy stay with her, maybe she would have told someone . . ."

"No chance." Lund tightened his hand around hers. "The Warwicks' maid said there was nothing that could break the sisters apart. Look at Clover. She went to the limit to protect Ivy from a murder charge. Even after Ivy shot her."

"If Wallace hired you," Patsy said, "he must have sent you to the house. Did you find anything?"

"I found evidence of some kind of harrasment, maybe blackmail," Lund said. "The harbormaster said he saw a woman in a hat walking to the boat the night of the party. He thought it was Coralee, but I don't. I'm certain it was Clover who took the *Fancy-Free* out that night. She dressed herself in Coralee's clothes and walked down to the marina in the dark—even waved at the harbormaster. It took nerve." He looked into the bottom of his glass as he spoke. "I spoke with a maid who used to work for the Warwicks. She found the hat and clothes Clover must have worn wadded up with her ruined party clothes, soaked through with saltwater. When the maid found them, Ivy almost beat the girl to death."

"You mean the maid who lost her eye?" Penelope put her whiskey down on a small table and watched Lund as he spoke.

"Her name is Eileen Fahey. I spoke to her this afternoon. She told me without Clover there to pull Ivy off her, she would have lost both eyes, or worse. The maid had seen the clothes, you see. Ivy thought their plan had been rumbled. When Violet found out what happened with the maid, she had her daughter sent away. This time for good. I can't think why they brought her back."

"I can answer that," Penelope said. "They couldn't afford it. Mary and Helen said Roger Warwick was flat broke. Clover's been raising money to try to leave town."

"That could explain why Clover resorted to blackmail." Lund nodded. "She needed money to pay the Faheys, money to get away. Money to take Ivy with her."

Penelope was silent. She stared into her glass.

Patsy began to speak, her voice so low she was almost talking to herself. "Ivy seemed to turn up everywhere last summer. She even came here. I don't know why I didn't see it, how I could have missed it. Now it seems so obvious." She downed her whiskey in one swallow and poured more into her glass.

"How did Ivy and Coralee meet?" Lund asked.

Patsy laughed bitterly. "That one's easy. They met at the sanitorium. It was her sister, don't you see? Lora was embarrassed by Coralee's homosexuality, said she was a deviant. Drugs, psychiatrists, Lora even made Coralee try shock therapy. That's what I thought happened when she didn't come home that weekend. I thought Lora had her stashed away in a sanitorium upstate. I raised hell with the police trying to track her down. But what would they do to help someone like me? Most of them think I'm a criminal. Then they found her body, said she had killed herself. I believed them. I tried to ask Lora about it, but she wouldn't see me. One morning I woke up and read Coralee's obituary. Said she had already been interred during a private service. Lora didn't tell me. The paper didn't say where they put her. I don't even know that. I had to have answers. Can't you see? I knew Ivy had known Coralee and I thought . . . I thought . . ." She focused on Lund. "Did I kill that poor girl? Tulip? I had to cast all three or Ivy wouldn't have come. It's what started it all, isn't it? That bloody opera!"

"It's not your fault." Lund was firm. "Tulip was leaving New York. She had gotten married, was starting a family with a lawyer in Philadelphia. She told Ivy so. That's why she died. Not because of an opera."

"I don't know. I feel it's my fault somehow. That poor girl. Tulip . . ." Barely in control of her voice, she continued, "It's too much. I feel as though I've lost Coralee all over again. I should have asked her. I should have paid more attention." She leaned her head on her hand and looked away. "I'd like to be alone now."

Lund and Penelope stood, walking past the broken window and down the hall. In Penelope's last glimpse of Patsy, she was sitting back in the chair, the decanter on the floor by her feet, one hand covering her eyes, the other gripping her glass as though it was the only thing holding her together, her mouth closed tight against a cry of grief.

THEY WALKED FROM THE BUILDING, the doorman leading them through a side entrance that opened into an alley. The snow was falling more heavily between the buildings. It would never stick, but the flakes were large and downy, like shredded cotton. Penelope lifted her face up to the sky and closed her eyes. She tried to think of something, anything, that had nothing to do with the Warwicks. Lund took her hand, his fingers warm. "Are you all right?"

"I'm fine." It was true. She was. Penelope opened her eyes, stared at the snow. "Ivy slept in my bed the day before yesterday. Now she's dead."

Lund put his arms around her, holding her close.

"I keep wondering if I hadn't brought Ivy home from the hospital, would she have done it? She used my gun to shoot Clover . . ."

Lund's voice rumbled, comfortably familiar. "Finding your gun was unfortunate, but she would have killed Clover in another way if she hadn't. Like she killed Tulip. Like she killed Coralee."

"I was looking through the photos Helen brought when I

remembered something Ivy said to me. She said Patsy hated her like poison." The photograph floated up in her memory: Coralee on a lawn chair, her face shadowed by a large hat; Ivy beside her on the ground, watching her. After spending hours with Ivy and Tulip, the scene of the two women at the party had been jarringly familiar. Coralee's face, pinched and uncomfortable; Ivy silently watching with the glass of lemon squash between them in the grass. The photo, Ivy's voice, and the memory of Tulip's pale, silent face collided, leaving only the memory of Tulip staring at Penelope from the clean white sheets of her hospital bed while the nurse asked her over and over what she had eaten and who had given it to her. Even Lund, who probably was in love with her, wouldn't understand the flash of truth. Coralee might not have known what was happening, but Tulip had. She had chosen to say nothing.

"I thought it was an odd thing to say," Penelope continued slowly. "It just—it just got me thinking. I went to find my gun, Thom. I knew right away who had it. She was the only one who could have had it."

"She was prepared to shoot Patsy." Lund's arm tightened around her. "As soon as it occurred to her that you would tell the police, she would have shot you too."

"Could she have not realized what she was doing?"

"No, I don't believe that." Lund pulled far enough away to look her in the face. "She knew." He looked away.

"What is it?" Penelope curled her hand on the lapel of his jacket. "You aren't telling me something."

"A man at the bank, William Bird, he was at the party the night Coralee died. Earlier tonight he confessed to helping Clover dispose of Coralee's body. Clover went to a lot of trouble to cover it up—posing as Coralee, taking the sailboat out by herself. He said she had an iron nerve about it. When he said he would go to the police, she braced him. She said she would kill him if he did, and he believed her. Believed her so well he let her blackmail him. Clover did that to him—and he was her alibi." He shook his head. "He spent the whole afternoon with her. William was the one man who could prove she didn't do it. Instead of going with him to the police, she forced him to help her. Tulip may not have known what Ivy was capable of, but—"

"Clover knew," Penelope finished for him, shivering. Lund removed his coat, draping it across her shoulders. "That's the second time you've given me your coat."

"You can keep it, as far as I'm concerned," he said lightly. "For the first time in my life, I know I'm a fool. But I don't seem to mind."

Penelope looked up at Lund. "What will happen to Clover?"

"If she lives? William says Coralee was dead when they took out the bilge bolts. It all depends on whether the court believes him. Clover went to a lot of trouble to cover up her sister's crime. And now, of course, they'll have to consider whether she knew about Tulip's murder. She'll need a good lawyer. William will too." A shadow passed over Lund's face. His sharp profile stood out against the alley brick.

"Was he a good friend?"

"I thought so." Lund glanced at her. "He stopped me in the stairwell on Friday morning. I think he would have told me then, but I was in a hurry. That's the thing about murder. You wonder what you could have done to stop it. Now I'll always wonder if Roger and Tulip Warwick would be alive if I had just taken a moment to listen."

"Did he kill Roger Warwick?"

"William says Warwick slipped and fell."

"Do you believe him?"

"That's not up to me, thankfully. A jury will decide. William had been gathering evidence against her for months. He's handed it all over to the police. Maybe that will help him. Who knows? Either way, Clover won't be as lucky. She might not have known what Ivy had planned for Tulip, but she must have had an idea Ivy was responsible after Tulip died. It was too similar to what happened to Coralee."

Penelope looked down at the pavement as they walked down the alley and wasn't sure if she would ever forget Clover's entrance with the champagne. She saw it all differently now. Instead of happiness, Penelope saw desperation. By then, Clover must have heard how Tulip had died. Maybe she had even spoken to Ivy and forced her to confess.

They reached the top of the alley, pausing for a moment to watch the scene in front of Patsy's building. The street was well lit, streetlights and car headlights illuminating passersby gathering on the street. Penelope couldn't see much of the policemen other than the bright brass fittings on their caps as they held back the crowd. For a moment, she thought she heard the lieutenant's voice shouting something about clearing the street of cars, but a blaring horn blocked it out. The snow was heavy, collecting on the hats and shoulders of the onlookers, melting as soon as it touched the pavement. The police pushed forward, the mass of bodies shifting to reveal a strange tableau: steam rose from the hood of a taxicab at a sharp angle across both lanes of traffic. As they stood there, an ambulance arrived, the horn sounding to clear the bystanders blocking the street. More shouting. The crowd cleared enough to reveal the taxi headlight shone on a crumpled sheet.

Lund's hand tightened on hers. "In Clover's purse, when Ivy asked you, were there two tickets?"

"Yes." Penelope answered. "There were two." Somewhere, a train was leaving the station with two empty first-class seats. A budding starlet would never arrive for her screen test. She remembered Tulip's lawyer in Philadelphia, waiting for a wife who was already late and would never arrive.

Lund took a deep breath. "McCain told me you can have your gun back after the trial."

"I don't want it." The words were quick. They raced ahead of the fear that surged around her. "It's been over a year since Kinkaid died. I've been telling myself for weeks that I should get rid of it. New York isn't Shanghai." Even as she said it, she wanted to take the words back. She'd have to find another way to feel safe, a better way. The crowd closed in around the scene. Penelope realized she had been holding her breath. She exhaled.

Lund turned toward her. "Does that include all your firearms? Or just this one?"

"Just this one." There were limits to how much change a girl could take at once.

Turning as one, they walked the block to the Excelsior in a comfortable silence, hand in hand.

Acknowledgments

Writing a book is not a solitary act. If it was, no book would ever be published—or read. I must thank my family first, for their tireless support and encouragement. Without it, I would have given up long ago: my father's encyclopedic knowledge of opera, my mother's tireless interest in books—especially mysteries—my partner's patience with hours and hours away from the family, and my kids, who gave me the biggest hug of my life when they found out I was working on this series. I thank them from the bottom of my heart. I also thank my editors, Sione Aeschliman and Lindsey Cleworth. *Murder at the Met* is a better book for their thoughts and insight. No book is ever produced perfectly on the first try. I must truly credit Sione and Lindsey with encouraging me to try harder and do better. Challenges are hard, but they always make for better writing. Not to mention Lindsey's divine cover design and miraculous line edit! Add to these two miracle workers proofreader Ellen Hornor checking my habit of abusing commas specifically and punctuation in general (not to mention countless misspellings), and the picture of just how many people require thanks begins to take shape.

I can't forget to thank author Marina Scott, without whose encouragement I would have never made it this far, or author Kelly Brackenhoff, who shared the inside scoop on book marketing. I must also thank Kathleen White, whom I will thank in every book from now until I stop writing because she was my first writing teacher and believed in me before anyone other than my parents. And thanks to extraordinary author May Cobb, who encouraged me to not be so shy at the very beginning of my career when I doubted myself.

I already mentioned him once, but I have to say it again. I must thank my partner, Tony Cooper. If he hadn't been a rock, if he hadn't encouraged me to dream, if he hadn't done a hundred other things just so I could write, this book would not have happened. Thank you for making my dream your dream too.

To all of you and many more, I offer my earnest thanks.

Historical Notes

Before embarking on some brief thoughts regarding the Metropolitan Opera House, or the "Old Met", I would like to comment on Danish soldiers in World War I. While it is true that Denmark was neutral in the conflict, it is estimated tens of thousands of Danish men joined the British, Canadian, and French armies (even the French Foreign Legion). Not much is known about these men. Amateur French and Danish historians have located mass military graves of many Danish soldiers and are hopeful in the years to come that we will learn more. After the war, many of these men traveled across Europe and to the Far East, where the French had military and police forces. My active imagination seized upon this idea for the first book in the series, *The Jade Tiger*, and I added it to *Murder at the Met* as well.

Now, on to the Met!

Built in 1883, the Old Met was located on a trapezoidal block at the intersection of Thirty-Ninth Street and Broadway. With sumptuous detail for the interior house and a double row of boxes referred to as the Golden Horseshoe, the Metropolitan Opera was the prize jewel in New York society's crown. Fifty-two families each contributed $10,000 (equivalent to $150,000 today) toward building the lyre-shaped opera house, with each promised a private box in return.

Unfortunately, the architects (who had never built an opera house or any type of performance space) designed the backstage areas with too little room to change costumes or wash; no room at all to store costumes, sets, or makeup; and no requisite heating and cooling. In fact, there was so little room backstage that during performances, large set pieces were moved out into the street until they were needed. During an ambitious staging of *Aida*, several camels and an elephant stood by on Seventh Avenue while waiting for the triumphant ballet that opens act three to complete.

The company began discussing a new facility as early as 1908. In 1929 a move to Rockefeller Center was planned, then abandoned after the stock market crash in October. In 1966 the Metropolitan Opera Company moved to Lincoln Center. A fierce battle to declare the Old Met building a historical monument, one of the first such efforts in New York City, began. The Metropolitan Opera Company joined the suit to raze the building, concerned that another operatic company would use the property to compete against them. The movement to save the building failed, the Old Met was torn down, and a large office building was erected in its place.

By 1935 the effects of the Great Depression had created a funding shortfall that threatened the existence of the Metropolitan. Board member Eleanor Robson Belmont suggested the formation of a guild to raise money for the opera company during the popular Saturday matinee radio broadcasts. With a good deal of hard work and an abundance of good ideas, early opera guild members covered the Metropolitan's shortfall and expanded audience outreach. (And not a single one of them murdered anyone to do it.)

These broadcasts continue to this day and are carried for free on National Public Broadcasting radio stations across the country. It was through these broadcasts that I heard my first opera. Many of my happiest childhood memories include these broadcasts, the sound blaring from all the open windows so my father could hear the music while he worked outside. Looking back, I am sure our neighbors were driven to distraction by it, but for me it was magical.

The fictional Hudson Valley Operatic Society is a poor shadow of the hard work done by opera guilds all over the world to promote and protect grand, comic, and modern opera. While the opera society in this book focuses on the sordid underbelly of high society, most organizations were truly invested in supporting opera. Opera was reaching a pinnacle of popularity and was growing in accessibility via radio and mass-produced long-playing records, and these guilds worked tirelessly to make the art form accessible to everyone no matter their background.

Finally, I cannot pass on the opportunity to share the soprano who inspired the hat trick pulled off by Valentina Carrera—Beverly Sills. *The Tales of Hoffman* is my father's favorite opera. From Olympia's "Doll Song" to the sublime Barcarolle, I had heard the opera perhaps a hundred times before I took one step inside an opera house. And every time we listened, my father reminded me of Ms. Sills's supreme accomplishment. I simply could not write another book about Penelope without including the music that so brightly colored my childhood. Ms. Sills may not have been the first (or the last) soprano to sing all three roles, but she is the one I remember best. To accomplish the feat, she wore all her costumes (including wigs) at once, removing one layer during each of the intermissions.

But my admiration of Beverly Sills does not stop at her *Tales of Hoffman* performance. Like the opera guilds I mentioned, Ms. Sills worked tirelessly to introduce opera to new audiences all over the world, and particularly to children. She was a delightful, caring person with the voice of an angel. I never met her, but I feel as though she was a member of the family; she was that much a part of our lives.

—E. W. Cooper

Questions for Discussion

1. When you think of the 1920s, what themes or stories occur to you? Did the representations in *Murder at the Met* surprise you? Why or why not?

2. When you think back over the book, what scenes come to mind? Which was your favorite? Your least favorite?

3. Throughout the book, Penelope makes a series of choices that have both good and bad consequences. What are some of these choices, and what are your thoughts about them?

4. Penelope decides to help a girl she hardly knows, Ivy Warwick, with disastrous consequences. Why would she consider doing such a thing? Should she regret it?

5. As the founder of the Hudson Valley Operatic Society, is Patsy Galton an enthusiastic supporter of opera? Why did she start the operatic society? And why did she allow it to continue after Coralee's death?

6. In *Murder at the Met*, Penelope finally has an audition without a member of the press breaking it up, but she

chooses to leave rather than pursue the opportunity. Why do you think she chooses to walk away?

7. Will Penelope and Thom ever have a real night out on the town where they aren't interrupted by a murder? Where would they go? What would they do?

8. What twenty-first-century art forms have similar influence and range as those of opera in the early twentieth century?

Excerpt from the Next Penelope Harris Mystery

"The nerve of Fred Mackey!" Mary crossed her ankles and settled back into the comfortable leather upholstery of the Staughton Daimler, dark mink swamping her petite frame. "Imagine giving you the cold shoulder for months, then suddenly demanding you drive all the way to Bay Cliff in weather like this!" She gestured toward the window without turning her head to look. Not that there was much to see. Grey clouds and heavy sleet swept away any roadside attractions in a blurry gloom. Penelope thought she could see a train station and a slash of dark brown that could have been trees. "If you hadn't called exactly when you had," Mary counted off on her fingers, "if I hadn't been reading a book instead of going to Nanette Winston's tea party, if Father hadn't left the Daimler, if Charles wasn't swanning about with Wally Phipps in his new racing car, we would have never made it in time."

And if the bank hadn't sent Lund off somewhere, Penelope would have been able to warm up her voice as they drove. She missed the comfort of his reassuring silence. Reminding herself it was a good thing that Mary knew every socialite and social calendar from Philadelphia to Boston, she asked, "Do you think we'll make it there on time?"

"Of course, darling. Didn't I just say so?" Mary patted Penelope's hand. "Don't fret. We'll get there. No thanks to Mr. Mackey and his last-minute telegrams."

"Fred's trying to be helpful, Mary. Every opportunity to sing is one where I might get some work." Penelope sighed. "Not that he has much pull these days. You know the Metropolitan replaced him as director after the news coverage of the Warwick murders. All he has these days is the chorus."

"The Metropolitan was only doing what it had to. Fred got himself caught up with that terrible female all on his own. It wasn't the opera's fault the papers had a field day describing their love nest. The Met has a reputation to protect as much as anyone else!"

"That just proves how he's sticking his neck out," Penelope said. "I spent more time on the front page than Fred. The prosecution didn't even call him to testify, while I got called 'the bad-luck broad' on the front page of the *Sentinel*. You'd think he'd want me as far from him as—"

"That's another one—Helen Mayfield! I thought she was your friend!" Mary's cheeks turned pink with anger.

"She's a journalist. She's just doing her job. Thom warned me it might happen. He was right." Penelope straightened the music in her lap. "In any case, the Metropolitan couldn't possibly be interested in the publicity I would bring to a production. He's sent for me in spite of the attention I might bring. It's curious."

"Could it be a solo with the chorus?"

"No. The chorus only sings once, at the end of act one." *Tosca*—the Metropolitan gave Fred Mackey the one opera with a chorus that only sang once; it wasn't a consolation prize.

The insult was so obvious even the newspapers had picked up on the slight. Moving music, certainly, but not the star-making turn Mackey had hoped for. It was a clear sign his days at the Met were numbered. Even with all that, Penelope still had the telegram in her pocket telling her to come. She couldn't help wondering what he could possibly want.

"What did it say, Penelope? Tell me again—the telegram?"

"Just 'Come to Old Chestnuts, Bay Cliff. 3 p.m. Bring Puccini.'" Penelope straightened the music portfolio in her lap for the tenth time. "He had to mean *Tosca*. It's what Carrera is here to perform. But why me? What could I do for them now?"

"Why indeed?" Mary replied coolly. "Maybe he doesn't have an audition in mind at all. Have you given that a thought? Maybe he wants to seduce you!" She straightened her back, turning to address Penelope. "Gil has told me terrible stories. They'd practically make your hair stand on end! But have no fear, I will not leave your side for a moment."

Penelope sighed, wishing Gil Richie hadn't supplied her cousin with so much backstage gossip. She had no doubt the stories were mostly false, just Gil's way of convincing Mary he was the only worthwhile conversational partner at an opening night soiree. Completely smitten with Mary, Gil had taken to following her around town and appearing at the most unexpected moments. His presence had become such a habit that Penelope half expected him to appear in the cushioned seat across from them as soon as they said his name. "Everyone knows the cast left the Met studios because the heat went out," Penelope said. "It was in all the papers. They packed up and headed for Old Chestnuts. There were photos. The de Vries wouldn't stand for that kind of nonsense, would they? Not when it could be in all the papers quick as a wink."

"You're probably right." Mary tapped her chin as she thought. "Margret did like a good joke once upon a time, but her precious papa couldn't take a scandal that might spook his board of directors."

Penelope raised an eyebrow and returned her attention to the subject at hand. "If this is an audition, it could be a lucky break for me. If I've got a chance to sing in the chorus, I'll take it. If it's a chance to sing, I'll do it." She stopped herself short, looked down at her hands. "I thought I could teach, but the newspapers won't let me do that. I could do any number of things, I suppose. But I keep trying to sing. It's ridiculous, to be honest. I keep trying when I shouldn't. I should leave it, but I can't." She wished Lund was with her. His steady belief a career would materialize if she only kept trying would buoy her spirits. "I should give up. I don't know what I'm doing here. Why do I keep throwing my hat into the ring when I already know the answer?"

"You must keep trying." Mary put her hand over Penelope's and gently squeezed. "It's been an age since I saw Margaret. You'll like the de Vries. A little eccentric but opera lovers from the very beginning. If I remember correctly, Margaret's grandmother had quite a bit to do with the Metropolitan." Mary leaned toward the front seat. "Parker, it's the next exit. I'll tell you where to go."

Parker exited the highway with a turn of the wheel, the silent Daimler sailing over the slick roads into the canopy of bare tree branches that stretched across the narrow road. The crack of the sleet against the windows slowed, while the temperature inside the car began to drop. Penelope shivered in her coat, wishing (not for the first time) that her mink had not been stolen and ruined at a party last October. Raising the collar on her coat, she watched the side of the road, looking for a clue of where they were and what sort of village Bay Cliff was.

Grey rock lined the streets as though carved from the side of a mountain, dark trees rising just behind like silent sentinels. Even without their leaves, the dense branches hid the grey light, what there was of it. It was a wild beauty, strange and silent. The road rose and fell, the rock giving way to the small village of Fox Hunt. Just a few buildings with white shiplap and green trim, a small grocery, a fire station, and a doctor's placard—all buttoned up against the wind and the sleet, the light behind the windows warm and inviting. As Penelope watched, the light behind the doctor's office went out, the shades folded shut against the street.

"Is Old Chestnuts nearby?" Penelope asked Mary as the Daimler coasted down through a narrow valley, the earth stretching up on either side.

"Yes." Mary did not turn her head. "You should see it in the summer, Penelope. You simply would not believe how green a place can be. We are just three or four miles from the water. It doesn't seem like it, does it? Feels like we're in another world." She sighed. "Parker, turn left at the bottom of the curve, then straight on until we reach the pavilion."

The rock and dense undergrowth gave way to a deep field of raw earth and straw-colored grass on either side. In the distance, tall chestnut trees lined the road, a flash of white standing at the aperture of their steady straight lines. Penelope's nerves began a faint staccato as her heart beat a little faster. Turning her head, she watched the fields beyond the trees for a distraction, any distraction. "Do the de Vries own all of this?"

"Yes, a hundred acres on either side and another hundred straight down to the water." Mary straightened her coat. "Margaret says her father likes the quiet. Slow down, Parker. They exercise the horses straight through here from time to time."

Penelope turned her attention to the building ahead of them, her stomach in tight knots. An arch over two stories high and the width of two cars stood clear and bright when they were still a half mile away. The pavilion, which had looked so small in the distance, rose up around them quickly. A wing buttressed the arch on either side with double garage doors on the bottom and small windows along the top. The closer they got, the more clearly Penelope could see. The wings beside the arch were covered in neatly trimmed green ivy with light sand-colored brick just behind. The arch was so bold in the gloom that the low buildings to either side seemed to disappear into the landscape. Penelope gasped. "Is that . . . marble?"

"Just wait. You haven't seen the house yet." Mary's words were crisp. "This is just for the servants."

The Daimler cruised through the arch with barely a sound and followed a curved drive wrapping around a garden. Roses, Penelope thought. Had to be a riot of blooms in the summer. There was no doubt the de Vries had enough money to ensure every rose bloomed vigorously. A gardener in a heavy coat moved about with burlap sacking, carefully wrapping the bushes from the ground to the top. Penelope noted the man was only a third of the way through the wrapping when she caught sight of two boys pushing wheelbarrows with more sacking and smudge pots.

"What's this, Parker? Is there weather expected?" Mary watched the gardener warily.

"Not that I heard, miss. But you never know about the country, especially this close to the water. Could be some ice." Parker continued his slow progress around the drive. "It will get worse when it gets dark."

"With any luck, we'll be long gone by then." Mary straightened her shoulders and stuck her chin out. "Are you ready, Penelope? Let's see what Fred wants with you."

About the Author

E.W. Cooper is the author of the Penelope Harris historical mystery series and the 2020 Booklife Prize finalist for mystery/thriller. A lifelong fan of classic mysteries and grand opera, Ms. Cooper is hard at work on the third book in the series. She lives quietly with her partner, children, three dogs, and one cat in a very noisy house in South Texas. To read more about the author and the other short stories and novels featuring Penelope Harris, visit her website at wswww.ewcooper.com.

CPSIA information can be obtained
at www.ICGtesting.com
Printed in the USA
LVHW032143240321
682338LV00009B/189